marry poppins

An Impossible Dream Novel

BETH CIOTTA

Marry Poppins
Copyright © 2016 Beth Ciotta

Cover Design © EJR Digital Art
Stock photo © stock_colors @iStock

ISBN-13: 978-0692620854
ISBN-10: 0692620850

ALSO BY BETH CIOTTA

Impossible Dream

BEAUTY & THE BIKER
ENCHANTING CHRISTMAS
MARRY POPPINS

The Cupcake Lovers

FOOL FOR LOVE
THE TROUBLE WITH LOVE
ANYTHING BUT LOVE
SOME KIND OF WONDERFUL
IN THE MOOD FOR LOVE

Peacemakers: Old West
LASSO THE MOON
ROMANCING THE WEST
FALL OF ROME

The Glorious Victorious Darcys
HER SKY COWBOY
HIS BROKEN ANGEL
HIS CLOCKWORK CANARY

For an extensive booklist, visit Beth's website
www.bethciotta.com

PRAISE FOR BETH CIOTTA'S NOVELS

"Deep love of family and strong dialogue bolster a refreshing romance that focuses on the emotional rather than the physical." –*Publishers Weekly* (on *In the Mood for Love*)

"Ciotta writes fun, sexy reads with a good dose of realism." — *RT BOOKreviews* (on *The Trouble With Love*)

"Ciotta's wit adds spark to this tale of extended-family joys and sorrows, smalltown living, and complicated characters." –*Publishers Weekly* (on *Fool for Love*)

"Enchanting contemporary romance." –*Publishers Weekly* (on *Charmed*)

"Ciotta's first steampunk series blasts off with this exhilarating riff on bodice-ripping romance, hurling 20th-century technology into an alternate Victorian England. Start of a delectable series." —*Publishers Weekly*, starred review (on *Her Sky Cowboy*)

"Ciotta has written another imaginative, whirlwind adventure, featuring a daring hero and a spirited heroine, incredible inventions, and übernefarious villains." —*Booklist*, starred review (on *His Clockwork Canary*)

DEDICATION

To my readers and fellow dreamers!

Prologue

Once upon a blustery day...
Nowhere, Nebraska

Georgina Poppins waffled through life like a leaf caught in the wind. Settling every so often, with a man or a job, then being swept back up into the chaos.

At first, she took the constant upheaval in stride. But then she turned thirty-one and was more than a little disillusioned. Two of her lifelong friends were engaged to be married. Another owned a successful business. Another juggled three fascinating jobs. Yet another was spiritually attuned and shrouded in a cloud of exhilarating mystery.

Georgie was floundering.

In spite of her dysfunctional upbringing, her deepest desire was to marry a local boy and start a family of her own. She'd been one of those girls who fantasized about the perfect man, the perfect wedding, the perfect family even before she wore a bra.

Unfortunately, Georgie suffered the same rotten luck with men as she did with jobs. Her friends had lost count of her defunct relationships and careers.

Georgie hadn't.

Her friends considered her ability to bounce back and adapt—time and again—impressive. They called her multi-talented and resilient.

Mostly she was just desperate enough to try anything once.

Georgie appreciated the positive spin on her inability to shine at any one skill and she did her best to affect a cavalier attitude regarding her string of professional flubs. Teaching assistant, tour guide, party planner, florist, ranch hand, bartender, the shall-not-be-talked-about gig as a lingerie model—to name a few. It's not that she'd bombed at any one of those things. In fact, she'd been fairly good at most of those things. But none had been her true calling and all of them had fizzled for one reason or another.

Just like her relationships with men.

Two days after her thirty-first birthday, Georgie hit a wall.

That particular morning, she found out the Nowhere Public Library was closing up shop—forever. That was tragic for a whole lot of reasons, but mostly Georgie hated that it meant one of her best friends was now unemployed. Fortunately, Georgie had been in the position to right Bella's world. Unfortunately, it meant Georgie was now the one scrambling for a job. Again.

Then, only a few hours later while she was stockpiling bargain buys at the grocery, Dirk Banning, a man who'd sworn he was head over heels in love with Georgie, sent her a text—a flipping *text*—announcing he'd kinda-sorta hooked up with someone else. NO HARD FEELINGS.

Seriously?

She held it together until she reached the privacy of her junker car then—man, oh, man—she indulged in a meltdown of epic proportions. Railing to the universe while strangling her steering wheel and punching her worn leather seats.

"I'm over trying to find my niche! I'm tired of struggling financially!"

And she had lost all hope of ever meeting Mr. Right.

At wit's end, that night Georgie threw caution to the wind. Like her longtime pals, Bella and Chrissy, she contacted Impossible Dream, an Internet company designed to match people with their most avid desire. Whether it be a dream job, dream partner, dream vacation, dream house—ID.com researched the best prospects. It was up to the applicant to follow through.

Bella and Chrissy had shot beyond the stars with their

farfetched requests and they'd both received guidance from Impossible Dream within a few days.

Mustering optimism, Georgie filled out the required data sheet then stated her Impossible Dream. In a world full of lonely people and single-parent homes, surely it couldn't be that hard to match her with her greatest desire.

Four months later... Georgie was still waiting.

One

Once upon a stormy wedding...

"How do I look?"

"Beautiful."

"Not too flashy?

"Nope."

"Or trashy?"

"You're wearing a designer silk dress, Georgie."

"Yes, but I bought it on eBay. Second hand. At a ridiculously low price."

Angel, one of Georgie's closest and most fashionable friends, smiled. "Everyone should be so resourceful and lucky."

Georgie studied her reflection in the full-length mirror attached to her closet door. The red dress popped against her lily-white skin. It complimented her emerald eyes and sable hair. The wispy silk draped gracefully over her slender form. The hem stopped modestly at her knees. Yes, the V-neck plunged, but she was only a 32B so it wasn't like there was any major spillage.

Objectively, she had to admit she looked darned close to spectacular. Certainly classy enough to attend the intimate wedding of her long ago unrequited flame and his present snooty fiancé. She just didn't look like herself. Granted that had been her intent when she'd scoured the internet for a bargain dress that would personify sexy sophistication, but now she simply felt like a screaming fake.

"It came without an interior fabric tag," she said. "It's probably a knock-off Valentino."

"So what if it is and since when do you care about designer labels?"

"Since I found out I'm on the verge of losing everything." Georgie closed her eyes and groaned. The last thing she wanted ever, but especially today, was pity. "Forget I said anything."

"You know I can't do that."

Her friend touched her shoulder and Georgie met her gentle gaze. Angel Drake was one of the kindest people Georgie had ever known. She was also one of the richest. Her second husband had left her a comfortable fortune. Even so, Angel worked full time. As the owner and lead stylist at Heavenly Hair, she was a creative dynamo and major contributor to the beautification—people and soul wise—of their hometown. She also championed local charities with selfless vengeance. She had a heart of gold. No way would she ignore anyone in need. Especially one of her oldest and dearest friends. Sidestepping Angel's concern was futile so instead Georgie turned away from the mirror and threw herself in front of the proverbial bus.

"My landlord's evicting me."

"What?"

"I'm behind in rent. Mr. Jones allowed me as much leeway as possible, but he's struggling to keep his head above water like most everyone in the county. He decided to sell the property."

Visibly stunned, Angel scrambled to absorb the severity of Georgie's plight. "How much notice did Mr. Jones give you?"

"A month. But that was two weeks ago." Georgie flushed, glancing around her bedroom and gesturing to the rest of the dinky modular cottage. "I know it's not much, but at least this place is...was affordable. I shudder to think what's available to me at this point. Forget forking over any kind of security or first and last month's rent. I don't have the cash

5

or the credit. I'm overextended, up to my eyeballs in debt, Angel."

"How is that possible? You're so frugal."

"I'm also perpetually in between jobs. What jobs I've had haven't paid all that much. Factor in my constant car trouble and also," she glanced away, "Mom needed a loan."

"She always needs a loan," Angel said. "Unbelievable. The woman moved to the Sunshine State and she still darkens your days. Why didn't she ask one of her other children for money? Or one of her ex-husbands?"

"She probably did. Never mind about that," Georgie said while stuffing away her own special brand of resentment. "It was just one of several contributing factors. The point is no matter how careful I was, no matter how frugal, once I got in so deep it snowballed. I'm a cliché. A poster child for a major faction of Nowhere—this side of destitute and a signature away from bankruptcy."

"Oh, Georgie." Angel hugged her now, somehow conveying empathy without pity. She smelled of herbal shampoo and earthy goodness—the perfect complement to her gypsy-chic maxi dress and fringed bohemian shawl. "Why didn't you say something to one of us?"

Us meaning The Inseparables. Angel, Emma Sloan, Bella Mooney, Bella's younger cousin, Chrissy Mooney, and their long-distance BFF, Sinjun Ashe. Friends since childhood. Soul sisters bound by a pact as well as ever-lasting affection.

Georgie returned the much needed hug, then eased away and perched carefully on her vanity chair, trying not to wrinkle her dress.

Angel settled on the second-hand trunk at the end of Georgie's bed. Anticipating a forecasted thunderstorm, she'd arrived early to allow extra travel time to the chapel. Since Georgie's car was presently suspended on a local auto repair lift—again—Angel had volunteered to be Georgie's ride and date for Bryce Morgan's wedding. A wedding that had taken Georgie and everyone else in Dawes County by surprise. Then again Bryce's life had taken one surprising turn after another over the last several months. Sort of like Georgie's. Only Bryce's life was on the upswing.

Battling a whirlwind of emotions, Georgie fidgeted knowing Angel was waiting for her to elaborate regarding her misfortune. "Did I mention how pretty you look?"

Angel had arranged her vibrant red curls in a sassy up-do. Her makeup was daring, but tasteful. Her appearance epitomized a free spirit, yet Angel was fiercely grounded. Although financially sound at present, she'd grown up in a low-income household. She'd also been widowed twice and she was only thirty-one. Her life hadn't been a bowl of cherries, yet she weathered every pit thrown her way with unflinching dignity.

Georgie, who had a habit of losing it big time—although always in private—aspired to such grace.

"You complemented my appearance as soon as I crossed the threshold," Angel said. "Thank you...again. Now stop stalling, Georgie, and tell me why you didn't reach out to us for help."

Georgie sighed knowing they wouldn't be going anywhere until she spilled the beans. As much as it pained her to see Bryce marry some big city snob, she didn't want to miss the vows. If she didn't witness it for herself, she worried her brain would keep dreaming the seemingly impossible—a future for her and Bryce. *Mrs. Georgie Morgan.*

"I didn't say anything because I wanted to turn things around on my own," she said. "I thought if I kept chipping away I'd eventually dig myself out of this mess."

"I respect that," Angel said, "but we could have at least offered moral support."

"Except none of you would have stopped at that. Chrissy would've told Mason and he'd want to help me the way he helped Bryce and everyone at the Coyote Club. Mason's a sweetheart, but I wouldn't feel comfortable taking his money. I feel the same about your money, and Emma doesn't have a dime to spare. Bella and Savage would have insisted on helping out by hiring me at Wonderland even though there's no open position."

"You'd already be working at Wonderland, earning a decent salary, I might add, if you hadn't bailed on the position Savage offered you four months ago. And don't bother telling me you weren't right for the job," Angel said with an arched brow. "We all know you stepped aside in deference to Bella."

Georgie didn't argue. Due to poor funding and dwindling

patronage, the Nowhere Public Library had closed its doors leaving Bella, the children's librarian and town's cherished storyteller, unemployed. Wonderland—an indoor learning and amusement center for kids, had been the brainchild of her fiancé, Joe Savage, and was a stellar venue for Bella's experience and talents. Georgie had never been perfect for that position, she'd just been in need of a job. So yeah, she'd bailed, but for good reason.

"The payroll could have accommodated you both," Angel said as if reading her mind.

"Only because you would have finagled it," Georgie pointed out kindly. Angel had a vested interest in Wonderland and therefore a small say in the distribution of funds. "Baxter left you a lot of money, but he didn't leave you a bottomless bank account. I don't want to be yours, or anyone else's, charity case."

"I don't think of you like that and you know it."

"I'd feel that way though." Georgie had vowed long ago never to borrow or sponge off of anyone. Ever. The line had blurred when it came to credit cards, but ultimately she and she alone would pay. It might take years, but she would make good on her debts.

Unlike her mom.

Squirming at the thought of being compared to Erica Jones, Georgie glanced down at her self-manicured nails. She itched to paint them black to match her present mood—and the skies. Three days of turbulent weather had only intensified her gloomy mindset. Instead, she'd opted for radiant red. She'd pull off confident sophistication today if it killed her.

"Does your family know?" Angel asked.

Georgie snorted. Her family—assorted half and step sibs, a disinterested father, three step-dads, and an irresponsible mother—had scattered, most of them anyway, to various other counties or states. As if any of them—except for one—could or would help her. As if she'd even ask.

"What about Ryan?" Angel pried.

Ryan McClure, Georgie's older half-brother, was the exception. He would move mountains to rescue her from a bad situation. Ryan, who served as Dawes County Sheriff, had a hero complex. He was also a super nice guy—newly divorced and in shared custody of a moody young daughter. "Ryan has his hands full."

"Yes, but—"

"Can we shelve this topic for today?" Desperate to shake the blues, Georgie forced a sunny smile. "I'll come clean with you and the girls when we meet for dinner on Wednesday. I should have a plan by then or at least a better grip on specifics. Today I was hoping to party as if I don't have a care in the world. Kind of a last hurrah. Once we get through the ceremony, we can cut loose at the reception. Now that I think of it, I'll probably get all sweaty from dancing." She ran her fingers through her long, silky hair. "I should have taken you up on your offer for an up-do."

Angel twirled her finger. "Turn around. I'll give you a ponytail."

"A sophisticated ponytail?"

"What's up with this sophistication kick?" Angel asked as she swept Georgie's hair off her neck. "Part of the last hurrah? Or are you trying to impress someone?"

Busted. "Like who?"

"Like Bryce."

Georgie grunted. "Get real." Meanwhile her stomach fluttered with a zillion butterflies. Bryce—The Bullet—Morgan. Georgie's first crush, not that anything had ever happened between them. Not even a kiss. Still. You never forget your first love and Georgie had never been able to shake the infatuation. Not that she ever talked about it. Pride and all that. "Bryce is getting married today. Hence our fancy duds, remember?"

"How could I forget? The mystery of the century. What does he see in that woman anyway?"

"You're kidding, right? She's beautiful and stylish and talented and successful and—"

"Shallow and bitchy."

"We only met her that one time."

"And she was on her worst behavior."

"Or having a bad day."

Angel frowned. "Why are you sticking up for her?"

"I'm not. I'm sticking up for Bryce."

Former pro football player. Present co-owner of the Coyote Club. That homegrown man had experienced a string of bad luck that outshined Georgie's, although things were turning around. If Kathryn Bellows, the producer of a popular cable sports show, could contribute to Bryce's good fortune then Georgie was happy for him. Bryce was one of the nicest men in Nowhere. Never mind that he'd broken her younger self's heart. Every man she'd ever cared about had broken Thumper. At least Bryce had been sweet about it.

"She's wrong for him," Angel said. "And she's wrong for those kids."

"I still can't believe Marla's gone. As in dead," Georgie clarified. "And given she'd been estranged from the family for years, it's downright incredible that she left her son and daughter in Bryce's care. From uncle to father in the blink of an eye. From single to married within four months. An instant family. If I didn't know better I'd think ID-dot-com screwed up and gifted Bryce with my dream."

Angel froze and Georgie winced. She'd tripped up twice in less than thirty minutes, spewing without thinking. At this rate she'd bare her soul to anyone who would listen by the time the bride cut the cake.

Angel swung around and perched on the edge of the rickety vanity. "You applied to Impossible Dream?"

Damn. "Yeah."

"When?"

"Four months ago."

"What did you apply for?"

"It doesn't matter. I didn't get it."

"The company rejected your application?"

"They said it's a work in progress. It's been four months. I'm not holding my breath."

Angel scrunched her brow. "You said Bryce got your dream. An instant family? You applied for an instant family?"

Georgie pushed to her feet and whirled away. "How hard can it be? A nanny position with potential for marriage. Or an amiable arranged marriage. There are a bazillion broken families in this country. Divorced men. Widowed men. Men with children and in need of a partner. Children in need of a mother."

"Your heart's desire is an arranged marriage?" Angel sounded incredulous. "What about love?"

"My heart's desire is to have a family. A husband and kids. Children to nurture and cherish. I'm tired of waiting for Mr. Right, Angel, and I don't want to go the single mother route and have a baby on my own. I want a partner. A family. A stable home and people to care for and laugh with and..."

Heart pumping, Georgie did a one-eighty, her modest hem-line brushing her knees, the ends of her ponytail swishing her bare upper arm. "I know. I sound like Suzy-freaking-Homemaker. A throwback to the 1950s. But what if being a wife and a mom... What if *that's* my calling? What if everything I've done up until now was training for being the world's most amazing homemaker? For making a positive, meaningful difference in some family's life? Is that so wrong?"

Angel smiled—a big, brilliant smile that lit up the gloomy room. "Actually, it sounds pretty perfect. Any family would be lucky to have you, Georgie. You're one-of-a-kind. Resourceful, resilient, loyal, kind-hearted, and *fun*. I could go on and on." She angled her head. "Maybe that's why Impossible Dream hasn't come through for you yet. They're not looking to match you up with any family. They're looking for the perfect family. For you."

Georgie's heart kicked. "Ya think?"

"I'd lay Baxter's money on it." After squinting out the window, Angel prodded Georgie toward the door. "Let's get a move on before those dark clouds burst. Don't want to be late for the ceremony. Who knows? Maybe Bryce will take one look at you in that spectacular dress and give Miss Snooty-Pants the boot."

Georgie smiled. "Nice try."

Angel shrugged. "Stranger things have happened."

Two

"You're joking."

"I'm sorry, Bryce. I thought I could go through with it. Then as the chauffeur was driving me here I realized I don't *want* to go through with it. I know this is short notice—"

"Short?" Bryce thumbed back the cuff of his jacket and glanced at his watch. "We're supposed to take our vows in eight minutes, Kathryn."

"It could be worse," she said in a tight, low voice. "I could have jilted you at the altar in front of your family and friends. Hell, I could have ordered the limo driver to pull a U-turn and not shown up at all. I wanted to give you the courtesy of telling you face-to-face so do me a favor and don't be a prick."

They were huddled in a cramped alcove of Grace Chapel. Kathryn in a classy light-blue dress and Bryce in a tailored navy suit. A small fraction of his family and friends were waiting patiently in the non-denominational nave, evenly dispersed on both sides of the aisle. The bride hadn't contributed to the guest list. Unless you counted her assistant who was standing in as her bridesmaid. Hannah, Bryce assumed, was waiting in the limo, weathering the thunderstorm raging outside instead of the squall brewing within.

If it wasn't for his dad, Bryce would have eloped per Kathryn's initial plan. But Arlo Morgan wasn't himself these days and the unexpected arrival of the grandchildren he hadn't even known he had only complicated an already tense situation.

Bryce had hoped an old-fashioned wedding would bolster the old man's spirits. He'd hoped it would help his niece and nephew to view Bryce and Kathryn as a couple dedicated to the long term—unlike their mother and her assorted *partners*. Kathryn, who'd yet to adjust to the idea of being a mom, had agreed to this small local ceremony under protest. He should have known her capitulating was too good to be true.

Never one to lose his cool, Bryce clapped a hand to the back of his neck and rubbed. *Relax. Breathe. Think.* "Are you saying you need more time? You want to postpone—"

"I want to break up. A clean break. Personally, that is. Professionally, we'll remain status quo. I still think you'd make a damn fine addition to any sportscaster team. You're the best thing that's happened for this year's charity circuit."

"But not the best thing that's happened to you."

When Kathryn smiled—a genuine smile—Bryce's pulse revved. This was not one of those smiles. This smile iced his nads.

"Circumstances were different when you proposed," she said.

"Actually, you're the one who proposed."

"Regardless, things were different. You were willing to relocate to Denver. Then your dad took that fall and you felt obligated to stay in Nowhere and commute to Denver on weekends. I could have dealt with that but then your sister died and you got saddled with those two..." She wisely bit off whatever derogatory thing she was going to say about Chelsea and Charlie and instead huffed a breath.

"I'm not ready to be a mom," she plowed on, "and I'm certainly not ready to mother twin five-year-olds with social and emotional issues. I'm not so heartless as to make you choose between them and me. Or maybe it's that I'm not that stupid. I know you won't desert them anymore than you'll desert your dad and his crippled ranch. And before you revisit the commuting thing, I have to tell you I've been offered an opportunity I can't pass up. I got a call from a headhunter," she rushed on, "offering me a position as co-producer for CSN."

"When?"

"I start next week."

"No, when did you get the call?"

"Last night." She laughed. "Talk about divine intervention. If you want to blame someone for nixing this marriage, blame fate. At any rate, you see why commuting is out."

What he saw was the tail end of his fleeting lucky streak. "CSN is based in Los Angeles."

"I know you want me to be happy, Bryce, and that job will make me very happy. You and I both know we wouldn't survive a long-distance relationship, so I'm cutting to the chase and calling it quits."

His mouth crooked in a self-deprecating smile. "It was nice while it lasted?"

Grasping the lapels of his jacket, she leaned in and nipped his earlobe. "It was fun while it lasted."

Right. The sex. The sex had been...adventurous. And plentiful. The sex had been the best thing between them and addicting enough to warp his senses.

Just then Bryce caught sight of Ryan McClure, Bryce's best man. Or rather his former best man. "Sorry to interrupt, but Pastor Dan asked me to find you. We're, uh, running a little late."

"Be right there," Bryce said.

Ryan, the soul of discretion, nodded then left.

"You'll forgive me if I bail now, right?" Kathryn asked while straightening his elaborately designed tie—a tie she'd bought, a tie he hated. "As for the honeymoon, feel free to cash in my ticket. Take your dad or maybe the kids. Maybe a trip would put a smile on those somber faces."

Bryce didn't answer. If she'd been listening when he'd first explained Chelsea and Charlie's background, as well as he knew it anyway, she'd understand that traveling to a new and strange place would only intensify their anxiety.

She fluttered a manicured hand toward the nave. "Feel free to throw me under the bus when you break this to your guests. It's not like I'll ever see them again. You, however," she said while turning on her designer heels. "I'll be in touch."

Just as she reached for the handle, the arched door flew open and Angel Drake rushed over the threshold, breathless and windblown. "Sorry," she said, swinging aside her soaked umbrella while sidestepping Kathryn.

Kathryn cursed but kept going only to slam into Georgina Poppins, who blew in with a gust of wind and sheets of rain.

Squealing an apology, Georgie wrestled with a mangled umbrella just as the door bounced off the wall and hit her in the ass.

On instinct Bryce lurched forward, catching Ryan's little sister as she slipped on the wet stone floor and wrenching his bad knee in the process. "Damn."

"Sorry. I..." Her wet front plastered to his now damp front, Georgie met Bryce's gaze and flushed. "Thanks for the save," she said while scrambling out of his arms. "I'm sorry we're late. Although..." She glanced toward the door then back to Bryce. "Did you already say your vows? Where did Kathryn go?"

"Back to Denver."

"Without you?" Angel asked.

Bryce ignored his throbbing knee, his damp shirt, and his dinged pride. He jammed a hand through his hair, cursing his pecker for getting him into this mess in the first place. "I don't suppose you know where I can find a warm and willing bride within the next three seconds."

"I'm available," Georgie said, causing Bryce to smile because, she was joking, right?

Eyes wide, Angel cleared her throat. "I'll, um..." She fluttered a hand toward the sound of the nondescript, pre-bridal-march song. "Meet you inside."

She scrambled away and Bryce turned back to Georgie, a bad feeling twisting his gut. Kind of like the time she'd declared her undying love for him. She'd been sixteen at the time. Bryce had been twenty-six. Ryan would have kicked his ass to the moon if he'd so much as kissed Georgie's sweet lips, and rightly so. "That was a rhetorical question, hon."

"I know."

Her cheeks burned red, matching the vibrancy of her dress, a rain-soaked, stylish number that clung to her gentle curves. Since when had he noticed Georgie in a sexual way? Although damn, between the thin wet fabric and the air

15

conditioning, it was hard not to notice certain things.

"But maybe I could stand in for a while," she said.

Bryce tore his gaze from her high beams and the tease of exposed flesh complements of the daring V-neckline of a very un-Georgie like dress. *Stand in?* "You're losing me."

"I'll just spit it out. Derring-do and all that."

"Whatever that means." His mind wandered to his dad and the "I-told-you-so" coming his way when he announced Kathryn's desertion.

Georgie swiped rain from her brow. "I need a job and a place to live. You need help with your dad and Chelsea and Charlie. My moving in with you guys, temporarily of course, would be mutually beneficial, don't you think?"

Bryce stared down at Georgina Lou Poppins, wondering if she'd lost her ever-lovin' mind. At the same time, he was just raw enough and desperate enough to take solace in the absurd. He glanced at the nave, knowing he had to break his news and pronto, then glanced back at Georgie. Shrugging out of his jacket, he draped it over her shoulders wanting to spare her from censure or smirks should anyone notice her chilled state.

He squeezed her shoulders. "Stay here and hold that thought."

* * *

Georgie stared as Bryce limped into the nave. She couldn't believe it. She just couldn't believe it. He'd been jilted. Bryce Morgan—gorgeous, sexy, kind-hearted, overly generous, once-upon-a-time football star, Bryce-The Bullet-Morgan—*jilted*.

That snooty, big-city producer was out of her gourd!

Georgie mentally kicked up her heels. She would have happy danced but that would be insensitive—Bryce had just had his heart crushed, after all—plus the floor was slick with rain. Just her luck she'd slip. This time Bryce wasn't here to catch her, and hadn't that been a heart-tripping thrill? No, he was inside announcing the cancelation of his nuptials to friends and family.

"Stranger things have happened."

Was Angel psychic or something?

Georgie wasn't and she wanted to hear what Bryce was saying.

She inched closer to the nave, holding the lapels of his big jacket so it wouldn't slide off. Bryce was known about town as a gentle giant. He was also the consummate gentleman. It was just like him to offer her his coat. Although how did he know she was freezing?

Oh, no.

She peeked down at her thin, soaked bodice.

Oh, yeah.

Cheeks hot, she finessed her arms into Bryce's super nice, super big suit jacket and hugged herself tight. In warming herself, she also breathed in his scent. Soap and woodsy aftershave.

Yum.

Feeling sort of pervy with her nose jammed in the crook of his sleeve, she shook off olfactory nirvana and crept toward the back pew, hunkering out of view as Bryce addressed his guests.

"I apologize for dragging you out late on a Sunday and then, well, fumbling the ball," he said. "Cake, refreshments, and music are waiting at Coyote's. No need to waste a party."

He gestured to his business partner who was sitting in the front pew, one arm around Chrissy and the other around their daughter, Melody. "Follow Mason to the club and I'll join you shortly."

After shaking hands with Pastor Dan, Bryce stooped to have a private word with his niece and nephew and his dad, Arlo.

Everyone traded stunned glances.

Mason stood and filled the awkward silence, re-extending Bryce's invitation to the Coyote Club.

Ryan squeezed Bryce's shoulder then helped Arlo with the cane he'd been forced to use ever since his fall.

Mumbling softly to one another, everyone shifted to their feet.

Georgie's phone dinged loudly with multiple texts. Cringing, she nabbed her phone from her purse and slid farther down the bench in an effort to disappear as people started down the aisle.

BELLA: *Where r u?*

EMMA: *Bryce just dodged bitch bullet. Party time!*
CHRISSY: *Bryce alert! Still hope 4 U, Georgie Lou*
ANGEL: *DID U JUST PROPOSE 2 BRYCE?????*

Pulse racing, Georgie hunched over her knees, head down, fingers flying.

TO BELLA: *Meet u @ Coyotes*
TO EMMA: *Show some sympathy. Poor Bryce. See u on dance floor.*
TO CHRISSY: *Since when R U a hopeful romantic, Christmas Joy? Oh, right. Since Mason.* ☺
TO ANGEL: *Sort of.*

"Everything okay down there?"

Startled, Georgie bumped her head on the bench in front of her. "Ow."

Bryce stood at the end of the pew. All six-foot-hunky-four of him, looking model handsome in his oxford shirt and the tie he loosened at his throat. She could have stared into those big brown eyes forever. Instead she scanned the room. Even Pastor Dan and Mrs. Barnaby, the ancient church organist with the perpetual silver bouffant and green cat-eye glasses, had vamoosed.

"Georgie?"

"I'm good," she squeaked. "You?" *Doh!* "Sorry," she added. "That was an automatic response. Obviously you're upset. I mean who wouldn't be, getting dumped like that. I mean..."

"I know what you mean."

She blew out a breath. "I'm a little nervous."

"That's all right. So am I."

"You nervous?" Even when he'd been on the verge of bankruptcy, right before Mason had stepped in and saved the day, Bryce had maintained an upbeat attitude and scary calm. Anxious didn't compute. "Why?"

"Because I'm thinking about taking you up on that offer."

"You are?" She barely heard her question above the blood roaring in her ears. Was this Impossible Dream in action? Although wouldn't they have given her a heads up? Or at least a cryptic clue? It's not like they could have known Kathryn would leave Bryce at the altar or however it had gone down. No, this was just some bizarre twist of fate. "Wait. The bride thing or the job thing?"

He angled his head. She knew that look. The same look he'd given her when she'd barfed up her teenage heart. The *you're-too-young-for-me-and-not-even-close-to-my-type* look.

Georgie snorted and waved him off. "Kidding. Jeez. You and me. As if. Right? Just trying to lighten the mood. Relax, Bryce. I'm so over you I'm on the far side of the moon."

Apparently he bought her lie because his broad shoulders relaxed and he smiled. Sort of. "Mind if I sit?"

His knee. He'd aggravated his famous football injury saving her from a tumble. Then he strode down the aisle and knelt to speak with his family. He had to be hurting, but Bryce never complained. Ever.

Instead of drawing attention to something she knew he was sensitive about, she skirted mention of his knee and gestured to the pew. As soon as he settled she slid closer so they could speak lower. It felt weird having this discussion in a church, but it's not like they were moving in together as lovers. She should be so lucky.

"Why do you need a place to live?"

"I, um..." Georgie straightened her spine. This admission did not come easy. Worse it summoned childhood memories that filled her with shame. *Just say it!* "I'm getting kicked out of my place."

"Why?"

"I'm having financial issues."

"I've been down that road."

"I'm a hard worker, Bryce."

"I know that."

"I'm a responsible person." *I'm not my mother.*

"I know that, too."

Summoning calm, she clasped her hands in her lap. She'd made some bold moves in her life, but this was a doozy. "I'm going to make you an offer you can't refuse."

He leaned back and crossed his arms and she swore she saw his lip twitch. "Dazzle me, Lou."

Her middle name. The nickname he used to tease her with when she was a little kid. *Great.* Determined to be seen as a woman full grown, Georgie slipped out of Bryce's jacket and passed it to him with an apologetic smile. "Sorry I got your coat wet."

"That's okay. Sure you don't—"

"I'm good." She waved off the jacket. "Thank you." She didn't look to see if there was any nip action. If there was, so be it. Further proof she wasn't a kid anymore. "To be honest," she lied, "I can only work for you on a temporary basis. I applied for a position through a company who sets people up with dream jobs. They're looking to place me with the perfect family. I should be hearing from them, oh, soon."

"Are you referring to Impossible Dream dot-com?"

Georgie blinked. "How do you know... Oh. Mason."

"Yeah. Mason told me about how Chrissy applied—"

"This is different."

"And Chrissy told me how Bella applied—"

"Way different." Georgie miraculously held the man's gaze. "I actually applied for a job. As a nanny," she clarified. "Which explains the placing me with a family part. While I'm waiting I figure I can practice on you. And the kids. And Arlo."

Bryce worked his jaw. "Chelsea and Charlie have only been with me for a couple of weeks, but it's clear they have issues. They're abnormally quiet."

"So far, my only one-on-one with the twins is when you brought them to Wonderland last week. Yes, they were very shy, but that didn't strike me as strange."

Since Bella had expected a large turnout for her Pajama-Rama event, she'd enlisted Georgie to assist with the festivities. Even though there'd been close to twenty kids to entertain, both Georgie and Bella had gone out of their way to put Chelsea and Charlie at ease.

"They're in a new environment, living with veritable strangers," Georgie went on. "Take it from someone who bounced from a string of homes and step-families... It ain't easy. And let's not forget the doozy of downers. They recently lost their mother."

"I get all that, but I'm worried it runs deeper."

"Maybe I can help."

"And Arlo," Bryce said. "The old man was a cranky cuss before he fractured his hip. Now..."

"Maybe I can help his cranky ass, too," Georgie teased with a soft smile.

"You don't mind cooking?"

"I'll even clean. But mostly I'll look after Chelsea and Charlie while you work and, well, try to mend things with Kathryn, I guess. The really great news is that all it will cost you is room and a nominal salary—just enough for me to squeak by. And just temporarily."

"Until your dream job comes through."

"Exactly. Which could be any day, but I promise to give you fair notice before I leave."

He rubbed the back of his neck. "I suppose we could give it a try."

Wa-freaking-hoo! She wasn't sure what she'd just talked her way into, but it felt incredibly right. She could control her lustful urges regarding Bryce. She'd been curbing them for fifteen years. At least she'd have a place to live and a chance to hone her Suzy Homemaker chops. She contained a giddy squeal, throwing back her shoulders and beaming instead. "You won't regret this, Bryce. I'm your dream come true. Temporarily."

Three

By the time Georgie and Bryce left Grace Chapel the pelting rain had eased. Georgie was glad for that, especially since her umbrella had bit the dust, mangled one too many times by monstrous winds.

Even though the storm had passed, she scanned the murky sunset as Bryce helped her into his pickup. Growing up in the northwestern corner of Tornado Alley, Georgie took thunderstorms in stride. Tornadoes were another matter. Unlike Emma, who rode shotgun with Chrissy's brother Zeke and the Z-Crew Stormchasers, Georgie had a paralyzing fear of twisters.

"Ryan know about your money troubles?" Bryce asked as he keyed the ignition.

"Not as much as you know. And no one, other than Angel, knows about my application to ID-dot-com," Georgie said as she tore her gaze from the gloomy horizon. "I'd appreciate it if you'd keep that under your hat for the time being."

If Impossible Dream did come through with her greatest desire, it might entail moving out of state or maybe even the country. When they were children, the Inseparables had made a pact to keep Nowhere on the map by sticking around and helping the town to thrive. Sinjun had already flown the coop, though not by choice, and Emma was itching to spread her wings. Georgie felt guilty about bailing on Bella, Chrissy, and Angel, but at least all three of them were making a positive difference in their hobbling town. Georgie was just...taking up space.

"Any other secrets I should know about?" Bryce asked in her contemplative silence.

Georgie's mind flew from her fantastic dream to her one fantastically, unbelievable bonehead indiscretion. Her one massive regret in life. So far anyway. She told herself not to blush but her cheeks burned all the same. Had Ryan broken his promise? Had he slipped one day and told Bryce about the time she'd posed in skimpy lingerie for what she thought was a legitimate fashion shoot. "What do you mean?"

Bryce shrugged. "You've been keeping a lot to yourself these days. I care about you, Georgie. If your troubles run deeper than finances—"

"What troubles? What have you heard?" Better to focus on potential gossip than Bryce's 'caring' reference. Of course, he *cared*. She was the younger sister of one of his closest and oldest friends. "Wait. Let me guess. You overheard Tom Rhodes badmouthing me."

"Parked his duff at my bar with a couple of friends last week. Got a lot drunk and a little loud. Couldn't help but overhear."

"He's mad because he wanted to get physical and I didn't. I'm not a prude but first date and a bad date at that. Hello?" She rolled her eyes. "He'll get over it."

"As long as he's not hassling you."

"Nice of you to worry, but that's not an issue. I'm sure Tom's already moved on to his next prospect." *They all do.*

Georgie shifted her gaze—to the faded line down the middle of the cracked road, to the assortment of rundown and abandoned stores lining Frontier Street, to anything other than Bryce. She didn't care that she'd been the star of Tom's trash-talk, but she did sort of care that Bryce had overheard.

Over the years she'd kissed a lot of toads, hoping to find her Frog Prince. Months ago she'd decided to swap the notion of happily-ever-after for happy-for-now. Lately she'd dated a couple of guys for pure escapism. A few hours of blissful distraction from her disastrous life. Emma swore by casual dating. It worked for her. Not so much for Georgie. She couldn't help wondering what else Bryce had overheard these last few months. Did he think she was promiscuous? A tease? Flighty? A chip off of her fickle mom's block?

"Big of you to carry on with the reception," Georgie said desperate to derail talk of her mucked-up affairs. "I'm sure the last thing you feel like doing is socializing right now. Although maybe that's preferable to wallowing in misery all by your lonesome."

"I'm only staying long enough to assure everyone I'm not..."

"Crushed? Depressed? Mortified? Ticked off and fed up with the entire opposite gender?"

"Something like that."

His expression hinted that she'd just betrayed her own mindset after her last dozen breakups.

Way to be transparent, Georgina. "I, um..." She nodded toward the bar as they pulled into the packed parking lot. Thanks to Mason's renovations and Bryce's revived star power, the Coyote Club was presently the number one watering hole in Nowhere. "I'm looking forward to chatting with Chelsea and Charlie," Georgie said as she primped her ponytail.

"They opted out."

"They're not inside with Arlo?"

"I tried to bribe them with cake and cola, but they didn't want to come. I'm not sure if they're blaming themselves for Kathryn's no-show or are just skittish about mingling with partygoers. They wouldn't say. Dad hitched a ride with Pastor Dan and took the kids home. Told me to take my time at the reception, to do right by the guests."

"Arlo's always been a stickler for manners." Probably one of the reasons Bryce was insanely nice.

"I'll do my bit then turn things over to Mason. Dad'll slap a bandage on this mess with cartoons and popcorn, but I'd prefer a heart to heart with the twins. I don't harbor ill thoughts about Marla, but what was she thinking dragging those kids all over, hopping from town to town, man to man. I..." He trailed off, eyes fixed on the bar he'd invested in shortly after being forced out of professional sports. "You don't want to hear all that."

"Actually," Georgie said, her heart aching for the entire Morgan family, "it would help if I knew specifics. Pertaining to Chelsea and Charlie that is. I'd hate to say or do the wrong thing out of ignorance. I'd hate to make matters worse."

"I don't see how you could make things worse. Also, unlike me, you empathize based on personal experience. Not that your mother was an addict, but she did..." He trailed off again, this time with a curse.

For once in this discussion, Georgie didn't flush. She wasn't fond of her upbringing, but it's not like she'd had a choice. If nothing else, she'd emerged from domestic dysfunction with mad survival skills and a heap of compassion.

"You don't have to walk on eggshells, Bryce. Everyone knows my mom bounced from husband to boyfriend to husband and that we lived in three different houses before I was eight. At least she kept our travels within the county. I had the stability of this town and my friends and their families."

"I'm guessing, but I'd wager," she went on, "that I had it better than your niece and nephew. We'll just have to turn that around. Make them feel safe, stable, and loved." Georgie beamed with sincere confidence. "It won't be that hard. You'll see."

Bryce stared.

Her stomach flipped. "Did I say something wrong?"

"You said everything right."

"Then why are you looking at me funny."

"Because I'm contemplating something crazy."

Georgie could scarcely breathe.

"I don't suppose you have a passport?"

* * *

"Run that by me again?"

"I invited your sister to London."

"That's what I thought you said." Ryan angled his head. "For your honeymoon."

"If it helps," Bryce said, "I didn't get married so it no longer qualifies as a honeymoon."

"It doesn't help."

Bryce hitched back his jacket and dropped onto one of the two club chairs in the cramped office he now shared with Mason Rivers, heir to the Rivers Audio Visual fortune. Even though he'd shut the door, the music blasting through their new state-of-the-art sound system seeped through the walls. Out there, thirty-some guests drank and danced in an awkward attempt to salvage Bryce's pride. In here, two old friends faced off due to Bryce's dinged perspective and gut instincts.

Instead of taking the seat next to him, Ryan perched on the corner of the desk. Even though he was off duty and out of uniform, he was still in protective mode—albeit as Georgie's big brother.

"So instead of canceling your trip you invited Georgie to stand-in for Kathryn. A knee-jerk reaction? A ploy to make Kathryn jealous?"

"Not my style," Bryce said, because normally it wasn't. Although he had to admit Kathryn's rejection stung and, God help him, he resented her freedom to indulge in wholly selfish opportunities.

"So what gives?"

Bryce shifted his thoughts from Kathryn—a woman who sailed through life on the winds of good fortune—to Georgie. Nothing came easy for Georgina Lou Poppins and she'd certainly never been handed a high-salaried dream job. Instead, she applied for her dream position—a nanny, of all things—through some sketchy matchmaking site. Given Georgie's history, Bryce could easily imagine her being placed as an *au pair* with the family from hell.

"I should have led off with the other portion of this unexpected development," Bryce said, struggling to keep his thoughts and emotions in check.

He'd been hammered with sympathetic smiles and encouraging words the moment he'd escorted Georgie into Coyote's. He was only now learning how many people considered Kathryn a bad match, which only made him feel like more of an ass. Blinded by mind-blowing sex and a selfish agenda. He could see that now and, damn, it was disturbing.

Deep down he knew he'd dodged a bullet. On the surface he felt gutted. And for all the wrong reasons. Doing something nice for Georgie helped to ease his smarting conscience.

"Let me back up," Bryce said. Georgie had given him permission to make her brother aware of her immediate needs—a home and a job—and their practical solution. Bryce filled his friend in on the temporary nanny bit without mentioning Georgie's bigger aspirations via Impossible Dream.

"I don't have to tell you that I'm struggling with this new twist in my life," Bryce said in reference to Chelsea and Charlie. "Dad's yet to adjust to forced retirement and I'm juggling responsibilities here at the club and new obligations regarding the sports charity circuit. Georgie's moving in to help with the kids is a Godsend."

"I'm sure she feels the same regarding the roof over her head," Ryan said then frowned. "I wish Georgie would have made me aware of her mounting debts."

"She didn't want to be a burden."

"She's always been self-motivated."

"Admirable trait," Bryce said.

"To a certain extent," Ryan said with a reflective expression. A heartbeat later he returned to the present. "The nanny arrangement. Sounds like some mutual ass saving. But the London trip? Just the two of you?"

"Kathryn suggested I take Arlo or the kids in her place. That's not happening. The twins need stability right now and Dad's hanging on to what's left of the ranch with an iron grip."

"Why not cancel?"

"Dad's idea. Told me to use the time to gauge the future. Reminded me this was his designated week to bond with his grandkids and that we already tapped Aunt Pauline to help out while I was away.

"In talking with Georgie," Bryce continued, "I realized I should fill her in on the kids' past. Explore some tactics on how to handle their future."

"I get it," Ryan said, "but why do you need to go overseas to have that discussion?"

"We don't. But Arlo's right. I've got some thinking to do. And I did promise him time alone with the twins. And Georgie... Hell, I know what it's like to be down and out. I almost lost this club and my shirt. Mason swooped in and cracked the gloom. I'd like to do that for Georgie."

"Crack the gloom?"

"Gifting her with an all-expenses paid vacation seems like a good start."

Ryan worked his jaw. "I have to admit, it's a nice gesture. Georgie's never traveled overseas. And she's been struggling a long time. A lifetime, come to think of it."

"We'll have separate rooms, of course," Bryce added as a last assurance. He hoped Ryan was on board now because Bryce was done explaining. He'd always been a man of few words and today he'd worn his throat raw with confrontations, explanations, apologies, gratitude, and plain ol' conversation.

"Still flying out tomorrow?" Ryan asked.

"We are."

"This will set a lot of tongues wagging."

"Let 'em wag," Bryce said. "Georgie's words, not mine."

Ryan threw up his hands. "If she wants to go, who am I to say, no, but be mindful, Bryce."

"Of?"

"Surely you know my sister's sweet on you."

She'd assured him she wasn't. "That ship sailed."

Ryan regarded Bryce with something akin to pity as they returned to the party. "When it comes to women, you're more clueless than me. Thanks for making me feel better, bro."

* * *

Georgie felt semi-ridiculous huddling in the ladies room with her friends and gossiping like teens, but that didn't stop her from spewing her saga in rapid-fire detail.

The Inseparables gaped in response, the amplified sounds of a Garth Brooks' song rattling the mirrors above the sinks, filling the silence until the first of the women recovered.

"I don't know what's more shocking," Chrissy said. "That you're moving in with Bryce to play nanny or that you're joining him on his honeymoon."

"Technically it's no longer a honeymoon," Georgie pointed out. Even so her heart fluttered like the besotted thumper of a new bride. Bryce had barely finished inviting her to accompany him to England before she'd pounced with an enthusiastic yes. Her life had been so crappy for so long, why would she refuse such an amazing and gracious offer? Kathryn Bellows may be out of her gourd, but Georgie was a smart—albeit crumbling—cookie.

Six days, seven nights exploring jolly old England with Bryce—The Bullet—Morgan?

Hellz yeah.

"I am green, absolutely raging jaded green with envy," Emma said.

"London, England!" Bella squealed. "How romantic! Do you know how many fairy tales and children's classics are rooted in Great Britain?"

"Paris would be romantic," Emma said, "but London is very cool. The history, the architecture, the museums."

Georgie frowned, realizing she was about to experience what Emma craved—an exhilarating adventure. "I'll probably be too jet-lagged to fully enjoy everything," she said. "The connecting flights alone equal fourteen hours. And then there's the time difference. And the language barrier. Okay, not the last part. But I hear the food's terrible."

Emma cracked a smile. "You'll be with Bryce. Food will be the last thing on your mind."

"It seems too good to be true," Angel said. "Several nights overseas with a guy you've had a crush on all your life."

"A nice guy who just had his pride trampled," Chrissy said.

"I don't like Kathryn, but I'm even less fond of seeing a good man like Bryce humiliated," Angel said.

"At least she dumped him in private instead of at the altar," Emma said. "It could have been worse."

"It doesn't matter when or where a person breaks your heart," Georgie said. "It hurts all the same. I should know. I've lost count of the times I've been the victim of romantic assault."

"Romantic assault." Emma snorted. "That's a new one."

"From what Bryce told Mason," Chrissy said, "his heart wasn't all that involved."

"This trip. You and Bryce. It was meant to be," Bella said, because Bella always spouted romantic clichés.

"A win-win," Emma said with a nod. "Either Bryce will realize how amazing you are and fall head over heels or you'll discover he works your last nerve on an intimate day-to-day and fall out of love."

Georgie peered over her shoulder. The bathroom door was still firmly shut, but another woman could walk in at any minute. She didn't want anyone to catch them gossiping about Bryce's misfortune although she knew full well the majority of the guests were, at the very least, whispering amongst themselves. Since the guest list consisted of Bryce's family and friends and a few of the club's employees, she doubted anyone was alerting the media. Regardless, by tomorrow morning the whole of Nowhere would know about the ditched groom, his runaway bride, and his last-minute traveling companion.

"I'm not in love with Bryce," Georgie whispered, "but I confess I've never really gotten over him."

"How is there a difference?" Chrissy asked just as her phone dinged. She peeked at the text. "Mason's looking for me. Mel wants to sit in with the band."

Melody was six-years-old and profoundly deaf, yet Mason and Chrissy—both talented musicians—had encouraged her love of dancing by helping her to focus on visuals as well as the vibrations of loudly cranked music. Watching Mel perform with her LED tambourine was a delight. Watching Chrissy and Mason perform with their daughter, seeing the love and joy in their eyes and hearing it in their music as they channeled their daughter's creative passion was exactly the kind of thing Georgie yearned to experience.

"I hate to miss one of your performances," Georgie said, "but I should get home. I have to pack. We're leaving tomorrow morning." Feeling woozy with wonder, she palmed her forehead. "I can't believe this is happening."

"If anyone deserves a vacation from reality," Angel said as she pulled Georgie in for a group hug, "it's you."

"Take pictures and journal your adventures," Bella said.

"Keep us posted via Party-Line," Chrissy said.

"Have lots of fun," Angel said.

"And lots of sex," Emma added.

"Bryce doesn't think of me in that way," Georgie said.

"Cram your suitcase with dresses like the one you're

wearing now," Chrissy said, "and he will."

"You know I don't own any more dresses like this."

"I do," Angel said. She hooked Georgie's arm and zipped past the stalls. "If we hurry we can sneak out before Melody takes the stage."

"Don't you mean before Ryan asks you to dance again?" Bella asked with a smile in her voice.

Georgie glanced at Angel who'd gone all red in the face. "Ryan asked you to dance?"

"She blew him off," Chrissy said.

"Wiser than tempting fate," Angel said.

Emma squawked like a chicken.

Angel flipped her the bird.

Georgie smiled as they skirted the dance floor and made their escape. Angel and her brother?

And just when she thought things couldn't get better.

Four

Once upon a jinxed ~~journal~~ journey...

FROM THE HEART OF ANGEL DRAKE
MONDAY, JUNE 15

Where to begin?

I've never kept a diary. I've never felt comfortable committing my innermost thoughts to paper. What if my musings, worries, and gripes fell into someone else's hands? Some things are better left unsaid. Or should I say unwritten? Especially if they'd hurt someone's feelings. I would never want to hurt someone's feelings. Most especially the feelings of someone I love.

Or in this case, the feelings of someone I could love—maybe—if I'd open myself up to the possibility.

I don't want to risk that. I won't risk that. Every man I have loved, every man who loved me... died. I've lost two husbands now and I'm only thirty-one. People whisper that I'm cursed. They joke that kissing me is the kiss of death. That jest was never meant to reach my ears, but it did. And it hurts because sometimes—on my darkest days—it feels true.

See what I mean about some things being better left

unsaid?

The good people, and they are good—mostly—of Nowhere didn't mean to make me self-conscious or superstitious, but they did. That's why I wouldn't dance with ~~Ryan~~ him. I can't go there. I won't go there. Not worth the risk.

Anyway, I'm rambling. Although, according to Sinjun, rambling is part of the process. Freethinking. Self-discovery.

"Journaling," she said, "is an ancient tradition and purported to have a positive impact on one's physical and emotional being."

Lately, I've been feeling confused and frustrated and a little, okay a lot, depressed. So I'm giving this journaling thing a crack and hoping no one ever discovers my... freethinking. My unfiltered thoughts and feelings, the ones I'd rather not share with the Inseparables. My friends have worried about me, consoled and supported me, enough for three lifetimes. They don't need to know I'm struggling.

I was doing pretty well until Chrissy slipped and mentioned ~~Ryan, Georgie's brother~~, he had a thing for me. That was almost a year ago. I was cutting her hair, giving her a makeover. She was nervous so I poured her a glass of wine, which might have loosened her tongue. We were talking about...him...and how...he...was having a tough time breaking off with his two-timing flake of a wife. I misunderstood something Chrissy said. I thought maybe she had the hots for ~~Ryan~~ him because most women in the county do. Yes, he has the man-in-uniform thing going for him but he's also handsome and down-to-earth and faithful. And, yeah, he's sexy. Alpha-sexy. Except Chrissy made it clear she only thinks of Ryan as a friend.

"Besides," she said, "he's too wrapped up in you and... Oh, shit."

Yup. There it was. The slip.

Ryan McClure has a thing for me? Since when? I wanted to ask, only I didn't. Better left unsaid. I'd rather not know.

Chrissy begged me to forget "the slip". I told her I'd try, but that hasn't been going well. Mostly—thanks to keeping myself insanely busy—I don't think about it. Unless I see him—like I did yesterday at Bryce's ~~lucky escape~~ canceled *wedding—then it's <u>all</u> I can think about.*

Speaking of Bryce... I'm feeling a little guilty about... No. I'm not going to write it. This is between ~~Sinjun~~ me and my conscience. I'll just trust that, in this instance, fate needed a little shove. Like Bella, I truly believe Bryce and Georgie would make a wonderful match. I just hope they fare better than me and Eddie (my first husband) and me and Baxter (my second husband). Fate cheated us of time and them of their lives. Which is why ~~Ryan~~ <u>he</u> and I will never be a "we".

Yours truly,
Angel Kane-Barnes-Drake

Five

Once upon a Trans-Atlantic disaster...
Jolly Old England

Georgie didn't know she was scared of flying until the plane's wheels left the runway. She didn't know she was prone to airsickness until they hit turbulence. She didn't know she was overly sensitive to motion-sickness medication until Bryce tried waking her to deplane.

It took several shakes and a lot of coaxing, or so he told her. She didn't remember much about disembarking. She was too sluggish. Too scattered. She could scarcely latch onto who or where she was and her limbs felt weirdly detached. She fumbled several apologies as Bryce half carried her through Heathrow Airport, explaining she was ill, not drunk, as they vied for their luggage then went through customs. She wilted in relief as he poured her into a big black taxi. She sighed with contentment as he settled in beside her. She must've conked out—again—because the next thing she knew she was staring at the back of a worn leather seat. Her head was in Bryce's lap and she was drooling on his pant leg.

Oh, God.

Georgie (ah, yes, *that* was her name) blinked and winced—her dry lids scraping over her bleary eyeballs, her mushy brain clearing just enough to remember three things.

She'd spent the first third of the twelve-hour flight battling extreme anxiety, the second third puking into an airsick bag or the teeny toilet in the tiny lavatory, and the last third zonked out on exhaustion and meds.

The only thing that would have made that flight more hellish was if they had crashed into the Atlantic Ocean.

Although death was quite possibly preferable to Georgie's present state. She felt like a zombie. A nauseous, hungover, jetlagged, mortified zombie.

"Sorry," she croaked as she forced herself upright. Averting her gaze, she palmed her clammy brow and licked her dry, tingling lips. "I'd kill for mouthwash and a bed."

"Fortunately, you won't have to go to that extreme," Bryce teased. "We're at the hotel."

Georgie peered out the window as Bryce paid the cabbie or whatever they were called over here. She'd missed the drive into London—the English countryside, her first glimpse of the historical city and any one of its famous landmarks. Had they passed Buckingham Palace, Big Ben, or Parliament? Even now she was too nauseous and out-of-sorts to appreciate the old buildings, the festive park, and the flurry of traffic and pedestrians. The sooner she escaped into her hotel room, the sooner she could recover in private. She didn't want to think about the embarrassment and hassle she'd caused Bryce, otherwise she might cry. And wouldn't that be icing on the non-wedding cake?

A bellman took their luggage and Georgie shielded her eyes from the bright sun. What time was it anyway? She felt like she'd lost an entire day. She knew she'd lost a good portion of the night—passed out in a first-class seat like a low-class lush.

"Good morning, Mr. and Mrs. Morgan and welcome to the Stratford Royal, the premiere boutique hotel in Leicester Square. Check-in is normally two pm, but happily the Royal Suite is available now. If you'd—"

"Excuse me," Bryce said, pulling Georgie into his side when she swayed on her feet.

Georgie palmed her brow, trying to ignore a dull headache, trying to focus on the sharp-dressed clerk. *Mr. and Mrs.? A suite?*

"I called late Sunday and altered the reservations," Bryce

said to the cordial, young man.

"Yes, sir. I see, sir. You requested the Royal Suite instead of the Bridal Suite. An excellent modification, by the way, as the view—"

"No. I requested two rooms. Separate rooms."

The clerk looked up from his computer terminal. "Separate rooms for you and your wife? I... That is..."

"I have an email confirmation." Bryce pulled out his phone and located the message.

The clerk scanned Bryce's screen. "Curious. I'm not seeing that exchange on our end." Then he looked back to his own monitor, tapped the keyboard and frowned. "I'm terribly sorry, Mr. Morgan, we have no other vacancies at this time and I dare say you and your wife will have difficulty obtaining similar lodging in the vicinity. There are several on-going festivals and—"

The man broke off and Georgie realized she'd groaned—out loud. She no doubt looked as awful as she felt, which would account for the sympathetic look on—she squinted at his nametag—*Malcom's* face.

Mr. and Mrs. Morgan. You and your wife.

Before Georgie could wrangle the words to set the clerk right, Bryce interceded. "We'll take the suite."

Going with the flow took a lot less energy than making a fuss. Georgie wanted a bed and she wanted it now, even if that bed was a sofa.

A short elevator ride and a long walk down the hall later and Georgie was almost in heaven. While Bryce tipped the bellman, she made a wobbly beeline toward the plush cream-colored couch which was just on the other side of the massive bed with the plum satiny bedcovers. The awful taste in her mouth prompted a detour. She angled into the bathroom—a room of horrors, thanks to a mirrored wall.

Georgie blinked at her full-length appearance—in all its shocking disarray—and burst into tears.

Swollen bloodshot eyes, smudged mascara, dried, crusty something on a hank of her messy hair. Her lips were puffy. Her complexion was waxy. Instead of her strappy sandals, she was wearing pink crocheted slippers. Red wine stained the flounce of her sundress and she'd misbuttoned her sweater.

She'd walked through Heathrow Airport looking like this? Bryce had seen her like this? Even worse were the fragments of memories tumbling back in mortifying Technicolor clarity.

"What the..." Bryce moved in behind her, looking concerned but one-hundred percent composed in his jeans and short-sleeved polo. No muss. No stains. He needed a shave, but instead of looking unkempt, he looked sexy. "What is it?" he asked. "What's wrong?"

Unable to bear their polar-opposite reflections, Georgie buried her face in her hands. "I'm a mess."

"You don't travel well, that's a fact."

"You saw me throw up."

"I partied with ball players, hon. I own a bar. I've seen lots of people hurl."

"On your boots?"

"That was new, but they cleaned up fine."

"Unlike me."

"You'll feel better after a shower. Or maybe a bath. Look there's some complimentary bubble stuff. Doesn't that sound good? A hot bubble bath?"

Georgie sleeved away tears and sniffed back snot. She risked meeting Bryce's gaze in the mirror and couldn't decide whether to be relieved or ticked that he was fighting a grin. "I bet you're sorry you invited me on this trip."

He squeezed her drooping shoulder. "You'd lose that bet." Then he passed her the bottle of bubble stuff and left her to her miserable lonesome.

* * *

Bryce didn't make it to the pros by second guessing himself. His gut and intellect made a killer team. His heart was the rogue player that occasionally wreaked havoc—mostly on his finances, but sometimes on his state-of-mind.

At the moment, he was staring at the closed bathroom door wishing he'd suggested a cold bracing shower instead of a soothing hot bath. What if Georgie fell asleep and slid under the water? Considering the calamity of events that had transpired thus far, it was damn well possible.

He knocked.

"Yes?"

"Are you in the tub?"

"Yes."

"I'm cracking open the door."

"Why?"

"I'm worried you'll fall asleep."

"And drown?" She barked a pathetic laugh. "Something tells me fate wouldn't be so kind."

He knew she was joking, still. "I'm opening the door."

"All right. But don't peek in."

"Wouldn't dream of it." Although maybe he would—*dream of it*, Georgie naked and neck deep in frothy bubbles—because he'd been surprisingly and annoyingly aware of her in a sensual sense from the moment he'd seen her in that red dress and heels.

Even though he'd been distracted by his home situation, that awareness had dogged him through the flight. He couldn't fathom how he could be sexually attracted to a woman who'd retched on his boots. Then again, he'd been off his game for weeks. Since learning about his sister and, even more so, his new role as guardian.

"Are you still there?" Georgie asked.

Bryce leaned against the door-frame and massaged his throbbing temples. "Yeah."

"Me, too," she said then gave another little snort. "It'll take more than medicated jetlag to fell Georgina Lou Poppins."

His lip twitched. "Glad to hear it." At least one of them was feeling better. Bryce was struggling with a truckload of guilt. The crux of his unease had been a mystery until midway over the Atlantic. The epiphany filled him with shame. He'd duped himself into thinking he felt bad about leaving the twins for a week. What he really felt was relief.

"About the suite," Georgie called out. "I'm sorry about the screw-up."

"Me, too. I don't know what happened."

"I just want you to know, if it's less of a hassle—financially and convenience wise—I don't mind sharing a room. I mean it's plenty big and I don't mind sleeping on the couch. Honest."

"If anyone sleeps on the couch, it'll be me." What was he saying? They weren't going to share a room. His goal had been to get Georgie settled—the woman needed to crash—and then to revisit Malcom and this rooming situation. The Stratford Royal had screwed up—royally—not him. There had to be a solution. "You almost done in there?"

"Would you please stop hovering? I'm trying to wash my hair and you're making me self-conscious. The sooner you leave me alone, the sooner—"

"Got it." At least she was talking coherently which was more than he could say a short while ago. "I'm stepping away to call Arlo. I don't know if you remember me telling you or not, but I already sent a message to Ryan letting him know we arrived safely."

"I, um...That part's fuzzy. Thank you."

"Want me to message one of the girls?"

"No, thank you. I'll do it when I get out, which is taking longer than anticipated."

"The hovering thing. Right." Bryce stepped away and crossed the spacious room, feeling confident Georgie was no longer in danger of sliding into sudsy oblivion.

He sat on the sofa, pulled off his boots and stretched out his legs. His damn knee throbbed like a mother. Massaging the ache, he focused on a plan. He'd check in with Arlo then, after he saw the whites of Georgie's emerald eyes, he'd head back to the front desk.

Arlo answered on the first ring.

"Sitting on the phone?" Bryce teased.

"Don't be a smartass, boy. Just glad to know you got there safe. You at the airport or the hotel?"

"The hotel." Bryce didn't elaborate. "How you making out with the kids?"

"Fair to middlin'. Chelsea's afraid of dogs. How you makin' out with Georgie?"

"Fair to middlin'. Georgie's afraid of flying."

"Did she scream in terror and try to squeeze under a chair?"

"No."

"You're one up on me then. Mason and Chrissy brought their little girl over for, what did they call it? A play date," Arlo said. "Brought their dog, too."

"Rush," Bryce said. A scraggly huge, but gentle, mutt.

"What kid doesn't love dogs?"

"Chelsea." Bryce squeezed the bridge of his nose. His niece was a skinny little thing with wide brown eyes and pale blond hair. She was skittish of just about everything. Including Bryce.

Instead of winning her over, he'd retreated to London. He'd told her he was coming back, but she didn't believe him. He'd seen it in her wary eyes. Given the revolving door of "uncles" in her history, Bryce couldn't blame her skepticism.

Disgusted with himself, he stood and limped to the window. "This trip was a bad idea."

"Ain't how I see it."

Instinctively, Bryce knew he'd be better off sitting for this one. He bypassed the sofa and dropped on the bed.

"I need you to do your grievin' away from these kids, son."

Bryce frowned. "Are you talking about Marla?"

"Marla. Kathryn. But mostly the loss of your freedom."

"If you mean the twins—"

"They're the tipping point, but by no means the root of it. Resentment's been simmering in you for years. Life's served you some blows, Bryce, and you've taken it on the chin. Or so you want the world to believe. It was fine when it was just you and me, but now it ain't. Bottom line," he said voice low. "You can't expect Chelsea and Charlie to accept you as a father-figure when you don't want the job."

"What the..." Coldcocked, Bryce fell back on the bed and caught his breath. "Don't you think that's a little harsh?"

"Show Georgie a good time," Arlo said. "She deserves it. Have some fun—if you remember how—and get your head straight about the future. If you want a second chance at a career in sports then grow some balls and go for it. We'll work out the family situation from there. Besides, we won't be alone now. We've got Georgie, right?"

"Right." Bryce noted the sound of a hair dryer. Georgie. Out of the tub, on dry land, and in the safety zone. The tension in his shoulders eased even as his headache raged. "Just so you know. Your pep talks could use some work, old man."

"I've been thinking on this a while. Wonderin' why you'd marry a woman with a stick so far up her ass—"

"Can we leave Kathryn out of this?"

"Gladly."

"We done here?"

"Yup."

"Call me if you need me."

"Yup."

Tossing aside the phone, Bryce stared at the ceiling. Reeling, the blow dryer lulled him into a trance like a rolling ocean of white noise. He felt himself succumbing to the long, harried travel day. He felt his world closing in and falling apart. He felt like a world-class bastard because Arlo was right. Part of him resented the new role of "dad". The timing couldn't be worse. Just as he was on the cusp of getting back in the game, albeit in a different way.

His knee twinged along with his conscience.

"Damn."

Six

Georgie woke with a start.

The room was tar black and she wasn't alone.

A man was in her bed and she was entangled with said man. The only thing that kept her from totally freaking was that she had him pinned with her arm and leg and not vice versa.

Who... What...

Her heart raced and her brain glitched. Disoriented. Woozy. Was she drunk? Hungover?

Not my room. Not my bed.

Then it hit her.

London. Hotel. Bryce.

Oh, no.

Face hot, Georgie tried to shift without waking her traveling partner.

"Welcome to the land of the living," Bryce said close to her ear.

She froze—partially out of embarrassment. Partially because his voice was deep and sexy and rumbled through her body like a vibrating sex toy. "I assure you this—me being in bed with you," she said as she scooted away, "is purely innocent."

"Never thought otherwise."

He meant that as a compliment. She got that. Plus, she had assured him she no longer harbored a crush. Still, it would have been nice if he'd voiced some sort of concern, suggesting her intimate proximity was somehow potent. As it was, she felt about as sexy as a ragdoll. A ragdoll with morning breath. *Eww.*

Her first thought was to escape into the bathroom—brush her teeth, comb her ratty hair—but that would mean leaving this bed. And Bryce. Rather than risk breaking this intimate moment, Georgie grappled for the breath fresheners she'd placed on the nightstand alongside her phone. She popped a brisk candy then passed the roll to Bryce, hoping he didn't take offense. "Mint?"

"Sure."

His fingers brushed hers. Zap. She imagined his hands gliding over her body...and flushed fifty shades of red. She stared into the dark, fantasizing about Bryce—naked—and wondering what floated his boat. A submissive partner? A bold dominatrix? Dirty talk? Sweet talk?

"You were out cold," she blurted. "What if I said I crawled into bed to take advantage of you? You know, sexually."

"I'd say I don't believe you. I venture sex was the last thing on your mind when you saw this big, comfy bed."

Georgie sighed. Sad, but true.

When she'd emerged from the bathroom in her totally non-sexy lounge wear, Bryce had been deep asleep—stretched out in his clothes, looking gorgeous, but mostly peaceful. She'd headed for the couch, but the bed—with its huge mattress and puffy pillows had beckoned.

Even though he was a tall, broad-shouldered man, Bryce only took up a modest region of that king-sized mattress. Georgie had settled softly on the opposite side. She hadn't even wriggled beneath the covers. She'd simply stifled a sigh of contentment while drifting into an exhausted slumber.

"I figured there was enough room for the both of us," she said.

"You figured right."

"I mean you were way over there and I was clear over here. I don't know how I ended up on top of you."

"It's a mystery."

Cloaked in darkness, she couldn't read his expression, but

he sounded amused. "Are you laughing at me?"

"Smiling because you're flustered. It's cute."

Cute? Great.

"It's not a big deal," he said. "You were dead to the world. I hated to disturb you."

Dead to the world. Dead weight. This just got better and better. She'd probably drooled on his shirt as well.

"Feeling refreshed?" he asked.

"Feeling weird."

"Like your brain's disconnected from your body?"

"Something like that." She popped a second mint.

"Fifteen hours—all tallied—travel. Jet lag. Time change. I'm feeling it, too."

"What time is it anyway?" Georgie asked as she fumbled her phone. "Oh, no. Ten-oh-five? At night?" She bolted upright. "We lost a whole day of sightseeing! I'm so sorry."

"Hey, I crashed, too." He caught her elbow and tugged her back on the bed. "Slow down. Relax. And stop apologizing for everything."

Her head hit the pillow and she sighed. "But this trip had to cost a fortune and so far I've made it memorable for all the wrong reasons. Also, I'm starting to feel guilty about gallivanting across Europe when I can't even pay my bills. I feel especially guilty about Mr. Jones. When I called him to tell him I'd be out of the country for a week, he didn't ask, "Where's my back rent?" He said, "Have a good time." And he meant it.

"If I'd been thinking straight," she went on, "I would have said no to this trip and stayed behind to pack up a week ahead of schedule. The sooner I move out, the sooner Mr. Jones can initiate repairs on the cottage. The sooner he can sell the property."

"First of all, I wouldn't call this gallivanting and London doesn't constitute the whole of Europe. Second, I'll advance you the money to pay Mr. Jones. We'll take care of it in the morning."

"I don't feel right about that."

"I do. And I need to feel good about something. You're not the only one wrestling with guilt."

Georgie's stomach dropped. She'd worried this would happen. "You're feeling bad about Kathryn."

"Feeling worse about Chelsea and Charlie."

Georgie blinked into the darkness. "About leaving them behind?"

"About not wanting to be their dad."

Surely she'd heard wrong.

"I can't believe I said that out loud. Let me rephrase. I'm not crazy about being a single parent." The mattress dipped as he rolled away with a groan. "Like that sounded any better." He flicked a switch and flooded the room with soft amber lighting. "Something about the dark... confessing ones sins... Maybe I'll shut up now. Otherwise you'll think even less of me than you do right now."

Heart pounding, Georgie frowned as Bryce gave her his back. She reached out and nabbed the hem of his shirt, thwarting his escape. "Not so fast. You can't say something like that and leave me hanging."

She released her hold when he dropped to the edge of the bed and dragged his hands through his messy hair. Keeping her distance, she infused her tone with firm compassion. "I've known you all my life, Bryce. You're a good man who's weathered a lot of bad. These past weeks alone have been a doozy. Even though you and Marla were estranged, I know you mourn her passing. You never even knew you had a niece and nephew and yet when you were informed, you flew across the country to bring them home to the Morgan ranch. To you and Arlo. To family. You told me you already initiated the paperwork for official guardianship. I saw your face and manner on Sunday when you talked to the twins after Kathryn called off the wedding. I know you care about them."

"They're blood. Innocents. Of course I care."

"Then what's the problem? The single parent thing? Or your single status, period?"

When he didn't answer, Georgie mused in the silence. "Did Kathryn break off because of Chelsea and Charlie? Was she unwilling to accept another woman's children as her own or did she resent the fact that it wouldn't be just you and her? She struck me as career oriented. Did she worry the twins would put a kink in her goals? Her lifestyle?"

"Yes."

"To what?"

"To everything."

Georgie frowned at the back of his head, the tense set of his shoulders. Bryce was famous for being closed-mouthed about his personal problems. She hated prying except she suspected he needed to vent. Maybe if she shut off the light.

She did just that then sat next to him—on the bed, in the dark.

"What are you doing?" he asked.

"Expediting this confession so we can go out for a late dinner. I'm starving." Bryce, like her brother, Ryan, was a tough cookie. Coddling wouldn't cut it, so tough love it was. "Did Kathryn ask you to choose between her and the children?"

"No."

"Because she knew you'd choose the kids," Georgie guessed. "Which means you do want them but you're bitter because they cost you the woman you love."

"I don't love Kathryn."

Georgie's heart bumped. That was a relief for a couple of reasons, but puzzling. "Then why did you ask her to marry you?"

"I didn't. She asked me."

Suggesting Kathryn loved him. *Enough to breech protocol, but not enough to make sacrifices?* "If you don't love her," Georgie figured if she said it enough times maybe she'd believe it, "why did you say, yes?"

"Weak moment. Selfish motivations." He shifted and, even though she couldn't make out his expression, Georgie felt the intensity of his stare. "I didn't realize how much I missed being submersed in the world of sports until I dipped my toes back in those waters. Kathryn navigates those waters."

Georgie could scarcely breathe. Maybe her close proximity didn't spark his interest, but his nearness set her senses ablaze. "Are you saying you were using Kathryn to...to what? Land a job on a sports show? Like an advisor or a sportscaster?"

"Seems like."

Not an attractive admission yet Georgie was attracted all the same. "Are you sure you don't love her? Maybe you're just ticked at her for jilting you. Maybe the jetlag messed with your senses. I can't believe you'd marry someone just to get back in the limelight. It's not you, Bryce."

"I don't love her, Georgie. I could kiss you right now and I wouldn't feel a lick of guilt."

"Are you sure?"

It was a rhetorical question—her head was spinning—but he took it literally. He kissed her—on the bed, in the dark. Not just a brush of the lips, but a melding of mouths and a hint of minty tongue.

Oh, my God. Oh, my God.

He eased away and it was all she could do not to follow.

"Feeling guilty?" she squeaked in the uncomfortable silence.

"No. But I'm thinking you're right about the jetlag messing with my senses." He reached around her and switched on the light. "Sorry about that."

"Don't be." Not wanting him to know she had a case of screaming thigh sweats, she feigned nonchalance and smiled. "Hungry?"

"Yeah."

Bryce held her gaze a little too long—just long enough to infuse Georgie with a sliver of hope. *Holy guacamole*, she thought as he excused himself to take a shower. Was he finally seeing her as a woman, a potential lover—and not as the little sister of his friend?

Georgie forced her tingling body upright, moving toward her suitcase in order to dress for a late dinner. With Bryce. Who'd just kissed her—on the bed, in the dark.

It was all she could do not to contact the Inseparables via Party-Line, their social media of choice. As much as she wanted to dish about that kiss—a kiss she'd dreamt about for years—it seemed like a breach of etiquette given Bryce had been in confession mode. Still her senses buzzed and her heart danced as she rifled through the clothes she'd borrowed from Angel.

Bryce didn't love Kathryn.

He was conflicted about his profession. He was conflicted about the twins.

But he didn't love Kathryn.

Georgie flashed on Impossible Dream.com. To the stock phrase included in emails received by both Bella and Chrissy when they'd been notified of their match.

Georgie hadn't gotten an email like that. But this trip, this opportunity with Bryce and the connected nanny gig, had to be a result of ID-dot-com's magic, right? This was the very thing she'd applied for. Her Impossible Dream. All she had to do was go for it, right?

She had an arsenal of derring-do—just one of the ID stipulations. Joining Bryce in the shower could be her first bold feat. She'd do it, too, except she sensed the timing was off.

She was a little short on patience—another stipulation—but she'd suck it up.

For once in her life, she felt like she was in the right place at the right time. With Bryce.

This, Georgie thought as she wiggled into butt-hugging jeans, *is my moment to shine*.

Seven

Bryce greeted the next day with a hard-on and a hangover. The hard-on compliments of the woman sleeping next to him. The hangover compliments of overindulging in an effort to dull his awareness of the woman sleeping next to him.

Georgie had surprised him with her easy, flirty banter over their late-night dinner. She'd wowed him with a sheer blouse and tight jeans that rivaled the low-cut dress she'd worn to his fiasco wedding. She'd charmed him with her beauty and wit. Her empathy and tolerance.

He was especially raw after admitting his reluctance to play dad to the twins. She'd somehow twisted his shameful confession into an honest apprehension. A fear of fumbling the responsibility. He didn't buy it, not completely, but he appreciated her faith in his innate goodness.

The longer they sat in that crowded pub discussing everything from their past jobs to their impending sightseeing agenda, the more Bryce succumbed to a mounting attraction. How could he have known Georgie all his life and not really know her at all?

Still. The urge to bury himself in all that sexy goodness was untimely and unwise for multiple reasons. Numbing his desire with too many ales had been a quick fix with unpleasant aftereffects.

Laying stock still as dawn filtered through a crack in the

hotel curtains, Bryce cursed his pulsing temples and the stabbing pain behind his bleary eyeballs.

He'd never been much of a drinker. Not even in his younger days. Alcohol muddled his judgment and reflexes and he'd always wanted to be sharp. For the game. For his parents. They already had one alcoholic in the family. Bryce had caught Marla sneaking booze when she was thirteen. That had been the start of their splintered relationship—big brother cracking down on little sister and little sister responding with equal doses of apathy and rebellion.

The last time Bryce had seen Marla she'd been twenty-two and wasted on vodka and crack. He'd tried talking her into rehab. Instead she'd left town and cut ties with the family.

A few years later, after his ball career had been cut short, he'd invested in the Coyote Club. Hawking booze wasn't his preference or his dream but it had made sense at the time. Now, especially in light of Marla's substance abuse related death, his role as bar owner weighed heavier on his shoulders by the day.

Just one of his current conflicts.

Careful not to wake Georgie, Bryce eased out of bed and escaped into the bathroom in search of aspirin and a bracing shower. Immediate remedies for poor choices and randy dreams. If only there was a miracle cure for a freaking pain-in-the-ass life crisis.

* * *

"What do you think?"

"I can't decide which is more impressive," Georgie said. "The London Eye or Big Ben." From their vantage point on the walking path alongside the Thames, she could see both of the iconic landmarks in all their majestic wonder.

The London Eye, Europe's largest Ferris wheel—a breathtaking ultra-modern ride also known as the Millennium Wheel—sat on the South Bank of the River Thames. Big Ben—historically known as the Clock Tower—rose high on the North Bank, bumped up against Parliament and just across the street from Westminster Abbey. A veritable cornucopia of cross-century architecture and legendary splendor.

Emma would be in her glory.

Vying for a prime position, Georgie took her bazillionth picture of the day. Later she'd post them on Party-Line, allowing the Inseparables to live vicariously through an assortment of cyber postcards. Maybe if she posted numerous stunning photos, her friends would bombard her with questions pertaining to the sights rather than prodding for juice about Bryce.

She still couldn't believe he'd kissed her.

She couldn't believe they'd slept together. Granted sharing a bed had been platonic, but it still gave Georgie a thrill...and hope. That lone brief kiss had verified a spark.

"Where there's a spark, there's potential wildfire," she could hear Emma say.

This morning, although Bryce had showered and dressed before she'd even stirred, he hadn't revisited the possibility of booking a second room. Instead of opening that can of worms, Georgie ignored it, assuming he'd resigned himself to sharing the suite...and the bed. Fine by her. She liked his company. She liked him. Even if sex wasn't in their future, there was something heady about their budding chemistry. Something that revitalized her flagging self-esteem.

Georgie tingled as Bryce caught her hand, guiding her through the thick of pedestrians. She could live off of this buzz for a long, long time.

"According to the guide book," he said, "because of the time of year we'll be fighting massive crowds, but if you don't mind a long wait, we'll squeeze in as much as we can before dinner."

"I don't mind the wait," Georgie said, "but do you think we could sit for a second? Soak in some of the wonder at a more leisurely pace?"

When Bryce's knee wasn't acting up, his stride was long and fast. Today his knee was fine and they'd been on the go since breakfast. They'd walked a good hour around Piccadilly Circus and Trafalgar Square before hopping one of those red double-decker buses for a city tour. Lunch in Covent Gardens. A scenic walk along Victoria Embankment, which had led them here. The frantic pace hadn't allowed for much talking—other than to comment on the sites.

Aside from needing a second wind, Georgie had a lot of questions about the twins and a small dose of anxiety about moving into the Morgan home as their nanny. Temporary or not, whatever time she spent with Charlie and Chelsea would make an impression. Whatever impact she made, she wanted it to be good. It was impossible to fully relax and enjoy this trip when her head was in Nowhere, sifting through memories of Marla Morgan and contemplating her children's issues.

How touchy would Bryce be about Marla's addictions and promiscuity? Was it even Georgie's place to go down that road? Would she ruin what had so far been a perfect day by introducing a subject that so obviously pained him?

"I know it's clichéd to talk about the weather," she said as they settled on a bench with a view, "but I thought it rained all the time in England."

"Not all the time. Just a lot of the time."

Georgie tucked her windblown hair behind her ears and tilted her face toward the clear, blue sky. "According to the weather forecast we're in for a week of sunshine and warm temps. I guess we lucked out."

"Guess so." Bryce glanced at her over the rims of his shades. "You really want to talk about the weather or is this a segue?"

"It's a warm up."

"For what?"

"Conversation. You're not much of a talker."

"But I'm a hell of a listener."

"Part of what makes you a good bar owner. I bet you hear all kinds of things at Coyote's."

He raised a brow. "You wondering about something in particular?"

"Just wondering how you'll feel when you overhear people talking about this? Us. In England. Together. On your honeymoon." Okay. This wasn't where she'd meant to steer this conversation, but now that she was here...

"Depends."

"On what?"

"On what they say."

"I don't expect they'll say anything too bad. Not to our faces anyway. Everyone likes you."

"Everyone likes you, too. 'Cept maybe Tom Rhodes."

Georgie scrunched her nose. "Why do you think that is?"

"You didn't sleep with him, remember?"

"No, I mean, why do you think people like me? What makes me special?" She could name at least three qualities that made Bella popular with the community. The same went for Chrissy, Angel, and Emma. "I'm not fishing for compliments," she said as she stumbled off track. "I'm just curious. Because mostly I feel like a screw up. Sort of like my mom."

Oh, crap. Did I say that out loud?

Bryce reached over and squeezed her hand. "You're nothing like Erica. You're a hard worker. Responsible and independent. You didn't run to Ryan when the bills piled up. You toughed it out. Considered alternate living arrangements. Applied for a dream job that could take you God knows where away from friends and family. You sure about that, by the way?"

Georgie didn't answer straight away. She was too transfixed by the feel of Bryce's warm hand wrapped around her fingers and the flecks of gold in his sexy, brown eyes. At some point, he'd slipped off his sunglasses, clipping them over the crew neck of his gray *Huskers* t-shirt. A well-worn, short-sleeved tee that showed off his tanned, muscular arms. Not overly beefed-up biceps, but toned from years of heavy-duty workouts and throwing a bullet-fast football.

"I, uh... What was the question?"

"That dream nanny job. What if it takes you to a place like this?" He jerked his chin toward the crowded skyline and hordes of pedestrians. "Would you want to live in a big city? A foreign city?"

"I'm not sure." She didn't think so, but... "I guess it depends."

"On what?"

The man. "The family."

He mulled that over, angled his head. "Seems to me a beautiful young woman would want to start her own family rather than looking after someone else's. Don't you want babies of your own?"

Did he just call her beautiful? And mention babies? Her ovaries fairly wept. Her libido revved. "Sure," she said, disguising her jitters with a teasing smile. "Know where I can find a warm and willing husband in the next three minutes?"

He smiled at that. "Any man would be lucky to have you, Lou."

Her childhood nickname. *Damn.* "Tell that to the bachelors of Dawes County. I've dated most of them and fell for more than half. Not that I'm promiscuous," she added. "Just perpetually optimistic. About love. Or at least I was." She squirmed and looked away. "But I'm over that eternal-true-love, happily-ever-after hooey. I'm all about happy-for-now."

"That so?"

"Yup." She didn't dare meet his gaze. Instead she used her phone and snapped a shot of the futuristic Ferris wheel and its gigantic, transparent passenger capsules.

"Those lines aren't getting any shorter," Bryce said, as he pulled her to her feet.

And just like that they were back in tourist mode—her chance to ask about the twins shot and her attraction to Bryce stoked.

* * *

Insomnia was a bitch.

Bad enough that his brain wouldn't shut down, but Bryce had a bone daddy that rivaled Clock Tower. For the third time in two days, he'd crawled into bed with Georgie. Strictly platonic. Although not without steely effort and a raging case of blue balls.

At least tonight, he hadn't overindulged at dinner. And later, after the concert they'd both enjoyed, he'd nursed one Guinness for a full hour.

Good news: He wouldn't suffer a hangover.

Bad news: His senses were sharp and trained on Georgie Poppins.

What the hell was wrong with him? As of three days ago, he'd been engaged to another woman. True, he didn't love Kathryn. Not in the eternal-true-love sense Georgie had mentioned earlier. But he had feelings for the clever, sexy producer with the (sometimes) killer smile. Their relationship had been based on sex, but they'd also had mutual interests and qualities. Kathryn was smart and interesting, definitely fun. She was quietly self-absorbed and obsessed with being in charge. They were—in almost every sense—compatible. And she circulated in a world—a sport—that he missed like a severed limb. Kathryn had crossed his mind more than once today—even though Georgie had monopolized his thoughts.

Was Kathryn battling regret? Wishing she'd gone through with their marriage or at least pursued an alternate plan based on her new job?

Meanwhile he'd already invited another woman into his bed, so to speak. He'd definitely invited Georgie into his life. When they returned to Nowhere, she'd move to the Morgan ranch to look after the kids and Arlo. They'd cohabitate, except when he traveled for charity. If he indulged in rebound sex it would bite him in the ass because, even though she touted that happy-for-now credo, Georgie was a nice girl. Strike that. *Woman.*

"Are you asleep?" she whispered from the other side of the bed.

Best not to answer. Best to pretend. "Nope." *Damn.*

"Can I ask you a question?"

Shut her down. "Shoot."

He felt the bed dip as she rolled to face him. Bryce didn't move. Just stared up into the dark. *Nuns and puppies. Nuns and puppies.*

"You mentioned Charlie and Chelsea are abnormally quiet," she said. "How much of the time?"

He hadn't anticipated talk of the kids, but it sure as hell dulled the sexual edge. "All the time. Since the moment I picked them up in North Carolina. I haven't heard them laugh once. Or argue or talk back. They don't ask for anything either. Just do what they're told—no fuss. That sound like a typical five-year-old to you?"

"Not really. I assumed they were overwhelmed at the Pajama-Rama event, so it made sense that they were reserved that night. However, I'm surprised they're consistently subdued at the ranch, especially after two weeks."

She paused for a second and Bryce fought the urge to shift closer. God, she smelled good.

"What are their interests?" Georgie asked, jolting him back to the subject at hand. "Do they play? Read? Draw? Sit quietly and stare into space?"

"I don't think they know how to play. Other than electronic games on their tablets."

"They own tablets?"

"I'm thinking Marla or one of her men bought them each one to keep them occupied. They both tend to keep their heads down in electronic games or the television."

Chest heavy, Bryce dragged a hand through his hair. "When I was a kid I was all about playing outdoors—sports, games, swooping skyward on a tire swing, climbing trees, riding horses. Charlie and Chelsea act like their allergic to the sun. Half the time, I think they're allergic to me."

"No social skills?" Georgie asked in a thoughtful tone. "Or do you think they're scared of you specifically?"

"A little of both maybe."

"Do you think they were abused? Physically, I mean."

Bryce hadn't seen any evidence of that. And according to social services, there hadn't been any records to support that scenario. He searched his memory and heart, saying, "No. Marla was a lot of things but she was never cruel or violent. On the other hand, my gut says those kids are strangers to affection and intellectual interaction. I hate to say it, but knowing Marla's addictions and lifestyle, they would have fared better if she'd given them up for adoption."

"Maybe," Georgie said quietly. "But now they have a second chance with you."

His gut cramped with an unwelcome twinge of dread. Of failure. What if they never warmed up to him? What if he did and said all the wrong things? Like he did with Marla?

"We'll figure it out," Georgie said as if reading his mind.

Arlo had said something similar. *"Trust in the team."*

When the going got tough, Kathryn bailed.

Georgie strategized.

Bryce was still at odds with the future. His agenda and goals specifically. But he didn't feel stranded in the end zone.

"Night, Bryce."

He smiled into the dark, resisting the urge to pat a butt cuter than any tight end he'd ever huddled with. "Night, Lou."

Eight

Once upon a non-traditional tradition...
Nowhere, Nebraska

The bad thing about conspiring with one friend to set up another friend for a potentially good thing was "not knowing" whether your meddling helped or backfired.

Angel had conspired with Sinjun (who Bella swore worked for some covert government agency—no one really knew) to tamper with Bryce's hotel reservation. Angel didn't know how she did it, but Sinjun, through some sort of cyber wizardry (aka hacking), altered the records so that one suite—not two rooms—was reserved under Bryce's name. In essence, Angel and Sinjun played matchmaker.

Angel felt a little wonky about their deceitful ploy. But she'd rather see Georgie living her dream in Nowhere with the Morgans (especially Bryce, a man Angel respected and trusted, a man Georgie adored) than some random family in Bumfart, Name-a-Country-Somewhere-Around-the-World.

Just because Impossible Dream had come through in spades for Bella and Chrissy, that didn't mean Georgie would enjoy the same stellar results. Most especially given her crummy run of bad luck. And Georgie—bless her heart—was so desperate, Angel feared she'd jump at anything that

Internet company offered. *If* ID.com ever came through with anything at all.

Going on Bella's theory that Sinjun dabbled in cyber intelligence, Angel had reached out and, although Sinjun had been hesitant, she'd agreed to manipulate those reservations. Georgie and Bryce had been in London for two days now and all Sinjun could tell was that they were indeed booked in that suite under the names Mr. and Mrs. Morgan.

But were they staying together? Or had Bryce booked an additional room at another hotel? If they were staying together, were they sleeping together? Were they hitting it off as a couple or playing it cool as friends? Were they happy? Miserable?

Angel didn't know because she hadn't heard a peep from Georgie other than Georgie checking in after they landed. Sinjun was in the dark as well. The suspense stunk. Did they screw up or did they do a good thing?

Angel hoped dinner with the girls at Café Caboose would distract her from the mystery of Georgie and Bryce, who'd gone off the grid.

She was wrong.

Emma and Chrissy didn't know about Sinjun and Angel's meddling, but they were every bit as curious about Georgie and Bryce.

Angel glanced across the table. "Anything, Chrissy?"

"Nope."

"Emma?"

"Nada."

While waiting for her burger and fries, Angel scrolled through her Party-Line feed, hoping to spy a missed note. Seated next to each other on the opposite side of the booth, Chrissy and Emma did the same. They'd received one group message from Georgie. A brief note letting them know she'd arrived safely in England.

Exhausted. Looking forward to sleep then a ton of sightseeing. More later!

That had been over a day ago and they hadn't heard anything from Georgie since.

"I'm sure she's fine," Emma said.

"She's with Bryce," Chrissy said. "Of course, she's fine. He's one of the most reliable people I know. Besides, if he allowed anything bad to happen to her, Ryan would kick his ass. And we've all seen Ryan kick ass."

"Forget Ryan," Emma said. "If anything bad happened to Georgie, Bryce would have to contend with us. The Inseparables on a rampage? Now that's scary."

Angel didn't want to think about Ryan kicking ass. She didn't want to think about Ryan period. And she certainly didn't want to think about anything bad happening to Georgie. "We're being ridiculous," she said while setting aside her phone. "Georgie hasn't checked in because she's busy having fun." *How's that for thinking positive?*

"Right now she's probably busy sleeping," Chrissy said. "England's six hours ahead of us, right? Over there it's past midnight."

"Unless they're cruising the pubs," Emma said. "That's what I'd be doing. That or having sex. That's if I were on vacation with a hot hunk. Not that Bryce does it for me, but he does it for Georgie. And in their case, we're not only talking vacation sex, we're talking rebound sex, which, in my experience, is hotter than kinky sex."

Angel shushed the wildest of their bunch as the waitress approached with a loaded tray.

"Three Choo-Choo Cheeseburger platters," Laura said as she served their plates. "You ladies should switch up once in a while. Try something different."

"Why?" Emma asked as she reached for the mustard jar. "No one flips burgers better than Russell."

Russell Levitt. The best short-order cook in Dawes County.

Laura Gantry, a long-time, part-time waitress at Café Caboose—the most popular eatery in Nowhere—shrugged as she served three milkshakes and extra spoons. "The Inseparables have been dining here once a week, every week for, what? Fifteen years?"

"Something like that," Chrissy said as she squirted ketchup next to her heap of fries.

"Seems to me you'd get tired of always eating the same thing."

"We experiment with desserts," Angel said. "But Choo-Choo Cheeseburgers are part of the tradition."

The exact night varied, but every week The Inseparables

had a standing date. Angel, Emma, Bella, Georgie, and Chrissy would meet for dinner at Café Caboose—a nineteenth-century rail car that had been converted into a popular dining venue. Although Sinjun, still technically an Inseparable, could never join them given she lived clear across the country.

Over the last year, various others in the BFF gang had started missing the occasional weekly dinner as well. More than ever life got in the way, especially for those who now had a significant other in their lives. For instance, tonight Bella had been waylaid with a deadline on a storybook project she was working on with Savage—who also happened to be an amazing illustrator. And Georgie was doing whatever she was doing in London with Bryce. Not that Bryce counted as her significant other, although after this trip, who knew?

At least that's what Angel and Sinjun were hoping.

"Not for anything," Laura said as she rearranged the condiments, "but, considering I rarely see all five of you in here together anymore, your tradition's unraveling."

"We're not unraveling," Angel said, taking offense. "We're evolving."

Chrissy pumped a fist. "Viva evolution."

"You can stop flashing that rock at any time," Emma said while batting away Laura's hand. The woman had rearranged the salt and pepper three times now. "You and Carson are engaged. We know."

Carson Anderson, the wealthiest man in Nowhere until Chrissy's fiancé Mason moved into town, was the proprietor of Anderson's Auto Family, the most successful car dealership in the county. The silver-tongued golden boy had once charmed Bella before she'd seen through his manipulative façade. Carson, who'd been in search of a trophy wife, had surprised everyone when he'd started dating Laura, a divorced, single mother of two, who, although by no means unattractive, was hardly what most men considered arm candy. She was, however, genuinely nice and—no doubt, most importantly to Carson—willing to bend over backward to please her man.

Angel gave Emma a subtle kick under the table. Laura couldn't help it if she was excited. Angel remembered well that giddy feeling of being newly engaged. She'd been there. Twice. Both engagements, both marriages, both husbands had been special. Each in their own way. She envied Laura who was about to embark on wedded bliss. Surely Cupid wouldn't smile favorably on Angel a third time and even if he did she feared that well-intentioned arrow would strike a deadly blow.

Shaking off morbid thoughts, Angel smiled up at Laura. "It's a gorgeous ring. Emma's just envious. As am I."

Emma grunted then bit into her juicy burger, sparing Laura her strong views on happily-ever-after versus happy-for-now.

"Have you set a date?" Angel asked.

Laura angled her head. "No. Has Bella?"

"She's thinking about December," Angel said.

"What about you, Chrissy?" Laura asked. "Have you and Mason set a date?

"Not yet. Why?"

"I'd hate to book the same weekend is all," Laura said. "It's a small town and we'll probably invite a lot of the same people. Speaking of weddings, can you believe that television woman jilted Bryce? The whole town's buzzing. And Georgie," Laura said, her eyes going wide, "running off with Bryce! Geez Louise!"

"Georgie didn't run off," Angel corrected, hoping to dampen town gossip. "Bryce had an extra ticket and he treated Georgie to a vacation. No one deserves good fortune more than Georgie, except maybe you," she said with a kind smile. "Congratulations again on your engagement to Carson."

Beaming, Laura admired her ring and sighed. "Thanks. Yeah. I really lucked out." Another sigh. "Guess I should get back to work, not that I'll be working here much longer. Holler if you need anything." Empty tray tucked under her arm, she bounced merrily away.

"You should be happy for her," Angel whispered, giving Emma another under-the-table nudge.

Emma rolled her eyes.

"Mind if I join you for a second?"

His voice revved her pulse, causing her to bobble a ketchup-drenched fry. Wiping goo from her sleeve, Angel stared across the table at Chrissy who—damn her—brightened while saying, "Slide in next to Angel. Plenty of room."

Ryan swept off his signature Stetson and settled into the booth. Angel had been so intent on her food and Laura, she'd been oblivious to the lean, mean sheriff's approach. She'd had no warning. No time to brace her senses. Even though she scooted as close to the wall as possible, Ryan's knee still bumped against hers. Awareness shot through her system as she gave another under-table kick, a harder kick, this time directed at Chrissy, who mouthed, "Ow."

"I'd like to ask you ladies something," Ryan said, except he was looking directly at Angel. "Do you think Sienna's old enough to get a manicure?"

Angel blinked. *He asked a question about his daughter. It's not like he asked you for a date. Say something, you tongue-tied ninny.*

Someone—Emma—returned one of those subtle kicks and said, "Sienna's nine now, right?"

"Just," Ryan said. "Every time she has a weekend visit with Lacey, she comes back wearing nail polish. She says her mom lets her do fun girl stuff. She mentioned manis and pedis and—hell—makeovers at some cosmetics place."

His words buzzed in Angel's brain and in the background she heard Emma and Chrissy reflecting on the first time they wore makeup and how Lacey placed too much emphasis on artificial beauty. She couldn't understand why Ryan's gaze was fixed on her when the advice was coming from the other side of the table. And she was more than a little stunned when he casually stole one of her fries, causing her core to ache with a jolt of desire. Since when was fry snitching an aphrodisiac?

"But I've given Mel a manicure for fun," Chrissy said, "and she's only six."

"If you really want to impress Sienna," Emma said, "book an appointment at Heavenly Hair. A professional manicure. And don't just leave her there. Stay and help her pick out the color."

"Maybe let her get a bright-colored feather extension," Chrissy said. "A temporary thrill. Angel stocks a fun selection."

Has Ryan always had amber flecks in his brown eyes? Why didn't I notice before? As always his uniform was neat and pressed. His strong jaw closely shaved. *What's that scent? A new cologne?* A masculine woodsy aura with a hint of fruits and herbs. Complex and intriguing—like the man who draped his arm on the bench behind her.

"Angel said something about having a light day on Friday," Chrissy said.

"Think you'd have room for the both of us?" Ryan asked while dragging his free hand through his short chestnut hair. "I could use a trim."

You could? His hair—and Angel was quite the critic—looked fine to her. Someone—Chrissy, maybe—gave her a swift kick, jarring the words, or at least one word, from Angel's constricted throat. "Sure."

"Great. I'll call the salon tomorrow and make an official appointment. Friday. Late afternoon. See you then."

He didn't wink, but he may as well have. His hand subtly brushed her shoulders as he slid out of the booth, electrifying her body with prickly sensual shocks. He pulled on his Stetson, tugged at the brim. "Ladies." And then he was gone.

"Gotta say, that was the weirdest set-up for a date I've ever witnessed," Emma said biting into her burger.

"Smooth, McClure," Chrissy said with a grin while spooning her thick chocolate shake.

Angel blinked, her body easing down from a sensual high. "What? Get real. That wasn't... We don't have a date."

"Yeah," Emma said around her toasted bun. "You kinda do."

Chrissy smiled at Angel, an ornery glint in her eyes as she squirted more ketchup. "You're welcome."

Nine

Once upon a whirlwind thrill...
London, England

Buckingham Palace. The Tower of London. Shakespeare at the Globe Theater. A Jack the Ripper Walking Tour, and the Victoria and Albert Museum.

Those attractions summed up the day's sightseeing highlights. Those were the places Georgie took selfies or surrendered her camera to Bryce who snapped shots of her. Or to a tourist who took photos of her and Bryce together, posing in front of one or another historical site. Those were the photos, along with the ones she'd taken the day before, that Georgie eventually posted on Party-Line. The extent of what she was willing to share with her uber-curious friends.

Hard to say who'd sent the most messages, begging her to touch base. Although Bella and Angel were definitely in the lead.

Except for one note—*Having a great time. Wish you were here. Bryce is the best.*—Georgie refrained from sharing details regarding her whirlwind adventure.

Most of her waking moments didn't seem real. Visiting places she never dreamed she'd see in person, alongside the man she once dreamed she'd marry. Not only that, they were rooming together and sleeping together—albeit platonically.

Aside from that one unexpected and amazingly perfect

kiss, Bryce had kept his lips to himself. Georgie would have been disappointed except his attraction was evident. She felt it. She sizzled with it. Something was building. Something was going to happen between Georgina Lou Poppins and Bryce-The Bullet-Morgan. The anticipation was exhilarating. The ultimate foreplay—and the most he'd done was hold her hand while navigating crowds. Or palming the small of her back while guiding her through an entrance.

His touch had been warm and welcome. He made her feel safe and cared for, as if she were his to worry about. Every brush of his hand felt like a lover's caress.

Maybe they weren't destined for forever, but they were destined for at least once.

She didn't want to jinx it. She didn't want to cheapen it with girlish, gossipy exchanges with her friends. She didn't want to rush it or force it—patience recommended—so she played it cool. No easy feat. Especially when they were first waking up or preparing for bed. Or basically anytime they were alone in the hotel suite—that king-sized, pillow-soft mattress screaming for action of the horizontal-mambo variety.

Sort of like now.

"Are you sure there wasn't anything else you wanted to do tonight?" Bryce asked as he shrugged out of a suit jacket and draped it over the chair.

A loaded question, considering, yeah, she'd like to jump his bones. Georgie answered cautiously as she sat on the sofa and unbuckled her left strappy heel. "Not for anything, but these shoes weren't made for walking."

"No, they weren't."

Georgie glanced up and caught Bryce staring at her legs.

The sexually charged air crackled and Georgie had to bite her tongue as she fumbled with the buckle of her other—not exactly, but as close as she owned—FMPs.

Bryce had treated her to dinner and a show. A musical playing in Leicester Square, which was sort of like New York's Times Square albeit it more quaint (according to Bryce, who'd been to New York City, unlike Georgie).

Even though Bryce had assured her not all people dressed up for the theater, Georgie couldn't resist going all out. Fortunately, Angel had supplied her with two dresses suitable for finer entertainment. Georgie had settled on a simple black halter dress and strappy red heels. The same heels she'd worn to Bryce's non-wedding. The difference was her non-wedding dress had skimmed her knees. *This* hemline stopped mid-thigh. So, yeah, her legs were on prime display.

Feigning innocence, she asked, "Anything wrong?"

"I should go."

"Where?"

"Anywhere. I need to walk this off."

It was all she could do to stay seated, to feign calm. He looked gorgeous and miserable and she wanted to tackle him to the floor. "Walk what off?"

Bryce palmed the back of his neck and rubbed. He blew out a breath. A tense breath. A *really* tense breath.

Georgie practiced extraordinary patience.

"That dress. Those shoes. You. The past few days." He stuffed his hands in the pockets of his trousers, studied the toes of his boots.

Georgie waited.

"You look hot, dammit."

Her pulse kicked. If only he didn't sound so disappointed. "Thank you. I think."

"I can't be here. This—and don't pretend you don't know what I'm talking about—can't happen."

Heart pounding, Georgie took a leap of faith. Enough patience. Time to initiate derring-do. She rose to her bare feet and closed the distance between them. "Okay. No pretending. Let's face *this* head on." She inched closer, pressing her body to his, acknowledging his oh-so-noticeable package. "Why can't *this* happen?"

He remained frozen, staring down at her in stoic silence.

"Because I'm Ryan's sister?" she prodded. "Because you're on the rebound? Because you don't love me and you don't want to complicate matters with meaningless sex? Because you're conflicted about the twins and your future and you need me to be there for them and for Arlo so you can honor your charity commitments and pursue whatever?"

She rattled off everything she could think of because there wasn't one forthcoming bone in Bryce's infuriatingly hunky body. The man guarded his innermost thoughts as if they were a flipping national secret.

He worked his jaw. "Yes."

"To what?"

"To everything."

She wanted to punch him—the big stubborn, noble, ex-jock. "What if I told you meaningless sex is all I'm interested in? What if I told you I have no intention of bailing on your nanny job—no matter if *this* happens or not—because that job is the only thing keeping me afloat until my dream job comes through. Which—in case I didn't mention it before—should be soon."

If she said it often enough, maybe it would happen. Maybe she'd get that golden email from Impossible Dream alerting her of a wondrous opportunity. As it was, the only notices she'd been getting were from bill collectors.

Jerking her thoughts back to pleasant ground, Georgie dug in. "Here's the thing. Ignoring this attraction won't make it go away, Bryce. Addressing it might. If it helps," she lied, "I meant what I said that day at Grace Chapel. This isn't a matter of the heart. *This* is purely physical."

And *that* was about all she could muster in the derring-do department without sacrificing her pride.

Bryce closed his eyes and cursed.

When he reached for his jacket, Georgie turned her back. He was leaving. Fine. "Go for your walk. Forget I said anything," she said while fumbling with the zipper at the back of her dress. "I'll be in bed by the time you get back, sleeping *this* off."

She heard the door open...

Don't cry. Don't cry. Do. Not. Cry.

...and shut.

"Dammit," she swore when the zipper wouldn't budge and her temper overflowed.

"Screw it." Bryce cupped her shoulders and turned her in his arms.

He'd changed his mind about leaving! He was touching her, holding her, and (*Oh, God. Oh, yes.*) kissing her!

Her anger melted. Her brain melted. Her knees went all wobbly and the little girl in her, the girl who'd once believed in true-heart-stopping-love, whooped with I-told-you-so joy.

Georgie poured a lifetime of longing into this kiss.

And (*thank you, thank you, thank you*) Bryce melded against her, holding her steady as the world fell away. One hand cradled her head, his fingers tangling in her hair. The other hand caressed her back as he kissed her...and kissed her...and (*holy smokes*) kissed her. The zipper easily gave way (*How did he do that?*) sliding lower and lower until he slipped his hand between the willowy material and her lacey black panties and palmed her bare butt.

Desire pulsed between her legs as she loosened his tie and jerked at his shirttail. She moved fast, fretting he'd succumb to second thoughts. She wanted this. She wanted Bryce. The down-to-earth jock who'd shined throughout high school and dazzled in his years as a pro. The guy who'd bailed his dad out of a financial crisis, not once, but twice. The man who'd paid his employees out of his own pocket when his business slid toward ruin. The man who'd forfeited his gorgeous, well-connected fiancé rather than abandon his orphaned kin.

She'd never known anyone kinder (*a massive turn-on*) or more resourceful (*also sexy*) and if this was to be their one and only time she'd be damned if she'd flub it.

To Georgie's immense pleasure, Bryce moved at his own feverish pace. Deft fingers released her zipper and clasps. Soon after, his trousers puddled on the floor along with her dress...and bra...and panties. Followed by his shirt and tie.

Naked. With Bryce Morgan.

Hellz, yeah.

Her skin sizzled from his touch—his hands, his lips, his tongue.

She didn't remember moving the party to the bed, but she was fully aware of skipping the appetizers in favor of the main dish. She rolled on top of Bryce, taking control and straddling his glorious body. In her impassioned mind, fifteen years of longing constituted fifteen years of foreplay.

Orgasm now. Thank you.

It's not like he argued when she lowered herself onto his impressive erection. Or when she rode him fast and hard. Or screamed his name. Or climaxed with the most intense and amazing orgasm ever.

His own release was fierce and wonderful and—*oh, my, oh, yeah*—one for her memory book.

Georgie collapsed on his heaving chest. She'd rendered

Bryce-The Bullet-Morgan breathless. Awesome.

"Damn."

She smiled against his shoulder, thinking he too, was in awe of their awesomeness.

"Please tell me you're on birth control."

Oh. He wasn't marveling at their lovemaking. He was fretting a glitch. In their lustful mania, they'd forgone a condom.

"I'm covered. And I'm clean," she added. "If that's what you're worried about."

"Same here. And no, that wasn't my worry. Not with you."

Even though she'd told him she'd fallen for half the men in the county. Not that she'd slept with them all. Not even close. But he didn't know that. He just assumed she'd been smart and responsible which she had. Up until now.

"I'm not always so desperate. But that was a long time in coming, Bryce Morgan."

"You call that a long time?"

"I mean—"

"I know what you mean." He smoothed her hair from her face and kissed her brow. "So. Got me out of your system now?"

"What would you say if I said it might take another time or two?"

"I'd say give me a chance to catch my breath. Damn, girl."

His teasing tone bolstered her joy. Stifling a sexy response, she smiled against his neck. She didn't want to talk this to death. Talking could lead to deeper thought. And regrets. Not hers. But maybe his. They'd return to reality soon enough. This was her fantasy come true and she wanted to wallow in wonderful and flirt with spectacular. Just now she was memorizing the contours of his body. The heat of his touch. The scent of his skin.

She wiggled against the connection she'd yet to break and felt Bryce twitching back to life.

"Let's continue this in the shower. Start fresh," he said. "Me licking my way down your curves."

Her heart sang. Angels sang. No wait. That was his ring tone.

"Could be Arlo. The kids."

She heard regret in his voice, but she also heard concern.

"You should take it." Georgie rolled away, covering her naked-self as Bryce's naked-self scrambled to find his phone in their mess of discarded clothing. She tried not to stare at his world-class sports-tacular butt. *Yeah, right.*

"Yeah. Hey, Dad. What's up?"

Bryce settled on the edge of the mattress and Georgie settled on admiring his muscular back.

"Who? Hold up," he said. "Let me call you back in five."

Sheet clutched to her breasts, Georgie sat riveted as Bryce pushed to his feet. "So..."

"Dad got a call from a man claiming to be the twins' father."

Ten

Bryce speed-rinsed and dried while Georgie lingered in the shower.

"Sorry to bail," he said.

"I hope it's not bad news," she said.

What would you consider bad news? he wondered while pulling on sweats and moving back into the sitting area. That the father wanted custody? That was the worry poking at Bryce. Although he'd been conflicted about being the soul guardian of Charlie and Chelsea, he'd be damned if he'd lose them to some asshole or addict. Even though Marla and Bryce had been at odds, she'd entrusted her children to him. Not their father. *Him.* For Bryce that spoke volumes.

Palming his phone, he called Arlo while sitting on the sofa. "I'm all yours, Dad. Do me a favor and start from the beginning."

"Got a call from a guy claiming to be the twins' father. Said his name was Jimmy Trent. Said he just learned of Marla's...of Marla's passing."

Arlo cleared his throat and Bryce knew the old man was stuffing down a sadness he'd yet to voice aloud.

"Said he learned his kids were with us. Said we need to talk."

"About?"

"Their future. I told him Marla already considered their

future and he wasn't in it."

"That was direct."

"I know a weasel when I hear one and I'm tellin' you, son, I smell a skunk."

"What else did he say?" Bryce asked.

"Said a father's got rights."

"According to that letter Marla left us, the twins' father abandoned her before they were even born. They weren't married and he wasn't supportive financially. Trent's got dick."

"Pretty much what I told him."

"And?"

"He said we'll be hearing from his lawyer. Unless..."

"Unless what?"

"Unless you meet with him in person. Before I could tell him to eat dirt and die he told me he knew meeting wasn't possible just now seeing you're shacked up overseas with some woman—a woman other than your fiancé. Said that oughta go over real well in court should he be forced to go that route."

"Son of a—"

"Weasel. Told you. Anyhow, he'd said he'd be in touch."

Bryce dragged a hand through his wet hair. "I already filed for guardianship."

"Trent could still make trouble."

"If he's got a legal leg to stand on."

"Even if he don't things could get ugly. He could sell a tale to a gossip rag. Bride dumps cheating groom at the altar. Former football star schtupps nanny under children's roof."

"That's a load of—"

"Stuff that sells papers and ruins reputations and careers. Mary Poppins."

"A nanny reference. I get it." The magical movie that had been a favorite of Marla's back when she was a doe-eyed innocent. Bryce could see the sensational headline as well as his old man. "The Bullet bangs—"

"No. M-A-R-R-Y. Marry Poppins. Georgie Poppins. Put a ring on her finger and nip this scandal in the bud."

Bryce felt sacked. "You're kidding, right?"

"Am I laughing?"

"Dad—"

"Never mind your own reputation—which if sullied could damage your work on the charity circuit. You want to risk Trent dragging Georgie through the tabloid mud? Some local folk are already speculating. Wondering if maybe you two had been sneaking around before... and then Kathryn found out. I know it ain't true," Arlo went on. "Most people know it ain't true. But all it takes is one ornery skunk to cause a stink. A skunk with a bee in his bonnet because you gave him hell for badmouthing Georgie, making him look bad in front of his friends."

"Oh, hell," Bryce complained, glancing toward the bathroom when he heard the blow dryer rev. "Tom Rhodes?"

"So I hear," Arlo said. "And believe you me, I got an earful from Ryan when I called him about Trent."

"Wait a minute. You called Ryan about Jimmy Trent before calling me?"

"Given he's the law, I figured he could run some kind of search on Trent. See if he's got a criminal record. Something we can use against the weasel. It's not like I was going behind your back. I was looking out for your ass. And Georgie's. Seeing Ryan's her brother I figure he's got a stake in this, too."

"Uh, huh." And a boot primed to kick Bryce's ass. Bryce couldn't even deny he'd shacked up with Georgie because he had. He couldn't refute his dad's crass schtupping crack because, as of a few minutes ago, guilty as charged.

"Tell me this, son. You and Georgie getting along?"

"Yeah."

"She's a pretty thing."

"Yep."

"And nice."

"Mmm."

"You already invited her to live with us and take care of the kids, right?"

"Right."

"Been good having Pauline around. This home benefit from a woman's permanent touch. Charlie and Chelsea—although they're warming up to me—would benefit from a doting mom. You'd benefit from a big-hearted gal—unlike that cold-hearted producer woman—and Georgie would benefit from a financially sound, smart, and decent man.

"I asked the kids if they remembered Georgie from that pajama shindig," he went on. "They said they did. Said she was nice. That's as good as a stamp of approval to me."

Bryce rubbed the back of his neck. "You about done?"

"Just say the word and me and Ryan will set things in motion. A quiet civil ceremony the minute you get back. We've got it all worked out."

"You and Ryan."

"Yep."

His dad and his friend—the rancher and the sheriff—matchmakers. Bryce almost laughed. Georgie poked her head out of the bathroom and he waved her on in. "How are Charlie and Chelsea doing?" he asked, hoping to swing Arlo to saner ground.

"Comin' along. Pauline and I gave them a few chores and engaged them in activities to build confidence. Seems to be working. They're still a mite backward, but at least they're peeking out of their shells. I won't speculate on why they are how they are. Not a place I wanna go. Just concentrating on mending what's broken and giving my grandchildren what they need. A family." Arlo punctuated the last part with fire. A fire he'd lacked since selling off the bulk of the ranch. "A real family. And no pissant like Jimmy Trent is gonna sabotage my efforts."

A grin got the better of Bryce. "That directed at him or me."

"Marry Poppins."

Bryce caught Georgie's gaze—a gaze full of curiosity, strength, and dammit-it-all affection. His gut kicked, telegraphing caution. Even so he could feel himself drifting toward the riskier play. "I'll get back to you on that."

Dressed in striped baggy pants, a faded tee, and the pink slippers she'd worn on the plane, Georgie sat at the opposite end of the sofa as Bryce signed off with his dad.

Looking only slightly self-conscious, she clasped her hands—hands that had recently been all over his body—in her lap. "That was a long call," she said.

"Arlo had a lot to say."

"Was it bad?"

"Wasn't all good."

"Not that it's any of my business—"

"Arlo and Ryan made it your business."

She blinked. "My brother?"

"You know how you said I'm not much of a talker? Brace yourself. I've got a story to tell."

* * *

Georgie had been knocked for plenty of loops, but this latest was a doozy. Bryce's words clanged in her head, inciting a barrage of emotions.

She couldn't decide which part riled her more. The bit about the twins' deadbeat dad threatening trouble or the part about Tom Rhodes instigating vengeful gossip. Never mind her and Bryce's reputations. What about the havoc their nasty meddling could wreak on two young innocents?

But it was the tail end of Bryce's story that flummoxed Georgie most. "Your dad and my brother think it would be best for everyone—you, me, and the kids—if we married?"

Bryce nodded.

"That's crazy."

"Is it?"

Georgie blinked. "Isn't it?"

"Unconventional. Absolutely."

"But you're considering it?"

"The notion has merit."

Georgie stared while struggling for words. Any words.

"You said you're all about happy-for-now. Are you happy?" Bryce asked. "Now? Here? With me?"

She nodded.

"Could you be happy with me and Arlo and the kids in Nowhere?"

Was that a trick question?

"We're a good match, Georgie. In temperament. In bed. And the benefits Arlo listed..."

"All true," she choked out as her thoughts and senses whirled.

"If you're not bothered by our age difference—"

"I was never bothered."

"Now that you're thirty—"

"Thirty-one."

"—ten years isn't a screaming taboo."

Her heart skipped a beat or three as she reverted to a besotted teen. "Meaning if I'd been older back then you might have reacted differently to my dramatic confession of love?"

Brown gaze fixed on her mouth, he crooked one brow. "Maybe."

Georgie squeezed her tingling thighs together, determined not to jump his bones before they sorted through this unexpected twist.

"Wait a minute," she said with narrowed eyes. "You're not suggesting this marriage thing just because we..." She gestured toward the rumpled bed. "Because that would be just like you. Marrying me to salvage my reputation. Not that I care what people say. But you do. As evidenced by you giving Tom hell."

"It wasn't as fiery as that."

"Still. And then there's Ryan."

"What about Ryan?"

"Knowing you, you're feeling guilty about boffing his little sister."

"I haven't thought of you as his "little" sister for days. And what happened in that bed, no matter how brief, wasn't as casual as you just suggested."

He sounded sort of ticked which was kind of sexy, especially since it intimated a connection beyond the physical. Respect and maybe, just maybe, a smidgeon of affection.

"On another note, if you're suggesting I'm motivated by something other than starry-eyed love, you're right."

Well, damn. She knew that. Still.

Bryce narrowed his eyes. "This chemistry. This bond. It's based on friendship and sex, right? You said—"

"Get over yourself, Bullet," Georgie teased with a crooked grin. Making light was easier than admitting she'd lied—a few times now—about her suppressed crush. "I'm into you—obviously—but I'm not in love." She refused to allow her feelings to run that deep. In her experience every time she loved, she lost. Surely wedded bliss was attainable without sacrificing one's heart and pride.

Taking a progressive view, Georgie gave a confident nod.

"The benefits Arlo mentioned were bang on, as they say over here. It's a logical and smart union."

One that would ease her financial woes and Bryce's stress as a single parent. One that could provide the best of circumstances for Chelsea and Charlie.

"Dad mentioned you to the twins," Bryce said. "They remember you. Said you're nice."

"That's sweet," Georgie said. "And encouraging."

"And it's your dream come true, right?" Bryce asked tentatively. "A family to nurture?"

Oh, right. And oh, wow. "Could you..." She pushed to her feet. "Give me a sec. Thanks."

Georgie rooted her phone from her purse. She scanned her inbox for an email from ID.com, looking for an alert similar to the ones received by Bella and Chrissy. A somewhat cryptic note directing her to Bryce. A note advising patience and passion and derring-do. Instead she saw junk mail and bills. Lots of bills. And a gentle, carefully worded nudge from her formerly patient landlord informing her he had an interested buyer. Code: *The sooner you're out, the better.*

The runner's high she'd been experiencing ever since Bryce mentioned marriage took a major dip. Georgie returned to the sofa, deflated and confused. "I thought this was it," she said. "The magic."

"Come again?"

She shrugged, feeling a little silly and a lot disappointed. Yet another example of a failed venture in her life. "When Bella and Chrissy applied to Impossible Dream, they received emails directing them to their greatest desire. I didn't get that prompt."

"Maybe because what you're looking for is in your own backyard."

She met and held his gaze. "It seems too good to be true. Too easy."

He grunted. "You're anticipating easy? Have you met Arlo? He comes with the package. At least for now. As for the kids, something tells me you'll wiggle your way into their hearts with minimal effort. As for me... This might be the time to dispel your romanticized version of me. I'm not perfect, Georgie."

"I don't think..." She stumbled and blushed. "Although maybe I do. But can you blame me? You always do the right thing, even when it's wrong for you. And don't pretend you don't know what I mean. Did you really want to move back to Nowhere after you left the pros? You could have lived anywhere. Opened a restaurant or some other business in a more profitable region. Instead you poured your energy and money into a local bar hoping to promote business in your dying hometown.

"And what about the blizzard that claimed two-thirds of your dad's cattle? Everyone knows you sunk the bulk of your savings into getting the ranch back up and running. You would have been sitting pretty financially for a long, long time if not for that. So yeah, it was the right thing to do for Arlo and the ranch-hands he used to employ, but not particularly for you. Should I go on?"

"Please don't." Visibly uncomfortable, Bryce braced his forearms on his knees and stared down at his bare feet. "I'm not a saint, Georgie. For every right there's a wrong. For one, I drove Marla away."

"She ran away rather than get help."

He shook his head. "I should have taken a different approach. I was harsh and impatient. I hated the turmoil she inflicted on Mom and Dad and, more selfishly, the potential scandal she posed to my football career."

"But—"

"Two. I was set to marry Kathryn to further a career in broadcasting. To immerse myself in a world I love. That's about as self-centered as it gets."

"Okay. But the work you do for the sports charity circuit—"

"Puts me in the spotlight. I enjoy being the center of attention. I always did. I liked being a source of pride and joy for my parents, for my team. I loved playing football. I lapped up the charge and respect I got from excelling on the field. It's like a drug. The challenge. The win. The adulation. In a way, I guess you could say I'm no better than Marla.

"When her kids dropped into my life, my second thought was how is this going to affect my shot at getting back in the game. Marrying you at least allows me to continue the charity work." He raised a brow. "Did I fall off that pedestal yet?"

Her heart swelled and ached. "Not yet. Although I admit it does make you more human."

He smiled at that. "What about you? Any skeletons in that closet of yours, Lou?"

"None that matter," she said because what good would it do to admit her one mega bonehead mistake of the past. A mistake she never repeated. A misstep Ryan had assured her he'd erased. Plus, she was too embarrassed. "But that's not to say I'm perfect by a longshot."

"Name a fault you're not proud of."

"That's easy. I'm prone to the occasional meltdown. And it's not pretty."

He scrunched his brow. "Like the one you had the first day we got here?"

"Much worse."

"Huh." He reached over and tucked a hank of her still damp hair behind her ear. "I can deal with that. Can you deal with me?"

"You're not nearly as scary as the pesky creditors," she said with a teasing smile. "Just saying, my motivations aren't entirely pure either."

"So should I put the call into Dad? Have him and Ryan lay the groundwork for a quickie marriage?"

"Sure. Why not?" Georgie's heart galloped, spurred on by a dose of old-fashioned faith and a spoonful of derring-do. Happy-for-now. *Hellz yeah.* "Sometimes you have to make your own magic."

Eleven

Once upon a freaky Friday...

FROM THE HEART OF ANGEL DRAKE
FRIDAY, JUNE 19

Life gets curiouser and curiouser.

Yes, I know. Curiouser is not a real word. It's from "Alice in Wonderland" which happens to be stuck in my head because Bella referenced it after we received a group text from Georgie asking for a mega-huge favor.

It wasn't the favor that struck us as curious, but Georgie's persistent reluctance to share details regarding her trip. We all want to know what's up with her and Bryce? Are they getting along? Getting it on?

I'm especially curious because I know they're staying in the same room. No one else knows that. Well, except Sinjun and we agreed not to spill that bean because we arranged that bean. Or whatever. Yeah. I'm a little wifty. Sleep deprivation will do that.

I've been indulging in late-night movie marathons, dodging sleep as much as possible or more specifically dodging dreams. Of ~~Ryan~~ him. Damn Chrissy and Emma for planting that date seed in my head. ~~Ryan~~ The exasperating sheriff booked a hair appointment, not a date. Still the possibility that I'd misread the situation ignited erotic thoughts of running my fingers through his thick brown hair. He-who-shall-not-be-named invaded my dreams. And in those dreams, he, we... I don't want to think about it. And I sure don't want to dream about it.

Hence the sleep deprivation, which led to me calling out sick today, which I never do, but hey it wasn't wholly a lie. I'm exhausted. Plus, I was dreading that appointment. I'd feel guilty about ditching him and his daughter except I asked Holly to handle Sienna's manicure and delegated the feather extensions as well as <u>his</u> haircut to Janeen. My two best gals. Father and daughter were in good hands, just not my hands. Thank God.

Where was I? Oh, yeah. Georgie's favor. So she asked the Inseparables if we would box up her belongings. Her clothes, her shoes, her cookware. Her everything. If we could label the boxes that would be great but beyond that she didn't have any specifics or bugaboos. She said she got an email from Mr. Jones. That he had an interested buyer and the sooner she cleared out of the cottage, the sooner he could start renovations and set the sale in motion. Yes, she'd be back in two days (tomorrow, in fact) but she was hoping to devote immediate attention to Charlie and Chelsea and to setting up her new home instead of lingering at the former.

<u>Her new home</u>.

Yeah. I know. Bryce offered her a job and a place to live so the Morgan Ranch <u>is</u> her new home. For the time being anyway. Still. I sense something more. Something's brewing and I don't know why I'm so unsettled by it. Maybe because I fear I set whatever's happening in motion and it's doomed for failure because I'm jinxed in the romance department. Playing matchmaker? What was I thinking?

Oh, well. At least I avoided my own potential disaster. For now.

Yours truly,
Angel

Just as Angel set aside her pen, a knock sounded at the door.

She assumed it was Holly or Janeen checking in before locking up the salon and going home. Even though she'd assured them she wasn't gravely ill.

So she swung open the door, dressed down in yoga pants and a flowery, spaghetti- strapped tunic, her unruly curls twisted in a top knot, her feet bare and sporting a chipped orange sherbet pedicure.

Him. "Ryan." *Busted.*

"Heard you're under the weather. Brought you some soup."

She glanced at the paper bag clutched in his hand—a bag bearing the logo of Café Caboose. They made the best homemade soup. And he brought some. For her.

Oh, God.

"So what?" he asked. "The flu? A cold?"

"Um, no." Rude of her not to invite him in, but she was not inviting him into her personal space. No way. No how. Even if he had come bearing a delicious smelling gift. Even though he was out of uniform—which only made him slightly less potent. The man was close to devastating in faded jeans and a black tee. And, even though he was off-duty, he still exuded an air of authority. Damn if she didn't feel like she'd just been caught playing hooky.

"Stomach bug?" he prodded. "Migraine?"

"Exhaustion," she managed, kicking herself for being so affected by the man. How could he make her stomach churn with guilt and butterflies at the same time? "I haven't been sleeping well."

"Restless. A lot on your mind."

She reached for the bag. "Thank you for the soup."

"Like how to avoid me."

Her hand froze on the crisp white bag and even though their fingers barely brushed, the skin-on-skin connection jolted her senses. "That's crazy, Ryan." Her cheeks burned. The confrontation. The touching. Why wouldn't he let go of the damned bag? "Why would I be losing sleep over you?"

"Because you know I'm attracted to you. That I've been attracted to you for a long time." He stepped forward, forcing her to back into her apartment otherwise they'd be flush. "Chrissy told me she unintentionally broke my confidence."

"When did she tell you that?" He knew that she knew? She felt blindsided and foolish. And trapped. Alone in her apartment with the first man since Baxter who'd made her stomach flutter in that oh-so-intimate way.

As if she wasn't rattled enough, Ryan set the food on her desk. Next to her journal. Her *open* journal.

"Last night at Georgie's cottage," Ryan said, forcing Angel to backtrack their discussion.

Oh, yeah, she thought. *The moment my rat-friend Chrissy betrayed me.*

"I showed up as scheduled along with Mason and Savage to transport boxes and furniture to the Morgans' barn. I was surprised you weren't there with the rest of the girls."

"I had to leave early."

"Before I got there, you mean." He cocked a hip on the edge of her desk which would have been sexy—given the way his jeans hugged his muscular thighs—except it put him that much closer to her journal.

"Look," he said. "I'm sorry I make you uncomfortable, but—"

"I..." All he had to do was glance down and he'd see the last penned page of today's "self-discovery". The part where she mentioned him invading her dreams! Heart pounding, Angel moved forward and snatched the bag. "I should put the soup in the kitchen. Want a beer?" She closed her journal as subtly as possible and scuttled past, praying he'd follow. Which he did.

"Is it because you're not interested?" he asked as she opened the fridge. "Or because you're scared?"

She froze. And it wasn't because of the brisk air wafting from the icebox.

"I've heard that insensitive rumor," he said. "Chrissy said you buy into it."

"Chrissy talks too much."

"You're not cursed, Angel."

Tense to the bone, she shut the fridge, sans soup and beer, and slowly turned. It was all she could do to meet Ryan's gaze but he needed to know the sincerity of her phobia. "Tell that to my two dead husbands."

He cocked his head and studied her hard.

She clenched her fists at her side, screaming at the universe for setting her up for yet another fall. She was perfectly happy—*mostly*—being single and celibate.

"I've been taking it slow for a dozen reasons," he finally

said. "The fact that both Baxter and Eddie met an untimely end isn't one of them."

Angel held her breath as Ryan moved in, trapping her between her stainless steel fridge and his iron-hard body.

"Maybe I should have been more direct," he said. "I'm out of practice."

Her throat clogged. Her heart raced. Her skin prickled with anticipation and dread and... Oh, cripes.

"I need to know something," he said as every molecule in her body zinged.

A rush of panic and, oh God, *lust* shot through her body, causing her to tremble as Ryan—a man she'd known all her life, a man she'd never been attracted to until very, very recently—blindsided her with a brief tender kiss.

Heart-stopping, sensual perfection.

A fatal attraction.

Stiffening, Angel shoved hard and followed through with a slap. An instinctual need to warn him off. *I'm dangerous. I'm deadly.* But even though she quickly rationalized her overdramatic reaction, the force of the slap shocked her. Seeing her hand's imprint on Ryan's cheek shamed her. "I'm sorry. I—"

"It's okay. Now I know."

If she'd hurt his feelings, he didn't show it. He even smiled a little as he dragged a hand through his hair. Hair trimmed by Janeen because Angel had been too much of a coward. Because she didn't want to touch Ryan in any way, shape, or form. Because she knew if they shared even a wisp of intimacy, she'd be tempted to play with fire.

And now this.

"Truth told," he said as he turned to leave, "this is a relief."

"It is?"

"I've been struggling with how and when to ask you on an honest to God date. I mean, do people even do that anymore? Go on dates?" He laughed a little. "Like I said, I'm out of practice."

Angel held her tongue as she followed him to the door. Her emotions and wits had yet to recover from that toe-curling kiss. And worse, that horrifying slap. "This is awkward," she said when he opened the door.

"Yep. But it'll get better. No need to lose anymore sleep," he said with a parting glance. "Take care, Angel."

Soon after she stared at a closed door, acknowledging the end of the shortest courtship of her life.

Done. Over. The man was moving on.

She should have felt better and yet she felt cheated.

And really, really angry.

$$\mathcal{T}welve$$

Once upon a logical liaison...

Given the time difference, sleeping on the long flight home would have been smart, but Bryce was too hyped. A victim of a nervous energy reminiscent of the pre-game jitters, only he couldn't work off the tension with a jog around the field. Even pacing the aisle was impossible given the turbulent flight.

So he toughed it out. Buckled in his seat, he watched a mindless movie while Georgie dozed. Even as the action exploded on the tiny screen, Bryce's thoughts overshadowed the convoluted film. His own life rivaled any cinematic drama.

As the hours passed he reflected on the string of events that had brought him to the threshold of a marriage of convenience.

Inviting Georgie to England.

Taking Georgie to bed.

Asking Georgie to be his wife.

For a man who once analyzed and rehearsed every play and alternate scenario to death, Bryce was now the king of kneejerk decisions. He'd given little thought to the various ways his actions could go awry. He'd trusted his gut. Trusted his dad. Trusted Ryan.

And Georgie.

"*Ours,*" she'd said, while they sealed their engagement

with a playful round in the sack, *"is a logical liaison. A perfect solution. A win-win. Starry-eyed love,"* she added with a teasing nip to his ear, *"is overrated."*

He didn't argue with that. Mostly because his mouth was busy otherwise. Partly because he agreed. He'd been head over heels a couple of times. Both times ended in heartbreak. Chiefly his.

So, yeah. The logical liaison thing. A marriage based on mutual respect and need and (bonus) satisfying sex sounded like a fair deal and Bryce rolled with it because it was the right thing to do for a whole lot of reasons. But the closer they got to Nowhere, the more he obsessed on potential pitfalls. He had an unlucky streak a mile wide. So did Georgie. This could very well be a futzed fiasco. Except he couldn't, wouldn't let that happen. Too much was at stake.

Just stick to the plan, he told himself while glancing over at Georgie. The plan they'd hashed out together. The arrangement she'd dubbed MFB. Married friends with benefits.

At that moment his bride-to-be shifted. Her lashes fluttered and her gaze locked with his. "As long as we keep our hearts out of the equation," she said as if reading his mind, "we'll be fine."

The voice of optimism—just as she'd been all through their time in London—except her tone lacked its usual conviction. Maybe she was tired. Or maybe she was having second thoughts. Like Kathryn.

Well, hell.

Being jilted twice in one week—the one pitfall he hadn't entertained. Talk about a sledgehammer to the ego. Worse, his Dad had already prepped the twins regarding an "unexpected but blessed" development.

"Don't borrow trouble," he heard a former coach say. Besides, he reminded himself, he was handing Georgie her dream on a platter. Why would she balk?

Beating back his own apprehensions, Bryce rallied and squeezed her hand. *Trust in the team.* "MFB."

* * *

Georgie's vacation from reality ended somewhere over

the Atlantic. Nothing in particular triggered the internal meltdown. The funk descended full blown—a hideous mass of doubts and dread that knotted her stomach and steamrolled her derring-do.

In London, she'd been a sunny-faced cheerleader, putting a positive spin on every negative scenario she and Bryce conjured. Even though this marriage-of-convenience was semi-random and this side of reckless, once they agreed to go for it, they backtracked and plotted a course. A logical, sensible, amicable, beneficial partnership.

MFB.

Now as they soared toward Nowhere, Georgie's optimistic resolve gave way to obsessive panic.

What if the kids hated her for stepping into their mom's shoes?

What if the kids loved her, but resented Bryce?

What if Bryce landed a sportscaster job? What if he didn't?

What if their mutual attraction faded and the sex fizzled? Could they be content as married friends *without* benefits?

Instead of voicing her worries, Georgie feigned sleep. The war within quietly raged for endless miles. When she finally dared to open her eyes, Bryce was studying her with an enigmatic expression. She registered a spark of worry and a flash of determination. She scrambled to stand by her man. Her friend. Her soon-to-be husband.

"As long as we keep our hearts out of the equation, we'll be fine."

Even as she said it Thumper rammed against her ribs, warning her to end things now. A clean break before she ruined the perfect affair they'd shared overseas.

"MFB," Bryce said, inspiring Georgie to sucker punch her demons.

So what if she had a crummy track record with men? So what if she'd fumbled dozens of jobs? This wasn't just any man or any job. This was her dream come true—even if not granted by ID.com. *Take that, you irritating funk.*

And yet the demons lingered.

"About the ceremony," Bryce said. "Are you sure—"

"I'm sure." She'd always envisioned a church wedding— the flowers, the music, the Inseparables standing alongside her in matching gowns. The reception, the cake, the band.

Part of the magic was in the planning. This civil service was a rushed affair and, truth told, she wasn't entirely sure her friends would approve. Bella, most especially, would balk at a loveless marriage. Emma wasn't a fan of hitching one's self to one man, period. Pragmatic Chrissy would ask, *what's the rush?* And Angel, though she'd probably be supportive, would insist on arranging an intimate union in the park. Angel was a hopeless romantic and this was a logical liaison.

Although Georgie knew he was being considerate—Bryce was always considerate—his efforts to personalize the ceremony tweaked her inner turmoil.

"I know we agreed to marry under the radar," he persisted, "but—"

"The goal is to seal the deal and to establish a stable home for Charlie and Chelsea ASAP," Georgie interrupted. *Please let it go.* "A quickie service at City Hall. No bells and whistles. No guests. Just Judge Loper and Arlo and Ryan as witnesses."

"I just don't want you to regret—"

"I won't." Unfortunately, her demons said otherwise.

* * *

Calling out of work two days in a row was a record for Angel, but her reasons—at least for today—were justifiable. She was exhausted and wired—a victim of another restless night. Her tense mood and wandering mind could prove disastrous were she cutting or coloring someone's hair.

As it happened, she'd only scheduled one morning appointment, intending to devote the rest of the day to ordering supplies and brainstorming a Christmas charity event. So after arranging Mrs. Barnaby's silver-blue hair in a dated beehive (the same style she'd favored for the last thirty years), Angel left the salon in the capable hands of Holly and Janeen and scooted over to Fanny Anne's Buds and Baubles.

The last person she expected to bump into at the floral gift shop was the man who'd contributed to her insomnia. Who was Ryan buying flowers for? Surely not her. *No need to lose anymore sleep*, he'd said—although she'd done exactly that. If he wasn't buying roses or daisies for her—he couldn't seem to decide between the two—then who? Considering he was in uniform—and yeah, that was a swoon-worthy sight—maybe he was looking to spruce up the stationhouse. Or not. Why did she even care?

Unfortunately the tinkling bell above the tiny shop's door announced her arrival, snagging his attention. Otherwise she would have backed out. Ignoring him would be petty, especially since he smiled. So she moved inside, hoping Fanny Anne—who was probably in the back artfully arranging bouquets—appeared sooner rather than later. Until then, unfortunately, small talk was in order.

"Hey," Angel said. "I'm here to buy flowers for Georgie." Not that he asked, but maybe he'd announce his intent in return. Because, damn, she was curious.

"So she broke down and told you," Ryan said. "Thank God. I can't decide if she'd prefer roses or wildflowers."

Angel frowned. "Told me what?"

"Oh, hell. I thought... Forget it."

Angel's senses sparked—and it wasn't because of Ryan's subtle, sexy scent. Or the gun resting against his sexy, narrow hip. Or the badge pinned to his sexy chest. Or maybe it was. Cursing herself for being so attracted to a man she'd rejected, Angel summoned casual indifference. "What's going on?"

"Why are you buying flowers for Georgie?" he countered.

"I thought I'd surprise her with a combo welcome home/good-luck-with-your-new-job bouquet. Why are you buying flowers for Georgie?"

He glanced from the back room to the front door. Even though they were alone, he jerked his head to the far corner, intimating they should move the discussion to a more secluded area. He didn't palm her back or take her elbow. There was no brushing of shoulders or hands as they slipped behind the display of decorative birdhouses. He took a dominant stance—legs apart, arms crossed. Not exactly aloof, but far from flirty.

And still her stomach fluttered.

"I'm going to tell you," he said in a conspiratorial tone, "because I think at least one of her friends should be there. Also, I could use some help."

Angel blinked, focusing on his words instead of his lips.

Lips that had kissed her dizzy.

"You can't share this with Bella, Chrissy or Emma," he said.

"For crying out loud, Ryan. Just spit it out."

"I need your word."

"What are we, kids?" Her nerves were shot. Her patience was nil. When she hadn't tossed and turned and obsessed on her "break-up" with Ryan, she'd tossed and turned and obsessed on her attempted matchmaking with Georgie and Bryce. "Fine. You have my word."

He dropped his voice even lower. "Georgie and Bryce are getting married. Today. A civil service at City Hall."

Angel stared.

"Out of left field, I know. Then again my sister's always had a thing for Bryce."

"And he finally fell for *her*? Wow." If she weren't so stunned, she'd kick up her heels. Her matchmaking efforts had paid off in spades! "But why is it a secret? And why today? What's the hurry? Georgie's always dreamed of a beautiful church wedding. Why City Hall?"

"Considering Bryce's brush with marriage last week, to another woman, no less, they want to keep the nuptials low key. Also, at this point it's more of an arrangement than a love match, but I have faith that will change."

"An arrangement? What, like a marriage of convenience?" Bryce needed a mother for those children. Georgie wanted a family. Had Impossible Dream finally come through for her friend? Or was this the work of Angel and Sinjun? Did it matter?

"It was Arlo's idea. Genius if you ask me. I'm tired of seeing Georgie struggle and, if left to his own devices, I'm worried Bryce will gravitate toward another gem like Kathryn. At least one of us should end up with a good woman."

Angel blinked. Was that last bit in reference to Ryan's two-timing flake of an ex-wife? Or a slipped reference to Angel?

"I offered to expedite the legalities," he plowed on.

Her thoughts hopped around like a jacked-up jumping bean.

"They're perfect for one another, don't you think? Bryce

and Georgie," Ryan added when Angel failed to respond.

"I'm sorry," she finally said. "This was Arlo's idea?" Why did she feel robbed of the credit? Why should she care who got Georgie and Bryce together as long as it happened? They were perfect for one another. Then it hit her. "Wait. Why doesn't Georgie want us there?"

"Don't take it personally."

"One of my closest friends doesn't want me at her wedding and I shouldn't take it personally?"

"I told you it's not a traditional—" His phone rang. "I need to take this," he said after glancing at the screen. "I'll be back. Pick out something nice," he said gesturing toward the cut flowers. "Something for a bride, but not too traditional."

Angel stared as he ducked out the front door.

Just then Fanny Anne appeared with a potted plant and a basket of flowers. "Sorry I took so long. Have you decided... Oh, hi, Angel." She glanced around. "Did the sheriff leave?"

"He'll be back. Meanwhile could you whip me up a small bouquet of sunflowers and lavender? Maybe add a couple of poppies and bind them with a pretty ribbon?"

"Sure, honey," she said while plucking flowers from various vases. "Give me a couple of minutes."

"No problem." Angel looked out the window and saw Ryan talking on his cell. Pulse racing, she scooted back to the corner and dialed Sinjun. Thank God her friend answered on the first ring. "Have you heard from Georgie?"

"No. You?"

"No. But Ryan has." Angel shared the news about the civil ceremony as fast as she could, trying to keep her voice down as her excitement welled. "Can you believe it?" she squealed. "We were right to finagle their room situation."

"No. No we weren't," Sinjun said, sounding somewhat panicked. "It was a mistake. Bryce and Georgie are a mistake. He's not the one."

"What are you talking about?"

"She must not have checked her email today."

"She's on a plane. She... Why does it matter if she checked her email or not? Did you write to her? Do you know something I don't? Something bad about Bryce?"

"I should have trusted my instincts. We shouldn't have pushed them together."

"I don't know whether to be worried or peeved," Angel said. "You're talking in riddles, Sinjun. And you're making me feel like I did something wrong."

"I'm the one who messed with the hotel reservation."

"I'm the one who asked you to." Sweating now, Angel glanced toward the door. "Oh, crap. Ryan's coming and this is supposed to be on the QT. I have to go."

"You have to stop the wedding," Sinjun said. "Or at least make sure Georgie reads her email before she says "I do" so she has a chance to say "I don't.""

Angel disconnected just as the bell tinkled and Ryan strode back inside. She couldn't remember the last time she'd felt this flustered, this clueless, this busted, and sick with dread.

He narrowed his eyes and angled his head. "Everything okay?"

Absolutely not. "Everything's peachy."

Thirteen

Rolling into Nowhere after spending several days in London was a bit of a shock. Sure, most of the stores and houses were old, but nothing dated back to Medieval times. And even though the former library and barely-hanging-in-there drug store were historical, they hadn't been lovingly preserved or restored.

In kind, there were no modern skyscrapers. No herds of pedestrians. No gridlocked traffic. No theater district or world-famous landmarks.

There was, however, a museum and when Bryce drove his pickup past the rinky-dink historical site, Georgie slid fast and low in her seat.

"What are you doing?" he asked.

"I can't remember if Emma's working at the museum today. I can't keep her schedule straight."

An assistant curator at Nowhere's Historical Museum, a trail guide for Eagle Butte's Hiking Tours, and a photographer for the Z-Crew Stormchasers, Emma not only juggled three jobs, she excelled at and had been employed at all those places for years. Georgie had always been intimidated by her friend's ability to thrive in multiple careers. And now that Georgie was embarking on the most challenging job of her life, she needed all the confidence she could muster.

"I don't want her to see me," she said, contorting her body even more. "Oh, and do me a favor. Make a left and go around the block so we don't pass Wonderland. Bella and Savage are definitely working and—"

"You don't want them to see you."

"They know we're returning today, but they don't know when. If they see me, they'll flag us down."

"And you don't want them to know where we're going."

"You're looking at me like I'm crazy."

"You're acting a little crazy."

She did feel like a human accordion just now, her body practically folded into the floor.

The truck hit a pothole and her head banged the dash. "Ow."

"For the love of—"

"I'm fine. I'm good." Brow throbbing, she shifted upward and heard a loud rip. "Oh, no."

"What now?"

"The hem of my dress was caught under my shoe and, *crap*, I tore the bottom ruffle." She couldn't believe it. She'd just trashed the only traditional thing about this ceremony— her long, white sundress.

"How bad is it?"

"Bad." A six-inch rip in the seam that left a gaping hole as the fabric sagged.

"At least no one will be there to see it," Bryce said.

Sarcasm didn't suit him, but he was entitled. His knee was acting up and he looked exhausted. Plus, she'd been less than congenial for the last hour. Hell, she was downright cranky. She kept waiting for something to go wrong. When it came to something she wanted heart and soul, something always went wrong.

You need an attitude adjustment pronto, Poppins.

She also needed a safety pin.

She dug in her purse, cringing when her hand brushed her phone. She'd purposely turned it off and kept it off for the entire journey. She didn't want to read any texts or emails or to hear any voice messages. She didn't want to out-and-out lie to her friends or to feel pressured into fudging a reply. So she'd unplugged. Only that felt weird, too.

"We're here," Bryce said.

Holy frick came to mind but instead Georgie begged a moment while she hiked up her skirt and weaved a safety pin through the underside of the fabric. "One more should do it," she said while popping open another pin and, "Ow," stabbing herself in the finger. "I'm fine," she said, even as blood oozed.

Groaning, Bryce reached past her and into his glove compartment while she nabbed a tissue from her purse.

"Could have been worse," she said as he opened a small first aid kit. "At least I didn't get blood on my dress."

"Maybe we should postpone—"

"It's just a pin prick!"

"You've also got a goose egg on your forehead," Bryce said as he cleaned and bandaged her wound.

"What?" Georgie flipped down the sun visor and gaped. "What the... Oh, cripes. I didn't realize I hit the dash that hard."

"You're a ball of nerves. Just tell me one thing. Nervous excitement? Or cold feet?"

"You'll think I'm screwy."

"I think you're flustered and I want to know why."

She glanced from her frazzled reflection to Bryce's handsome face. Her insides squished and her pulse revved. She'd crushed on this man all her life. "I'm worried this is too good to be true. That our noble intentions and heartfelt agreement are doomed even before they get off the floor. That something or someone is going prevent us—the two most unlucky people in Nowhere—from tying the knot."

His lip twitched and his tired eyes sparked. "Sit tight."

"What..."

He slid from the truck and hobbled around the hood.

Her door swung open and—*Geez, Louise*—he reached in and pulled her out, hauling her up and over his shoulder.

"I'm carrying you inside rather her than risk you tripping on the steps or bumping into anything or anyone that might postpone or prevent us from tying the knot," Bryce said as he limped toward City Hall. "Any objections?"

"Your knee—"

"To hell with my knee. We're getting hitched."

Georgie suppressed a girlish giggle as Bryce awkwardly

whisked her up the steps and into the small brick building. *I'm getting married*, she thought. *To Bryce Morgan. My dream man. My...*

"Typically the groom carries the bride over the threshold after the wedding," came a hushed but familiar voice.

Georgie shifted and saw Angel standing nearby, albeit upside down. Strike that. Georgie was the inverted party. "What are you doing here? How did you know about this? About us?"

"Ran into Ryan," Angel said as she rushed toward them. "He slipped about this, about you, and of course I had to be here. The least I can do is spruce up your hair and makeup," she said to Georgie then rounded on Bryce. "This is cute and all, but not exactly discreet."

Georgie looked over her friend's shoulder and saw Mr. Lockhart busying himself behind a desk littered with piles of pamphlets and forms. He'd been the resident notary public and go-to man for last minute fishing permits and such for the last forty years. His hearing was shot and his eyesight was iffy, but he was a Nowhere fixture—sort of like the museum.

"I think we're okay," Georgie said, "but good point."

"You're also wrinkling your dress."

"It doesn't matter," Georgie said as Bryce set her carefully to her feet. "It's already ripped."

"I can fix that, too," Angel said, patting the massive tote looped over her shoulder. "I'm loaded for bear. Borrowing your girl for a few," she said to Bryce while nabbing Georgie's hand. "See you inside Meeting Room A."

Georgie's stomach flipped when Bryce met her gaze. He didn't look keen on letting her out of his sight. All the same he smiled as Angel dragged her toward the ladies room. "Glad you could make it, Angel," he said.

"We'll see about that," she mumbled as she fairly pushed Georgie into the tiny green-tiled room. Once inside, she whirled—eyes wide, voice low. "I've been calling you. I left messages. I texted."

Confused, Georgie hugged her purse. "I shut off my phone."

"When?"

"Before we left London."

"And you haven't turned it on since? Never mind. Just...turn it on and check your email."

"Why—"

"I don't know why, exactly. Just check it."

"You're freaking me out."

"I know. I'm sorry. It's probably nothing. But it could be something. I just... Are you and Bryce in love?"

"No," Georgie blurted as her heart bumped to her throat. "But we're a good match."

"What if you aren't?" Angel asked. "What if you're meant for someone else? Not just a good match, but a love match? Please check your email."

Angel's desperate expression cramped Georgie's already knotted stomach. "I'm afraid to look."

"Then let me."

Dizzy now, Georgie snatched her phone from her purse and passed it to her friend. She broke into a cold sweat as Angel powered up.

"Oh. Oh, no," she said as she scrolled. "Oh, wow."

"Wow what? What are you reading? Who's it from?"

"ID-dot-com."

"Impossible Dream? I got a note from Impossible Dream?" Georgie could scarcely breathe. "Is it a rejection?"

"Nope. A prospect. Your dream nanny position with potential for marriage. To a widower with three young children. A wealthy doctor. A surgeon, no less. Wait. There's a photo attached." Angel clicked over and whistled.

Georgie palmed her clammy brow, wincing when she connected with the goose egg. "What? Handsome?"

"Gorgeous. And what a smile," she said, even though she was frowning.

Georgie couldn't take it. She grabbed her phone, glommed onto the guy's face and, after registering the swoon factor, clicked over and focused on the body of the email. "It gets worse," she said with a groan. "We have a lot of common interests and he's relatively local. Just north of Chadron. Which means I'd still be close to you and the Inseparables. I wouldn't have to breach our pact."

"What are you talking about?"

"Bryce wants to be a sportscaster."

"Don't get me wrong," Angel said with a raised brow. "He

has the looks, the charm, and the knowledge, but he's not technically trained and sportscasters are motor mouths. Bryce doles out words with an eyedropper."

"Except for when he talks about the game. He gets into this animated zone. Trust me. I've seen it. Anyway, if he's lucky enough to land a job, I might have to relocate to who-knows-where."

"Oh, Georgie."

"Oh, God." Georgie scrolled through the email, reading beginning to end, her pulse pounding when she spied the golden phrase.

Impossible Dream offers the most likely prospects based on data, research, and ID-tuition. It's up to the applicant to follow through. We provide the magic. You provide the derring-do. True passion and faith required. Patience recommended.

The words that had steered Bella toward Savage and Chrissy toward Mason. True love and a promising happily-ever-after.

"What are you going to do?" Angel asked.

"Marry Bryce."

"But what if—"

"We made a deal. Plus, Arlo already told the twins. They need me. Bryce needs me."

"Yes, but what about you? What if Dr. Benjamin Ryder—"

"We'll be okay. It'll be okay," Georgie said, as she stumbled toward a stall. "We have an arrangement. MFB's," she said, then promptly hurled into the toilet.

* * *

Bryce got a bad feeling when Angel dragged Georgie into the john. He got even edgier when the only one waiting for him in the meeting room was Arlo. According to his old man, Frank Loper, a retired judge who officiated occasional ceremonies, had encountered car trouble. Ryan left to pick him up.

Bryce, who'd never been prone to pessimism, envisioned several scenarios, all resulting in something or someone sabotaging the nuptials. Georgie's screwy worry come-to-life. At least Arlo had assured him the twins were on board with the proceedings. That was something.

Even so, Bryce limped back and forth in an awkward attempt to walk off his jitters. He passed Arlo (who'd engaged in his own brand of stilted pacing) twice. At least Arlo had a cane.

"Don't we make a pair?" Bryce quipped.

"Maybe we should sit before we fall," Arlo suggested.

Instead they met in the middle and leaned against the conference table.

They both eyed the door.

"What's taking them so long?" Arlo asked.

"I told you. Angel offered to do Georgie's hair and makeup, and to stitch up her dress."

"I thought Georgie wanted to keep this simple."

"She does. Speaking of..." Bryce tapped the jeweler's box in his pocket. Arlo had slipped it to him when he'd entered the room, saying, *She'd want you to have it.* Then he'd barreled into an update regarding Charlie and Chelsea.

"I'm not sure how Georgie's going to feel about Mom's ring."

"It's not all that fancy," Arlo said.

A silver band with an amethyst heart. Beautifully understated and especially designed by Arlo for Shirley to celebrate their twenty-fifth wedding anniversary. "But it is sentimental," Bryce said. His mother had treasured this ring and had intended to pass it down to Marla. "You should save it for Chelsea."

"Georgie can pass it on to Chelsea when the time's right. Today you need a ring and this ring represents a long, happy marriage. Think of it as a good luck charm," Arlo said then glanced toward the door. "Maybe you should check on those girls. Make sure they're okay."

"I'm sure they're fine." Only he wasn't. Given her recent clumsy streak, he imagined Georgie slipping on the tiled floors or Angel accidentally branding her cheek with a curling iron.

The door swung open and Bryce braced for the Bride of Frankenstein.

Instead, Ryan strolled in with the retired judge in tow.

Wearing a sportsman vest and a canvas cap, Loper looked more suited to fishing on the lake rather than officiating a wedding.

"Everything in order?" Bryce asked.

"Hello to you, too," Ryan said with a crooked grin.

"An eager groom," said Loper. "Now all we need is a bride."

"I'm here!" Georgie blew into the room, looking beautiful and bride-like in her white ankle-grazing dress.

The distance from the door to where Bryce stood with the judge was a few scant feet and Georgie was moving at a good clip. But, just like in one of those heart-stopping moments when he'd thrown a pass to a wide receiver in the end zone, everything moved in slow motion. Senses heightened, Bryce noted details as Georgie closed the gap.

Her long, dark hair—now braided and accentuated with small red flowers.

Her white-knuckled grip on a wildflower bouquet.

Her wholesome, pretty face.

Miracle worker, Angel, had camouflaged the swelled bump on Georgie's forehead by drawing attention to her lush pink lips and striking emerald eyes. Eyes that had yet to meet his.

She was beautiful and she was nervous.

Gone was the easy, flirtatious moment they'd shared when he'd carried her into the building. What had happened in that bathroom? Had Angel filled her head with second thoughts? Was Georgie gearing up to ditch him at the altar?

He balled his fists at his side and acknowledged a kick in his gut. Even though they'd only bonded this week, Bryce knew Georgie's rejection would bother him far more than Kathryn's.

Ryan nudged him in the side then addressed Georgie because, damn, Bryce was tongue-tied. "You look gorgeous," his friend said, then pulled her into a hug and whispered in her ear.

"I'm sure," she said then smiled up at Bryce—a smile that iced his nads because it was too bright. Too forced. "So," she said after wiggling from her brother's embrace. "What do we need to get this ball rolling?"

Ten-minutes later, in a whirlwind rush from securing the

license to taking their vows, Bryce slipped his mother's ring on Georgie's finger. A ring that represented a long, happy marriage and bone-deep love. The logic and practicality of this union, every mutual benefit he'd discussed ad nauseam with Georgie, blurred.

"I now pronounce you man and wife. You may now kiss the bride."

Bryce had kissed a lot of women, but he'd never kissed his wife.

He felt another nudge from Ryan and saw Angel elbow Georgie.

He cupped her forearms, leaned in, and, after they both angled this way then that, they sealed the deal with something between a peck and a brush.

The kiss was awkward. The whole ceremony was awkward.

Chiefly because Georgie was so damned wired. Angel, too. Now Bryce had a tension-induced kink in his neck to go with the twinge in his knee.

If Ryan and Arlo were conscious of any tension, they didn't let on. Nope. They were grinning like idiots.

Maybe Bryce's perception was skewed because of the way he and Georgie had been all over one another in London. Maybe awkward and tense was normal when pledging "for better, for worse, for richer, for poorer". Hell, he'd never even made it to the altar with Kathryn. This was a first.

As if to confirm his tunnel vision, Judge Loper blew out a breath and laughed. "I've never seen two people more anxious to tie the knot! And I never pegged you two as a couple. But I see it now," he added with a slap to Bryce's shoulder. "You got yourself a homegrown beauty, Bullet. And you," he said to Georgie, "you got yourself one heck of a standup man and a hometown hero to boot. Forgive my swift exit, but I need to scoot to Tank's garage. Of all the days to have car trouble. Ryan?"

"Be right there, sir," Ryan said as the judge strode out. "This will be rushed," he said to Bryce and Georgie. "Hell, this whole thing was rushed. Just want to say, it does my heart good to see two of the nicest people in my universe together. And that," he added with a smile, "is as sappy as I get. I'm hoping we can have a celebratory dinner or barbecue. Something."

"I second that," Angel said. "I'll happily arrange it. Just tell me when."

"On another note," Ryan said. "I'm still verifying info on Jimmy Trent. I'll give you a call when I have a full report, but I can tell you one thing. I can't imagine any court awarding him custody of those or any other children."

"Hold up!" Arlo butted in as Ryan turned to leave. "You can't leave us hanging! If you have specifics on that vermin—"

"I'll be in touch. Relax and enjoy the day."

"Who's Jimmy Trent?" Angel asked after Ryan left.

"The twins' birth father," Bryce said.

"A skunk," Arlo said.

"He's threatening to make waves," Georgie said.

Angel narrowed her eyes. "Which will be harder now that you and Bryce are married and can offer the children a stable home with two parents."

"And a grandpop," Arlo added.

"We're a team." Georgie looked up at Bryce, her emerald gaze brimming with grit and optimism. Then she linked hands with him and Arlo, adding, "We're a family."

And—*bam!*—there it was. The first dent in Bryce's MFB armor.

Fourteen

Angel walked out of City Hall with the rest of the wedding party—sparse as it was—not knowing what to think or feel. She wanted to believe that Georgie and Bryce had a fighting chance and that, even if they didn't love one another now, maybe love would bloom in time. Ryan had faith that it would, but Ryan didn't know about Impossible Dream or Dr. Benjamin Ryder. And even though Georgie made it clear that she was fully committed to Bryce and his family, historically her personal and professional ambitions imploded, exploded, or fizzled within months. Sometimes weeks.

After assuring Angel she'd break the news about her semi-spontaneous marriage with the rest of the girls pronto, Georgie drove off with Bryce. Arlo—who'd only recently started driving again—trailed after in his own truck.

Angel sat in her sporty two-door—an overly generous gift from her late husband Baxter—too distracted by chaotic thoughts to hit the road.

If she hadn't meddled in the first place, Georgie and Bryce wouldn't have been forced to share a room in England, they wouldn't have gotten so cozy, and more than likely Bryce would have laughed at Arlo and Ryan's suggested marriage match.

Bryce and Georgie would have returned to the states as friends—period—and Georgie would have been free and clear to pursue the eligible and wonderfully suited doctor as suggested by Impossible Dream. The company that had led Bella to Savage and Chrissy to Mason. Two perfect, loving matches.

Had Angel unwittingly botched Georgie's happily-ever-after? And how did Sinjun figure in? She'd known about that email from ID.com, but how? Had she hacked into Georgie's email the way she'd hacked into the hotel's? Maybe she was hoping to find an email from Georgie that held some sort of clue as to how she was getting along with Bryce. All the Inseparables had been dying of curiosity and frustrated by Georgie's silence. Still. Would Sinjun invade a friend's privacy to that extreme? Although if she was in the spy game, like Bella often suggested, maybe her code of ethics was skewed.

Angel keyed the ignition and kicked up the air. It was a hot summer day made hotter by a rush of panic and guilt. She'd already speed-texted Sinjun.

GEORGIE CHOSE BRYCE

Then she'd silenced her phone for the ceremony. Checking now, she saw that she had a response.

CALL WHEN U CAN

Which was better than texting because, yeah, boy, Angel was bursting with questions.

Sinjun answered on the first ring. "So is it a done deal? Did Georgie marry Bryce?"

"Via the shortest, most unromantic ceremony ever."

"Crud."

"Crud?" Angel repeated in the silence that followed. "Georgie married the wrong guy—maybe—because of us—partially—and all you can say is *crud*?"

"I'm a little out of sorts."

"Welcome to the club." Angel wiped sweat from her brow then aimed all the air vents directly at her face. "How did you know about the email, Sinjun?"

"I'd rather not say."

"Do you work for the CIA?"

"Bella asked me that before and the answer's the same. No."

"Are you saying that because it's true? You really don't? Or are you saying that because you signed some sort of confidentiality agreement?"

"I don't work for the CIA."

"FBI?"

"What makes you think I work for a government agency?"

"You're always so close-mouthed about your life."

"I'm a geeky loner who works long hours," Sinjun said. "Trust me, there's not much to tell."

"A geeky loner who's scary gifted with computers. Did you hack into Georgie's email account?" Angel plowed on. "I could almost understand. Since Georgie wasn't giving up much about her trip with Bryce—"

"I'm not a snoop," Sinjun said, sounding insulted. "Or a spook."

"Then how... Oh, wait. No. That would be weird. Although..." Retracing Bella and Chrissy's ID experiences, Angel narrowed her eyes. "Do you work for Impossible Dream?"

"I'd rather not say."

Angel thunked her forehead with the heel of her hand.

"And I'd really appreciate it if you wouldn't share your theory with the rest of the Inseparables," Sinjun said. "Or anyone else for that matter."

"I can't believe this."

"It would be better if you didn't."

"Why? What do you do for the company?"

"I'm their secret weapon."

Angel shivered and cranked the air back a notch. "Meaning you possess some special skill?"

Sinjun didn't answer.

"What? If you tell me, you'd have to kill me?"

Crickets.

"Aw, come on!" Angel cringed at the sound of her raised voice and instantly cooled her jets. She should probably drive home, continue this discussion in total privacy, except she was pretty sure she'd expire of curiosity by the time she got there.

"I won't tell a soul," Angel said, sinking slightly in her seat.

"If this gets out—"

"It won't."

"Cross your heart?"

"Oh, for...Yes. Cross my heart. I'd spit and shake on it if

you were here, but you're not."

Sinjun sighed. "All right. We call it ID-tuition."

"A spin on intuition?"

"Code for psychic."

Angel blinked.

"I have visions," Sinjun added.

"I'm sorry, but, seriously?"

"This is why we opt for the pseudo-scientific term. No one rolls their eyes at ID-tuition."

"I'm not rolling my eyes."

"But you are skeptical."

Angel massaged her temple. "More like shocked. I mean, this is huge, Sinjun. Have you always had psychic abilities?"

"I started having visions when I turned twelve."

"And you never confided in any of us?"

"Actually, if you think back, I did tell you about a freaky dream I had involving the church organist and preacher man."

Angel scrunched her brow. "Oh, yeah. Mrs. Barnaby and Pastor Dan. We laughed our butts off. As I recall you laughed, too. And, by the way, they still aren't and never were romantically involved."

"Not that you know of, anyway." Sinjun cleared her throat. "Listen, I can't really get into this now. Maybe I shouldn't get into it at all. Maybe we should hang up and forget we ever had this discussion."

Angel frowned, bothered by her friend's stressed tone. "No, no. I'm sorry. I just need to absorb, that's all. So, you have visions. Like a prophet? A seer?"

"I prefer the term facilitator, but only because I've yet to clearly define my gift. It's a multifaceted process," Sinjun said in a hushed voice. "And, no, I don't use a crystal ball. I see and sense people and events via my dreams."

As hard as she tried, Angel was having a hard time connecting her mousy, soft-spoken, scary-smart friend with anything supernatural. For some reason, it had been easier thinking she was a tech geek for a covert agency.

"So. You had a prophetic dream about Bella and Joe Savage? You saw them together?"

"Yes."

"And Chrissy and Mason? You dreamed about them, too?"

"Yes."

"But not Georgie and Bryce."

"No."

"Then why did you mess with the hotel reservations? If he's not "the one" then—"

"Georgie had me stumped. Where she was concerned, my dreams had gone dry. Four months and no vision. How do you think I felt during some of our video chats, seeing and hearing how miserable she was?

"I had concerns about pushing her and Bryce together," she went on. "Trust me. Major gut twinge. But I knew Georgie carried a smoldering torch for Bryce and I thought maybe, well, maybe he'd be a nice distraction until the real thing came along. And considering he'd just been jilted, I figured Georgie would be salve for his wounded ego."

"And then out of nowhere, you dreamed about Georgie and that doctor?"

"Yes. Listen. I have to go. I'm on the clock and someone's coming. I have to tell you, Angel, I'm relieved you guessed my ties with ID-dot-com. You can't imagine how frustrating and lonely... never mind. Let me simmer on Georgie's situation. I'll be in touch. And remember," she added in a whisper, "you crossed your heart."

"Right. Wait!" Angel said as a panicked thought welled. "Did you ever dream about me and Eddie? Or me and Baxter? Did you... Did you foresee their deaths?" *Could I have prevented their deaths?*

"No. Oh, Angel, no. I swear I never envisioned their deaths. I don't see everything and everyone. It doesn't work like that."

"Okay." Angel blew out a tense breath. "That's good. I guess." Just then she caught a glimpse of the Sheriff's truck in her rearview mirror. "Have you dreamed about me at all lately? Envisioned me with anyone specifically?"

"You mean like a love interest?"

Angel swallowed. "Yes."

"No."

"Oh."

"The dreams don't come willy-nilly, Angel. For the most part, they're triggered by the applications. If you want me to point you toward the best prospect—"

"I don't!" Every man she loved died. That was fact.

"About Georgie and Bryce... I could have misinterpreted my dream."

Angel perked up. "Does that happen a lot?"

"No."

"Oh."

Fifteen

Georgie spent the first few minutes of their drive staring at her ring. Or rather Shirley Morgan's ring. It was simple and lovely and Georgie knew it had meant the world to the woman who, some say, died of a broken heart.

If only Marla had kept in touch. A phone call here. A letter there. But instead the troubled rebel had cut her family off cold. In losing her daughter, Shirley slowly lost her spark.

Even so, the matriarch of the Morgan Ranch soldiered on, upholding tradition by organizing annual barbeques and holiday parties. The guest list was always long and Georgie, by extension of Ryan, was always invited. Throughout the years, Shirley had gone out of her way to make Georgie feel welcome and to shield her from gossip regarding her irresponsible mother.

In kind, Georgie had tried her best never to gossip about Shirley's daughter. Even as Marla turned older and more troublesome, Shirley made it a point to celebrate family and friends with her festive affairs. Since Shirley's passing, the parties had stopped. Although for Georgie and most anyone who'd ever attended, the warm memories lingered.

Georgie's heart had bumped to her throat when Bryce slid his mother's ring on her finger. She'd always looked up to Shirley. Now, as Bryce's wife, she was in the position to bring those happier days back to life. Even though she relished the opportunity, her shoulders tensed with a heightened sense of responsibility. She could manage the household. She could organize parties. But could she recreate Shirley's glitch-free magic?

"About the ring," Bryce said as she thumbed the sparkling heart, "if it makes you uncomfortable—"

"I'm honored to wear it, Bryce. Your mom meant a lot to me. Although, it should really go to Chelsea."

"That's what I said to Dad. For now, he wants us to have it. Thought it might bless us with good fortune."

Meaning Arlo thought they needed all the help they could get. Georgie forced a smile. "It was a kind gesture."

"For a cranky cuss he has his moments."

"It's been a few rough years for Arlo."

"Yes, it has."

In addition to losing his wife and daughter, he'd skirted bankruptcy twice. And even though he and Bryce presently had their heads above water, you never knew what fate had in store. Luckily, Georgie was used to living on a shoestring.

As they sailed out of town, they fell into silence, lost in their thoughts and companionable exhaustion. Nowhere faded in the side-view mirror and miles of nothing stretched ahead.

After spending a week in congested and majestic London, Georgie had forgotten the beauty and serenity of wide-open spaces. Lush green grass, scores of trees, rocky ridges and sparkling creeks.

Spying Eagle Butte in the distance, she tingled much as she had when she'd first spotted Big Ben. The historic clock tower had offered new thrills, but Eagle Butte triggered a lifetime of fond memories. Hiking, camping, wildlife sightings. There was also the nearby reservoir. Swimming, boating. She couldn't wait to introduce Charlie and Chelsea to some of the outdoor fun she'd had as a child. Bryce had never heard the twins laugh.

New goal: Make twins laugh.

Soon after, her mind jumped to additional goals—all of them revolving around the wellbeing and happiness of the Morgans. Oh, to be part of a thriving, loving family.

And just like that her mind jumped tracks. To the smiling surgeon and his grounded children.

"*For the love of God,*" she could hear Chrissy saying, "*stop doubting yourself.*"

All through the ceremony, Georgie had mentally recited a

one-note pep talk. Shaking her virtual pom-poms, she repeated that mantra now.

I made the right choice. I made the right choice. I made the right choice.

The next thing she knew they were only a few miles from her new home. So much for contacting the Inseparables pronto.

"I'm not sure if it's jetlag or the whirlwind wedding," Georgie said as they whizzed past the turnoff to her former cottage, "but I'm feeling a little dazed."

"It's been a hell of a day," he said while massaging his knee. "And it isn't over yet."

"Yeah." Eyeing his tight expression, she casually popped the glove compartment. "The whole greeting Charlie and Chelsea thing and settling into the house as their future guardians." *No pressure there.* Was he feeling it, too?

"Mr. and Mrs. Bryce Morgan," he said as if trying it on for size.

Mrs. Georgie Morgan, she thought to herself while snagging pain relievers from the first aid box. At the height of her teen crush, while daydreaming about Bryce, she'd doodled that very name—wishful thinking—a million times.

Out of all of her presently single girlfriends (except maybe Emma), Georgie had been the most unlikely to marry any time soon and she'd married first. It didn't seem real, but the ring on her finger, the bouquet in her lap, and the vows echoing in her ears proved otherwise.

All that was missing was a sense of giddy happiness. She blamed that damned email.

Impossible Dream had taken four months to match her with a family—a family perfectly suited to her. She'd rejected Dr. Ryder and his children in a heartbeat. She couldn't decide if she'd been a maverick or a fool.

"*Given my history of poor judgment*," she mentally fired back at Chrissy, "*I have every reason to doubt myself.*"

Temples throbbing, Georgie washed down an aspirin with a swig of bottled water then passed two capsules to Bryce. "I need to let the girls know I'm back in town," she said without remarking on his knee. "And about, well, us. I'll send a quick text."

He accepted the capsules with a grateful nod. "A text?"

"I know," she said, ignoring the heady brush of his hand. "It seems impersonal, but I'm not up to long discussions right now. Between waiting for news from Ryan about Trent and feeling anxious about meeting Charlie and Chelsea..." Not to mention the ID bombshell. "...I'm distracted."

"Dazed and distracted."

His teasing tone and sexy grin prompted another kind of thrill altogether. Even if she'd chosen the riskier family, there was no denying her physical attraction to Bryce. Surely that counted for something. "I'll make it up to them in person," she said while suppressing an urge to scoot closer. "Or in a video chat so we can include Sinjun. They'll understand."

I hope.

Georgie palmed her phone and thumbed a tab for a group text. *The Inseparables.* Angel, Chrissy, Bella, Emma, and Sinjun. Her oldest and dearest friends. None of whom she'd invited to her wedding. She decided to take an airy approach, hopefully bowling them over with calculated zeal.

TO INSEPARABLES: *Great news! I'm home! And...brace 4 it... I'm married! To Bryce! Can U believe it? Me neither. One thing led to another and we took the nanny position to the next level. 4give me 4 not inviting U 2 whirlwind ceremony. We sort of eloped. Only it was here. Ryan, who arranged the license, slipped 2 Angel so she was there. No one else though, except 4 Arlo. Angel can fill U in a little. I'll fill U in more when I can. Swamped with settling into new home with new family. Plz B happy 4 me. Luv U all!*

It was, by far, the longest (and most faked cheerful) text of her life.

Georgie held her breath as she waited for the replies to roll in. A quarter mile later, her phoned chimed three times.

CHRISSY: *What the... Seriously? U go, Georgie! Did Bryce tell Mason? If not, can I?*

EMMA: *One thing led 2 another? So vacation sex demolished your sensibilities?*

BELLA: *It was meant to be! Over the moon happy 4 U and Bryce!* ☺

Georgie gave it a second but when she didn't hear back from Angel or Sinjun, she fired off a response.

TO INSEPARABLES: *U can tell anyone. Not a secret. Just unexpected. Mutual, spontaneous attraction with common needs and goals.*

More dings.

BELLA: *Is that anything like spontaneous head-over-heels love?*

EMMA: *Interesting.*

CHRISSY: *Hmm. Can't wait 2 hear more. Vid chat later?*

BELLA: *It's her wedding night.*

EMMA: *Considering how AWESOME Bryce is, pretty sure she'll be otherwise engaged.*

CHRISSY: *Dinner tomorrow @ Caboose?*

ANGEL: *Sorry 4 late reply. Just got home.*

BELLA: *Yeah. From the wedding of the century!*

EMMA: *U & Ryan hanging out now, Angel? ;)*

ANGEL: *Coincidental crossing of paths.*

CHRISSY: *Where's Sinjun?*

ANGEL: *Working. So dinner tomorrow?*

BELLA: *I'm in!*

CHRISSY: *Ditto!*

EMMA: *With bells on. You still there, Georgie? Or can't U keep your hands off The Bullet?*

Their enthusiasm brightened her spirits like a shot of sunshine. Georgie rolled her eyes, but smiled.

TO INSEPARABLES: *Making dinner 4 the family tomorrow. Afternoon java and sweets @ Buzzbees?*

Everyone agreed then signed off with various emoticons.

"Considering that smile on your face," Bryce said as she ditched her phone, "I take it no one balked at not being invited."

"They were too stunned to be insulted. Although I might get an earful after it sinks in. I told them I'd meet them tomorrow for coffee. After that I'll grocery shop for the household."

"I think we're pretty stocked."

"I have some special meals in mind. Plus it will give you a couple of hours alone with the kids. That might be a good thing."

"You're probably right."

"Speaking of food," Georgie said in an attempt to keep things light, "I'm hungry. You?"

"Starving. Lucky for us, Pauline is cooking a welcome home dinner. Should be close to ready by the time we get to the ranch."

Although they were a few miles away, Georgie could envision the rustic coziness of Bryce's family home. She'd visited the Morgan Ranch on several occasions throughout the years. She knew the house and land well, even though much had recently changed.

Over the last decade the cattle operation had suffered considerable hardship and this past year, Bryce—who'd never had an interest in ranching—finally talked Arlo into cutting their losses by selling the livestock along with the vast portion of land that supported the working operation. Calving barns, corrals, equipment sheds, machinery—sold lock, stock, and barrel to a transplant from Wyoming who'd built a house on the far western end of the property.

The proceeds had left Arlo with money to retire on. He'd also retained twenty acres of pasture and pines at the east end, along with his two-story home, a rickety horse barn, and a small guest cabin.

"When we get there," Bryce said as he made a right onto Eagle Butte Road, "I want you to make yourself at home." He glanced over. "Could be me but things felt awkward between us at the ceremony."

Georgie straightened in her seat. Time to man-up and shove off her insecurities. Time for a dose of honesty. Mentioning the ID email didn't seem wise, so she focused on another worry. "I might have been a *tad* uptight," she teased, then palmed her throbbing forehead and sighed. "I'm sorry for being a basket case today. It's just... This is my moment to shine—as an MFB, as a caretaker and homemaker. I want to get this right."

"You already have."

Pulse tripping, Georgie held Bryce's gentle gaze.

"When you declared us a team and a family," he said, "you scored with me. And Arlo. You got it right with us and I know you'll follow through with the kids. I just hope we score with you. That we'll be all you dreamed of."

Georgie colored at the mention of her dream. More than ever she was determined to strike that email from her mind. She'd sworn Angel to secrecy about Dr. Ryder and, as soon as she grabbed a private moment, she intended to contact ID.com, informing them of her changed status so they could steer the man in a different direction. Surely she wasn't all that special. There had to be alternate prospects equally suited for the doctor and his children.

Her place was with the Morgans.

I made the right choice.

"Brace yourself," Bryce said as they rolled through the open iron gate bearing the Morgan brand. "We're here."

* * *

What the hell?

Gone was the carefree, confident woman he'd been with in London. Yes, Georgie had gone a little squirrely when they'd rolled into Nowhere, but he'd pinpointed the source of her anxiety and he'd teased her back from the edge. The bond they'd forged overseas had been intact when he'd carried her into City Hall. But then Angel had whisked her into the bathroom and—*What the hell?*—now there was an ocean between them.

She may not have had cold feet before they'd said their vows, but now she was shaking in her boots. He kept waiting for her to spill about whatever transpired between her and Angel. He'd grown used to Georgie speaking her mind—a refreshing, if not sometimes unnerving, stream of verbal freethinking. Instead, she'd been pretty tightlipped while driving through the countryside. He'd almost asked straight out about her sudden skittishness. Then it occurred to him, maybe he was blowing things out of proportion, reading things into her private moments with Angel. So he'd skirted the awkwardness of the ceremony and—finally—pegged the problem. She was uptight about getting things right in her new role as wife and mother.

As a first-time husband and father figure, Bryce commiserated.

Trying to relax for both their sakes, he flexed his hands on the wheel as he navigated the private road that led to his childhood home. Surrounded by sloping hills and sky-reaching pines, he rolled down his window and breathed the familiar scents of fresh country air. Gravel crunched under the truck's tires as they rounded a bend and then—bam!—there it was.

117

The rustic two-story cabin with the emerald green roof.

The home he'd grown up in. The home he'd be sharing with Georgie.

For the last few years, he'd been living in a modest apartment above Coyote's. He'd moved back to the cabin after Arlo had broken his hip, nursing his old man back to health as well as overseeing the partial sale of the ranch. Then the children came. Bryce had no intention of raising those kids in a man-cave above a bar. The ranch—what was left of it—was the natural choice. At least for now. Who knew what the future held?

Bryce braked, and Arlo, who'd been following the whole way in his own pickup, parked alongside. Pauline was sitting on the shaded porch along with Chelsea and Charlie. A suitcase and a satchel were parked nearby.

His aunt shot to her feet.

"Something's up," Bryce said as he pushed out of the cab.

Georgie didn't wait for him to come and open her door. She was on the ground and moving by the time he was halfway around the hood. Arlo joined them and they met his sister on the expansive, lush lawn.

"What's with the suitcases?" Arlo asked.

"Samuel's in the hospital," she said while wringing her hands.

"My uncle," Bryce clarified for Georgie then turned to Pauline. "What happened?"

"Heart attack. He says he's fine, but they're keeping him overnight for observation so how fine can he be? I'm so sorry," she said, glancing at each of them. "I need to go home."

"Of course you do," Arlo said.

Bryce tensed at the possibility of losing another family member. They'd barely absorbed the loss of Marla. "Why didn't you call us right away?"

"I didn't want to ruin the ceremony." She grabbed him in a brief hug. "Congratulations, sweetheart. Take good care of our boy and those kids," she said to Georgie in a quivering voice.

"I will." Brow scrunched, Georgie gestured toward the suitcases. "So you're driving back to Chappell now? Alone?"

"Not alone," Arlo said. "I'm goin' with."

Bryce frowned. "Dad—"

"Don't give me any guff," Arlo snapped. "I'm fit enough to drive, at least part of the way. And I can keep Pauline focused and calm."

"I'd appreciate the company," Pauline said to Bryce then turned to her brother. "And Samuel would delight in a visit. It's been a while since you boys spent some time. Maybe you could stay for a few days and then I can drive you back."

"I can take the bus home."

"Maybe I should drive," Bryce said as he eyed his aunt and her nervous actions. Between her distracted mindset, Arlo's healing hip and advanced age, he couldn't imagine them undertaking a three hour drive without incident. "I'd feel better seeing Sam with my own eyes. Humor me. Short visit. In and out. I'll return later in the week for Arlo."

The old man glared. "Or I could take the bus home."

"Or you could take the bus home," Bryce conceded. *Prideful bastard.*

"I couldn't impose," Pauline said. "Not on your wedding day. Besides you must be exhausted from your flight."

Georgie touched his arm. "We could give Ryan a call. I'm sure he wouldn't mind—"

"Ryan's driving Sienna to Lacey's tonight." Bryce searched his new wife's gaze. Was she worried he'd fall asleep at the wheel? Scared to be alone at the ranch? Maybe she thought he was jumping on an excuse to delay his reunion with the kids. Considering all he'd confessed in London, he wouldn't blame her for making that assumption.

"I'll be back before night's end," he said. "Dad, go pack a bag. Aunt Pauline, let me talk with the twins then I'll load your luggage and we'll hit the road."

"If we take my car," she said, "how will you get back?"

"I'll rent a ride."

"I'm telling you, we can manage," Arlo said, even though he was leaning heavily on his cane.

"Yes, we could," Pauline said even as she eyed he brother's cane, "but I can tell Bryce is set on this. If you're sure," she said to him then turned to Georgie. "And if you don't mind."

"I just want everyone safe and well."

"All right then. Thank you. And thank you for the time

with Chelsea and Charlie. They're good kids," Pauline said to Bryce. "Shy, but good." She gestured toward the house. "I'll give Samuel a call. Let him know we're on our way."

Arlo waved to his grandkids then hobbled inside. Pauline hurried after.

Georgie started to follow, but Bryce held her back. "I'm not happy about leaving you and the kids alone."

"We'll be fine," she said in a hushed voice. "I didn't mention Ryan because of us. I'm worried about you. Did you sleep at all on the plane?"

"I should be running on fumes, but I'm stoked on adrenaline. I'd feel like hell if Sam took a turn for the worse and Pauline wasn't with him."

"And if you don't drive her, Arlo will. Cranky *and* stubborn." Swiping her palms down her dress, Georgie glanced toward the kids. "I feel like I'm being tested," she said under her breath.

"Tell me about it." What were the chances that a crisis would pull him away from his new family on day one?

"Never mind me," Georgie said while straightening her spine. "Pulling on my big-girl-nanny panties. Let's do this."

A glimpse of the confident girl he'd known in London. The timing couldn't be better.

Relaxing a little, Bryce clasped Georgie's hand and, together, they approached the porch. Maybe their rocky start would smooth out from here. Setting an example, he summoned calm and an easy smile.

"Hi, guys," he said as they neared the swing. "I'd ask if you missed me, but I'm thinking you were too busy having fun with Grandpop and Aunt Pauline."

Brother and sister looked up from their laps. Both were small for their age. Both were blond and pale. Both had huge brown eyes, only Charlie kept a bead on you while Chelsea snuck peeks through lowered lashes. He was wary. She was skittish. When Charlie took his sister's hand, Georgie palmed her heart. Bryce knew her mind. She had the same kind of protective brother in Ryan.

Bryce thought about the last time he'd held Marla's hand, the last he'd had her back, and how easily he'd allowed her to slip away. Guilt robbed him of words.

So much for suave nonchalance.

"Speaking of fun," Georgie intervened. "Those are interesting projects."

Chelsea had a coloring book and Charlie had a sketchpad. A shoebox filled with crayons was wedged in between their scrawny little bodies. Basic pastimes in place of electronic games. Fresh air and—if the porch swing counted—outdoor activity.

Progress.

Chelsea didn't make eye contact with Bryce, but she did speak up albeit it in a hushed voice. "You came back."

Was she glad? Disappointed? Confused? How would she feel when he drove away ten-minutes from now? "I'll have to go away on occasion, sweet pea. Like now," he said while gently touching her bowed head. "I need to drive Aunt Pauline home. It's important. But, I'll be back. I'll always come back."

When she didn't respond, he settled next to Charlie. "Whatcha drawing there, bud?"

Charlie shrugged, his right hand clamped hard around a green crayon.

"Looks like some sort of dinosaur to me," Georgie said as she sat next to the boy's sister.

Bryce angled his head and looked closer. "Stegosaurus?"

Another shrug.

"Do you remember me from the Pajama-rama Party?" Georgie asked.

Charlie nodded. "Grandpop said you'll be living with us."

"That you need a family," Chelsea said. "Like me and Charlie."

Georgie squeezed the bridge of her nose, presumably blinking back tears.

"Told you, Arlo has his moments," Bryce said, his own chest tight with emotion. Knowing Georgie's past and knowing what she'd applied for with that matchmaking site made this moment all the more intense. If he didn't think the kids would be spooked, he'd initiate a group hug, physically bonding them as a family. If only it were that easy.

Instead, he leaned forward, forearms braced on his knees, hands loosely clasped. "What else did Grandpop tell you?"

"That you need a good woman," Charlie said.

Georgie smiled.

Bryce cleared his throat. "Yeah, well, Georgie's a good woman and we're a team now. The four of us and Grandpop. Thing is, teams stick together and work together and I could sure use your help."

Charlie and Chelsea perked up at that and Georgie leaned in, too.

Bryce pitched a strategy, affording the twins an all-star role that would hopefully build their self-esteem. He finished with, "Can I count on you to make Georgie feel at home?"

Two nods.

Game on.

Relatively confident that things were stable on the home front, Bryce succumbed to a sense of urgency regarding his uncle. Excusing himself, he transferred his and Georgie's luggage from the truck to the house. Seeing that his aunt was still on the phone, he nabbed two of the souvenirs he'd purchased in London and hurried back to the porch.

"We thought you might like these," he said while placing a bear in Chelsea's lap and passing a double-decker bus to Charlie.

The twins murmured a respectful, "Thank you," while eying their presents like ticking bombs.

"They came all the way from England," Georgie said.

"There's a story about that bear," Bryce said to Chelsea.

"The book is in my bag," Georgie said. "We'll read it tonight."

"Okay," was all the little girl said. She'd yet to make eye contact with Bryce. Was she worried he expected a hug? Was she unaccustomed to presents? Wary of men bearing gifts?

Arlo hobbled out, juggling a suitcase and his cane. "I got it," he barked before Bryce could intervene. "You grab Pauline's gear. She's right behind me." His expression softened when he looked at the kids. "See you in a few days. Be good for Georgie."

Pauline blew out the front door with her purse and a raincoat. She kissed Charlie and Chelsea on the head. "I'll wait in the car," she said to Bryce. "Take your time."

Translation: *Hurry up.*

"I'll see you in the morning," he said to the kids, then nabbed Pauline's suitcases and gestured for Georgie to follow.

"No wonder you made such an effective quarterback," she said as they crossed the yard. "Asking Charlie and Chelsea to show me around. Putting them in the driver's seat. Implying trust. Well played, Bryce."

"You weren't so shabby yourself."

"I can do better," she said while hugging herself. "I'm off my game."

"Jet lag will do that to you. Unless there's something else—"

"I thought they'd be more excited about their gifts. You're right," she said, sounding distracted. "They're abnormally subdued."

"Actually, they've come a long way in the week I've been gone."

"Really? Wow. Okay, well, onward and upward."

Her enthusiasm was forced. Her attention scattered. "Feeling overwhelmed?"

"Feeling challenged. Today isn't going like I imagined."

He tried not to read into that. "Maybe you and the kids should come with."

"Let's not complicate matters just because I'm jetlagged. I've got this."

"If you're sure."

"Positive."

"If you need me for anything," Bryce said as he loaded the luggage in the trunk, "don't hesitate to call."

"We'll be fine."

"If there's an emergency, call Ryan or Roger Mooney. He lives—"

Arlo laid on the horn, adding to the tension.

"For crying out loud," Georgie grumbled. "I know where Chrissy's dad lives. Also Bella and Savage are only a few miles away. Plenty of people to call should the need arise. Which it won't."

"Yeah, well. It's pretty isolated here. Easy to get spooked—"

"If you don't trust me with the kids, Bryce—"

"Of course, I trust you, dammit. I wouldn't have married you otherwise." Closing the trunk with more force than necessary, Bryce turned and faced Georgie who'd gone all red in the face. "I didn't mean that like it sounded, Lou. I'm sorry. I'm tired. We're both tired. And stressed."

"Any day now!" Arlo shouted.

Bryce pulled Georgie into his arms. "Let's backup and take a breath."

She rested her head on his shoulder and sighed. "You're right. I'm tired and I'm stressed, but I've got this."

"I believe you." Smoothing a palm down her back, he kissed the top of her bowed head. "We good?"

"We will be." She gave him a squeeze then eased back just as Arlo gave the horn another blast. "You best get going before he steps on the gas and leaves you in the dust." She crooked a shaky smile. "I'll think positive thoughts about your Uncle Sam."

Unsettled, Bryce stole a parting glance before opening the driver's door. "I'll think positive thoughts about us."

Sixteen

"You, Georgina Lou Poppins-Morgan, are a neurotic, delusional, immature mess."

Okay. Maybe she wasn't quite that screwy, but she was definitely in over her head.

For one, she was pretty sure she and Bryce had had their first fight while standing in the driveway behind his aunt's dusty, old car. And *she'd* been the instigator.

Even though she knew he was doing the right thing by looking after his elders, she'd been unable to temper her intensifying angst. Overwhelmed with exhaustion and doubts and disappointed with her less-than-stellar interaction with the twins, she'd twisted his caring words and taken them as an attack on her capabilities. She'd been impatient and oversensitive. She'd snapped and he'd snapped back.

Because she knew Bryce to be a good and kind man, Georgie knew he hadn't meant to hurt her feelings. He'd stated a hard fact—*I wouldn't have married you otherwise*—not a cold dig. Yet the words and the notion burrowed deep.

A dozen what-ifs dogged Georgie, nipping at her conscience in the wake of her mini-meltdown with Bryce. A meltdown triggered by that untimely email from Impossible Dream.

What if she'd sabotaged his happily-ever-after by jumping on the happy-for-now train? What if fate had intended him to patch up things with Kathryn thereby, ultimately, securing him a notable job in sports casting? Or if not Kathryn, what if Bryce was destined to meet his true love at the next charity event? A woman who loved children, a woman capable of making the twins smile from the get-go—unlike Georgie.

Historically, she always made the wrong choice and, instead of bowing out gracefully and accepting the dream job with Dr. Ryder, she'd chosen to marry Bryce. Just because they were friends, just because he cared about her, and just because he gave her the thigh sweats, that didn't mean they were suited as man and wife. That didn't mean she'd make the best caretaker for Charlie and Chelsea.

As if to confirm she'd acted rashly and perhaps recklessly (yet again), fate intervened, stealing the groom away from the bride and forever tarnishing what should have been their first night together as a family. Instead of settling in with the twins as a couple, Georgie was struggling to make the transition on her own.

In London, she'd imagined herself blowing into the children's lives like some sort of super nanny—transforming them into joyful, carefree beings with a spoonful of enthusiasm and a dash of derring-do.

In reality, there was no magical insta-bonding between her and the kids.

No doubt about it. The universe was testing her.

She realized early on in the evening that it would take far more than a cheery smile and sweet disposition to win the trust of Charlie and Chelsea Morgan. When it came to conversation, the twins were mini-clones of their uncle. Getting them to express their wants and needs and opinions was next to impossible. Their favored response—a shrug—was disappointing and, by night's end, frustrating.

At least the tour of the massive two-story cabin had been a mild success. The kids led their new "aunt" from room to room, explaining who slept where and noting the locations of linens and cookware and such—just as Bryce had asked.

Although their social skills lacked, they excelled at following dictates. They even helped her unpack and settle into Bryce's room and they didn't seem to mind when she rattled on—about their trip, about her friends, about her past adventures at Eagle Butte.

Instead of asking the twins if they'd like to explore the wonders of the surrounding land (and thereby risking a *shrug*), she simply listed her planned excursions. Plans that included them and lots of fun.

Georgie talked and kept on talking—all through supper and the cleaning up after. She chatted away as she finessed the children into a bath and then their pajamas. She tore through three storybooks, reading with animated enthusiasm, even as the fog of jet-lagged exhaustion thickened.

It wasn't until she tucked Charlie and Chelsea into their beds that she allowed her mind to veer fully to her marriage-of-convenience and her botched opportunity with Impossible Dream. Even though she was determined to honor her commitment to Bryce, she couldn't stop pondering the timing of that email and the awkwardness should her computer generated "dream match" show up on her doorstep. Her life, thus far, had been riddled with dodgy luck so naturally she assumed the worse.

She'd already fired off a quick response to ID.com, alerting them of her new relationship status and informing them she was no longer in need of a job. That had been four hours ago and she had received a brief confirmation, but she didn't trust it. She didn't trust fate. Not when it came to her and Bryce and their mutual tales of woe.

She'd feel better if she spoke to someone from the company in person. Perhaps there was a phone number buried somewhere on the webpage in tiny print.

After changing into her pajamas, Georgie slipped into Bryce's—their—bed and snuggled in with her laptop. Connecting to the wireless internet, she clicked over to Impossible Dream.

She saw the slogan...

ImpossibleDream.com
"Making magic since 1956"

...and the whimsical wand beneath. Which usually made her smile. As if a Fairy Godmother was putting the "possible" in "impossible" instead of some data analyst. Except now, the magical logo competed with a big, ugly hardhat bearing disappointing news.

SITE DOWN DUE TO CONSTRUCTION

"Are you kidding me?"

Georgie cursed the inability to click onto any one of the site's pages. No matter how many ways she searched for alternate contact information, she couldn't find it. She sent another email only this time she got an automated response. *Temporarily unavailable. Correspondence to resume ASAP.*

Frustrated, Georgie speed-dialed Angel. "Sorry to call so late."

"It's only eight-thirty."

"Oh, right. Sorry. My body clock's off. Actually, my everything's off," Georgie said. "Jetlag stinks and so does this ID thing."

"What do you mean?" Angel asked, voice tight. "Are you regretting your decision to marry Bryce instead of nannying up with Dr. Ryder?"

"No. I want this to work. I really do, Angel. But I can't help feeling the cards are stacked against us. For one, I'm worried Dr. Ryder might follow through on his end. I mean if he applied for a nanny-slash-potential wife, and Impossible Dream sent him the same email they sent me... What if he tries to get in touch?"

"So what if he does? Just tell him about Bryce."

"But what if Bryce is standing there when he calls? Or shows up? I don't want Bryce to know that ID-dot-com came through. He's always putting other people ahead of himself and there's a chance he'd insist I'm better off with the affluent surgeon."

"I don't know about that," Angel said.

"I sent ID-dot-com an email asking them to cancel the match," Georgie plowed on, "and they said they would. But what if I fall through the cracks? I'd feel better knowing it's a done deal. I'd feel better talking to an ID representative one-on-one. Verbal reassurance. Just now I tried to pull up their website in order to find a phone number but the site's down."

"I know."

Georgie scrunched her brow. "You went to the ID website?"

"Tried to, yes."

"Why?"

"Just curious."

"Are you thinking of applying? *Have* you applied?"

"No and no." Angel cleared her throat. "So where's Bryce while we're having this discussion about Dr. Ryder?"

"There was a family emergency with his uncle. Supposedly he's on the mend, but Pauline was upset so instead of letting her behind the wheel, Bryce and Arlo drove her home."

"She lives in Chappell, right? So I guess Bryce won't make it back until tomorrow? Not much of a wedding night. Not much of a wedding period. Please take me up on the offer of throwing you and Bryce a party."

Georgie thumbed her ring, anxious to make her mark as a Morgan. "I'd like to host a reception here. At the ranch. Something to celebrate family and friends."

"Like Bryce's mom used to do," Angel said. "Nice."

"I'd appreciate your help and I'd like to get the twins involved in the planning as well. Maybe it will help to reshape their warped concept of family. Something tells me Marla pretty much ignored them."

"Like your mom ignored you?"

Resentment welled and, because she was already in a crummy mood, Georgie wallowed. If it wasn't for her friends' parents, she never would have known the joy of baking Christmas cookies or going on haunted hayrides. Her mom couldn't be bothered. She was too focused on herself and her man of the moment. From what she'd learned about Marla, Georgie suspected the twins' mother had been equally self-absorbed.

"I can't turn back time," Georgie said. "I'll never make popcorn balls with my mom, but I can make them with Charlie and Chelsea."

"Just don't expect too much, too soon," Angel said. "From the kids or Bryce. The man had fatherhood foisted on him. Unlike Dr. Ryder."

Georgie tensed. "Are you saying Bryce isn't capable of loving those children like his own?"

"No. But there's no guarantee he'll love being a dad." Angel sighed. "Remember. An instant family was your dream, not Bryce's."

Georgie's gaze bounced from her laptop to the framed photos and trophies adorning Bryce's shelves and walls. Evidence of his glory days in football—from high school to the pros. A reminder that his dream was to get back into sports and that he'd been prepared to marry a woman he didn't love in order to achieve that goal. "You think I made a mistake."

"I'm worried you're trying to force something."

"Something that would've come naturally with Dr. Ryder and his kids. Maybe." Georgie's temper flared along with the nasty doubts that had been simmering all day. Doubts she wanted to slay. "Just because Impossible Dream steered Bella and Chrissy right in matters of the heart, that doesn't mean the company gets it right every time."

"I just want you to be happy."

"I *am* happy," Georgie insisted even though she was gritting her teeth. She refused to believe she was being overly confident about her future as Bryce's wife. She'd make her own magic if it killed her. "The only thing that would make me even happier is knowing for certain Dr. Ryder knows I'm off the market!"

At wit's end, Georgie typed the doctor's name into the search field. "You know what? I'll just call him directly. I have his name and location. Even if his home phone's unlisted, surely there's a number for his office. Shoot! Call waiting. Hold on. It's Bryce."

"You've got enough on your plate," Angel said, sounding anxious now. "Don't worry about Ryder. I'll make that call."

"Are you sure?"

"It's the least I can do for... for upsetting you. I'll touch base in the morning."

Angel signed off and Georgie palmed her brow. Her head was spinning.

"Everything okay?" Bryce asked.

"What? Oh. Yes." *Deep breath.* "Sorry I didn't answer right away. I was on the phone with Angel." *Talking about another man.* "How's everything there?"

"Not as good as Sam led Pauline to believe, but it could have been worse. He'll need to make some lifestyle adjustments."

"How's Pauline holding up?"

"Pretending to be a rock."

"Arlo?"

"A pain-in-the-ass. So far he's insulted one doctor and two nurses. But he did get Sam the ice cream he wanted."

Georgie smiled a little. "There's a softie underneath all that cranky-ass guff."

"A softness prompted by Marla's death," Bryce said, sounding especially subdued. "He doesn't talk about it, but I know he wishes he'd worked harder to keep her close. That makes two of us."

Georgie blinked at his raw admission. It wasn't like Bryce to bear his heart. Everything she'd been obsessing on for the last hour flew out the window as she narrowed her focus to diminishing her husband's stress.

"Listen, Georgie. I want to apologize again for losing my cool today."

"I lost mine first. So much for grace under pressure." Grappling to set things right, she bared her own heart—or at least a slice of it. "I have to confess something, Bryce. I didn't get on as well with the children tonight as I implied. I mean, we got on fine but we didn't, well, click."

"You mean you didn't have them laughing and doing cartwheels before tucking them in bed?"

She appreciated the good-natured rib, but she had imagined accomplishing something similar. "I feel like I misrepresented myself over in London."

"Because you didn't work miracles with Chelsea and Charlie on day one? It's not like I made it any easier by not being with you this evening."

"You're where you need to be. Speaking of... If you need to stay a day or two, don't hesitate. I know your family's still adjusting to the loss of Marla. This thing with Sam obviously pushed some buttons."

"Along with Chelsea and Charlie."

On pins and needles, Georgie waited for Bryce to elaborate. When he didn't, she shared the high note of her tense evening. "You know the bear you gave Chelsea? She took it to bed with her."

"She did?"

"I read her the story and, even though she didn't say

anything, I think she connected with the premise."

"Settling in with an adopted family," he said. "Trying to do the right things. Wanting to fit in."

"Wanting to be loved." Regardless of Angel's cautionary speech, Georgie had faith that Bryce had the insta-father gene. While waiting to board their plane at Heathrow, he'd read that storybook front to back. And although he'd itched to buy Charlie a rugby ball, not wanting to force sports on the boy, he'd opted for the toy bus.

In the three times Georgie had seen Bryce interact with the twins, she'd witnessed extraordinary patience and compassion. All-consuming devotion couldn't be far behind.

"Even though you don't think you clicked," he said, "I have no doubt you made a positive impression on the kids, Georgie. You must be exhausted."

A transatlantic flight followed by a whirlwind wedding followed by a trial by fire evening with the twins. Georgie would have laughed if she had the energy. "Feels like the longest day of my life."

"It should have been the happiest." He paused then blew out a breath. "Not much of a wedding or wedding night. I'm sorry about that, hon."

In addition to apologetic, the man sounded bone-tired. "Don't give it, me, the day, a second thought," she said a little too brightly. "I mean it's not like this is a love match. It's a friendly arrangement, right?"

"Right."

The tension in that one word reply knotted her stomach. What the—

"I should go," Bryce said.

"Give my best to Pauline and her husband. And Arlo. And remember if you need to stay, stay."

"Thanks, but, I want to be there when the kids wake up. Night, Lou."

"Night."

Georgie powered off, sensing she'd fumbled the conversation with Bryce. Sort of like she'd fumbled the evening with the kids. In trying to make things better, she'd only made them worse.

Normally, she'd call an Inseparable to lament her mostly sucky day, but that would mean admitting her worst fear.

When it came to nurturing healthy relationships with men and children, Georgie was no better than her mom.

Seventeen

Once upon a derailed dream...

As spent and cynical as she'd been the night before, Georgie greeted the dawn with renewed optimism. Her first full day in wife and mother mode and she was starting that day nestled against her husband. A man she'd almost assaulted with a hefty championship trophy when he'd crept into the house in the dead of night.

"What the hell?" Bryce asked, flicking on the stairway light just as she poised to strike.

"I heard a car and then doors and floors creaking and stuff," she said in a hushed squeal. "Like someone was sneaking in."

"Yeah. Me. I didn't want to wake you." He frowned up at her as he scaled the stairs. "I told you I'd be back before morning."

"It's two a.m."

"I'm aware." He relieved her of the trophy. "You're trembling."

Heart pounding, she sagged against his chest. "I thought you were Trent."

He tensed. "Why? Did he call or—"

"No, no. It's just I was sleeping hard and dreaming and... I got spooked. I thought he was after the kids."

"And you were primed to bust one of my favorite trophies over his head."

"I couldn't find a baseball bat, so yeah."

He laughed a little, pressed a kiss to her forehead then, after looking in on the kids, steered her back into their bedroom. "Come on. Let's get some sleep."

And that's exactly what they'd done. No wedding night sex for the newlyweds. Bryce had pulled Georgie into a spooning position and, three seconds later, he was snoring softly in her ear. Instead of disappointed, she'd been ecstatic. Although their phone conversation had ended on an awkward note, Bryce hadn't shied from sharing their bed. Maybe things were wonky between them, but wonky wasn't broken.

Noting the early hour and knowing the extent of his exhaustion, Georgie resisted snuggling deeper into Bryce's embrace. Instead she eased out of bed and slipped quietly from the room.

Wrestling with the surreal feeling that this was her new normal, Georgie showered, then roused and dressed the kids. They were midway through eating breakfast when Bryce ambled into the kitchen with a hitch in his step.

"Morning," he said with a ragged voice and a tired smile.

Chelsea and Charlie answered in tandem, "Morning, Uncle Bryce," although they didn't meet his gaze. As a result their greeting sounded more dutiful than sincere. Much like their expressed gratitude when he'd presented them with the souvenirs.

As for Bryce, he could have moved in and kissed them on the head or ruffled their hair—some form of affection—but instead he kept his distance. Was he playing it safe? Waiting for them to make the first move? Or was he afraid of being rebuffed?

One thing was certain, the man was dragging. Unshaven jaw. Bloodshot eyes. He'd pulled on jeans and a wrinkled tee, but hadn't bothered to comb his hair. Exhausted? Try zombie-fried.

"You should have slept in," George said.

"I'm good."

"I'll set you a place. I wasn't expecting—"

"I can manage," he said, staying her with a brief squeeze.

She wished his hand would have lingered. Or that he'd kissed her cheek. Or better yet, her lips. She ached for a wisp of the physical intimacy they'd shared in London. Her heart skipped as she watched him pad barefoot across the kitchen. *Sexy.*

He nabbed creamer from the fridge, pulled a mug from the cupboard, then poured coffee from the percolator. *Also sexy.*

If they were alone, she'd pounce on him here and now. Kitchen sex was hot. Unfortunately she wasn't sure they'd ever have the opportunity to indulge in spontaneous lovemaking, let alone anything of a slightly kinky nature. How could they with two five-year-olds in the mix?

The kids devoured their second helping of pancakes while Georgie nibbled her fourth piece of bacon.

Bryce collected a plate and utensils.

Her gaze glommed onto his denim-clad butt.

She knew what she was thinking about (sex, sex, sex). But what were the kids thinking? What was Bryce thinking?

The silence made her twitchy.

A half-dozen conversation starters popped into Georgie's brain but they all felt forced.

Her first morning with her new family. She should have been on top of the world and yet she felt mired in mud, struggling to fill this home with carefree cheer.

Charlie and Chelsea weren't any chattier this morning than they'd been last night. And Bryce rarely prompted small talk. Yesterday, he'd at least tried to initiate conversation with the kids when he'd asked about their art. Today was a different story.

Bryce's phone rang and Georgie let out a pent up breath. At least someone had something to say.

"It's Mason returning my call," Bryce said. "I'll take it in another room. Be right back."

As soon as he left, Georgie's own phone vibrated against her hip. Since the kids were intent on their pancakes, she snuck a quick look. A text from Angel. Yes!

SPOKE W/RYDER. NICE MAN. KNOWS THE SCORE. YR OFF THE HOOK. TTYL

Georgie wished they could talk now instead of "later". But at least she knew her Impossible Dream was officially canceled.

So why did she still get a bad feeling when she thought about Dr. Ryder?

Did a small part of her worry she was sitting in the wrong kitchen? What were mornings like with the surgeon and his kids? Did they greet each other with affectionate hugs and kisses? Did they laugh and chatter like magpies during breakfast? Wayward thoughts about a fun loving, tightknit family caused Georgie to flush with shame. She'd chosen her family and just because it wasn't an instantly mushy, happy family, that didn't mean she couldn't turn things around.

"Don't expect too much, too soon."

Right.

Bryce ambled back into the kitchen sans phone.

"Everything okay?" she asked.

"Touched base with Mason about the club. Everything's fine. That man could run Coyote's solo with his eyes closed." Bryce settled in a vacant chair and smiled at the twins. "Those pancakes as good as they smell?"

Mouths full, they nodded. At least they didn't shrug.

The three of them focused on their food and Georgie swore she heard crickets chirping.

She was tempted to provide Bryce with a newspaper and the kids with their tablets. Then, at least, she'd feel less troubled by the lack of conversation. Growing up, her mom and assorted dads ate their meals in front of the TV. As an adult, unless she was meeting up with the Inseparables, breakfast had been a solitary affair. This moment she felt almost as alone as when she was alone.

Determined to engage with her family, even if she instigated shrugs and grumbles, Georgie filled the grating silence with a cheery announcement. "I'm throwing a big party and you three are going to help."

* * *

By the time Georgie parked her car in front of Buzz-Bee's Bakery she was hopped up on five cups of coffee, a boatload of syrup, and an ocean of nervous energy. More sweets and java were the last thing her system needed, but the Inseparables were waiting inside and she very much needed a dose of easy-flowing girl-talk.

Her mention of a party hadn't sparked a lot of feedback from Bryce and the kids, but they had responded to direct questions and they hadn't seemed to mind when she'd gushed about past parties thrown by Shirley Morgan. In fact, the kids had looked somewhat transfixed as Georgie described the grandma they never knew and the rollicking affairs she was famous for.

The good times and memories had flowed and every time Georgie noted a theme or a game or a delicious homemade dish, it spurred an idea for future parties of her own. By the time they finished washing the breakfast dishes, Georgie had committed to hosting five festive affairs before the end of the year.

"Let's tackle the wedding reception first," Bryce had gently suggested, *"and take it from there."*

Assuming he'd been worried about the amount of work or maybe even the cost, Georgie had assured him she'd operate on a shoestring budget, and handle the bulk of the planning. If that made him feel better, he didn't say.

Georgie chose to believe that Bryce was on board. She needed this party. Planning it made her feel like a Morgan as opposed to the Morgan's nanny/housekeeper. She'd felt like the odd-man-out at breakfast. The only person in the room who craved emotional and physical engagement. It was one thing not to expect too much too soon, but what if Bryce never grew comfortable with showing affection? What if the kids never broke into excited chatter? What if they never burst into uncontrollable giggles or begged Georgie to take them on a hayride? What if they didn't want to be nurtured? And how would cranky-ass Arlo play into things once he returned?

Georgie's *Suzy Homemaker* fantasy faded with every projection.

Had she survived the indifferent family she'd grown up with only to sign on for dysfunction of another nature?

"Stop it. Stop imagining the worst." *What is it with you?*

Disgusted by her negative thoughts, she flipped down the mirrored sun visor and gave herself a pep talk.

"You will not have another meltdown. You will rally. In fact, you're going to brighten the lives of Bryce and the kids so much they'll have to wear sunglasses 24/7!"

After swishing on fresh lip balm, she nabbed her purse, and pushed out of her car.

"I don't expect too much," she grumbled as she hurried toward Buzz-Bees. "I expect a miracle. Georgina Lou Morgan. Making magic since...today."

Spying her friends seated across the crowded bakery, Georgie brightened. She craved and needed her friends' support. She needed positive energy. She needed them to believe that she was walking on sunshine otherwise they'd worry she'd bungled yet another life choice. Better to pretend everything was hunky dory.

See it. Be it.

I am Suzy Homemaker and I have the perfect family.

Catching their attention and seeing their smiles, Georgie waved. "Sorry I'm late!"

Mrs. Wickham, one-time teacher, now owner of the bakery, wagged an admonishing finger as Georgie zoomed past the black and yellow tiled counter. "Why don't you announce it to the world, Miss Poppins? And slow down before you break your neck!"

Georgie didn't slow, but she did correct the raspy-voiced senior. "I traded Poppins for Morgan, Mrs. W. Just so you know. For future reference, I mean. I got married yesterday!"

"Cheese and crackers," the woman said as other locals traded looks and whispers. "You and The Bullet got hitched?"

"Yup!" And with that she plopped in an empty chair between Angel and Bella. They, along with Emma and Chrissy, gawked at her like a school of open-mouthed bass. "What?"

"You're as high as a kite," Chrissy said.

"High on love!" Bella said.

"Or sex," Emma said.

"Actually," Georgie said, "I'm jazzed on caffeine, sugar, and adrenaline. I've been up since six a.m. Cooking and cleaning. Getting the kids dressed and motivated and mapping out our week. Bryce drove me to Tank's garage so I could pick up my car which," she said while looping her purse over the back of the chair, "is still making weird sounds. Although don't tell Bryce. He'd want to buy me a new ride and he's done enough already. Can you believe he paid Mr. Jones everything I owed in back rent? I wish he wouldn't have done that. I mean I'm glad for Mr. Jones, but now instead of being indebted to him, I'm indebted to Bryce."

"I'm sure Bryce doesn't look at it that way," Angel said with a raised brow. "You're his wife now. Partners in life and all that entails."

"I know. I just don't want him, or anyone," Georgie said with a quick look over her shoulder, "thinking I'm taking advantage of Bryce's giving nature."

"I can't imagine anyone who knows you thinking that," Bella said.

"Not to mention, he's getting a housekeeper and caretaker for those kids and Arlo," Angel said. "That's a hell of a tradeoff."

Just then Mrs. W ambled over with a tray of fat, gooey cinnamon buns and a pot of fresh coffee. As always she was wearing a sparkly hairnet over her silver curls and a pair of oversized novelty earrings. Today's lobe oddity: Porcelain bumblebees.

"Buns and coffee on the house," she said while handing the goods off to Chrissy who, up until a few months ago, had been a longtime employee of Buzz-Bees. "Congratulations, Mrs. Morgan," she said to Georgie. "I'm not one for gossip, but other people are and let me tell you tongues wagged while you and Bryce were away. Now they'll wag even more." She patted Georgie's shoulder. "But in a good way."

She tottered off and Chrissy snorted. "Not one for gossip, my eye. But whatever," she said while pouring coffee for everyone. "Let's back up to something you said, Georgie. You were behind in rent? How far? Why didn't you say anything before now? Maybe Mason and I could have helped."

"Hold up," Emma said while scanning her phone. "In yesterday's text, you mentioned *mutual, spontaneous attraction with common needs and goals.* Is this—"

"A marriage-of-convenience," Georgie said in a rushed, low voice. "Yes. But it's okay. Honest. There are perks."

Emma grinned while trading her phone for a bun. "Perks meaning hot sex?"

"We are sexually compatible. Absolutely," Georgie said. Although there'd been no sex last night.

Chrissy scrunched her brow. "Compatible, huh?"

"Well, more than just compatible," Georgie said, cheeks heating as she tore into her own warm confection. "But I'm not giving up details so don't ask. Let's just say hooking up with Bryce is everything I ever dreamed it would be and more." That much was true. The sex in London had been off-the-charts fantabulous.

"That's great and all," Bella said with a frown, "but what about love?"

"She's better off without it, if you ask me," Emma said. "Love complicates matters and when it goes wrong, things usually get ugly. Take Ryan for instance. Lacey put that man through the wringer for years, but because he was stupid in love—for reasons I cannot fathom—he forgave her cheating, fickle ass every time."

"Yeah," Georgie said, thinking back on her brother's misery. "That was the worst. But now he's free and able to date a genuinely nice woman. I was hoping that might be you, Angel. But things seemed a little icy between you two at the ceremony."

"That's because Angel's freezing Ryan out," Chrissy said.

"I'm sorry," Bella said. "But I'm still trying to wrap my mind around the marriage-of-convenience thing."

Instead of talking in circles with a woman who was fixated on fairy tale romance, Georgie turned the spotlight back on Angel. "But Ryan's a great guy. Why not give him a chance?"

"Because of the jinx thing," Chrissy answered.

"But you're not jinxed," Georgie said to her tense-shouldered friend. "What if Ryan is perfect for you? What if you were meant to be? What if—"

"What if you were meant to be with Dr. Benjamin Ryder?" Angel snapped then slapped her hand to her mouth.

"What?" Emma asked, looking from Angel to Georgie.

"Who's Dr. Benjamin Ryder?" Bella asked.

"I'm so sorry," Angel blurted.

Georgie wasn't sure what surprised her more. Her friend's loose lips or her obsession with Dr. Ryder.

SPOKE W/RYDER. NICE MAN.

So nice that Angel truly believed Georgie belonged with him and not Bryce?

Rallying, Georgie sipped coffee then cleared her throat. "I, um, might have applied to Impossible Dream a few months back and, well, they might have emailed me yesterday with their suggested prospect."

"Wow," Emma said, looking injured. "You're full of secrets these days, Georgie. First the back rent then the wedding. Now this?"

Georgie's cheeks burned.

"What did you apply for?" Bella asked.

"A nanny position."

"And it took them months to find you one?" Chrissy asked.

"As dreams go," Emma said, "you being a nanny seems awfully doable. I thought ID-dot-com specialized in farfetched dreams."

"I was pretty specific," Georgie said as she twirled her wedding ring. "A nanny position with potential for marriage. Essentially, I applied for an instant family."

"Which you got with Bryce," Chrissy said.

"It had been four months. Four long months without a single prospect." Twirl. Twirl. "And then Kathryn jilted Bryce and I saw an opportunity." She shrugged. "I made my own magic."

"But Impossible Dream has been making magic since 1956," Bella said in an almost reverent tone.

"Did you get the email about the doctor before or after you married Bryce?" Chrissy asked.

"Just before."

"And you chose Bryce—a man with notoriously bad luck and sporadic financial issues—over a stable, successful doctor?" Emma asked.

"But I'd already agreed to an MFB arrangement with Bryce, and Arlo had already prepped the kids and—"

"What's an MFB?" Chrissy asked.

"Married friends with benefits."

Bella gawked. "You turned your back on your potential Prince Charming for friend sex?"

Temper flaring, Georgie clenched her fists in her lap. "We're talking about Bryce here," she said in a hushed tone. "We've known him all our lives. He's a good man and I've crushed on him for a long time. He needs me. Charlie and

Chelsea need me. I wanted a family and now I have one. In my own backyard."

"Where does the doctor live?" Chrissy asked.

Georgie frowned. "Just north of Chadron."

"That's almost our backyard," Bella said.

"I can't believe you're questioning my judgment," Georgie said. Everyone responded with raised brows and she sighed because, yeah, historically her judgment sucked. "I'm going to make this work, but it would be nice to have some support."

"Of course we support you," Emma said. "And we all agree. Bryce is a nice guy. A good man."

"It's just that Chrissy and I are with Mason and Joe because of Impossible Dream," Bella said, "and what we share goes so far beyond 'mutual attraction with common needs and goals.' To think that you're missing out..."

Chrissy nudged her cousin. "Leave it be, Bella."

"Not to mention Bryce was on the rebound," Emma said. "Turning to you so quickly after Kathryn, how can you trust—"

"He didn't love her," Georgie blurted.

Bella blinked. "Then why marry her?"

Georgie hesitated. Sharing that he'd been seduced by Kathryn's role in the sport's world seemed like a betrayal. Mentioning he was intimidated by the single-parent issue didn't seem fair either. "Bad call." Like that was much better.

An awkward beat later, Chrissy smiled and squeezed Georgie's arm. "Far be it from me to cast stones when it comes to relationships. I mean, look how I misjudged Mason the first time around."

"And thanks to ID.com," Bella said, "you got a second chance."

More awkward silence.

"Maybe Impossible Dream got this one wrong," Georgie said. "What the heck is ID-tuition? It can't be one-hundred percent on target all the time, right?"

"She has a point," Emma said then glanced over to Angel. "You're being awfully quiet."

"I've said more than enough today." Face burning as red as her fiery hair, Angel—who usually ate like a bird—stuffed her mouth full of a glazed bun.

Unsettled by her friend's tense mood, Georgie shifted. "Maybe we've all said enough. On this subject anyway. Let's forget about Doctor what's-his-name and the ID email. I made my bed and believe-you-me I don't mind laying in it."

Everyone nodded a pledge of silence and Georgie scrambled to leave this get-together on an uplifting note. "Remember those awesome parties Shirley Morgan used to throw? I'm going to reboot that tradition, starting with a post-wedding cookout. You're all invited and I might even ask you to wear matching dresses. You know. Something bridesmaid-like. Shiny pink with lots of ruffles."

Bella clapped. "I love it!"

"Over my dead body," Emma said.

"Okay. We'll nix the ruffles," Georgie teased.

"And the pink," Chrissy said.

"What's wrong with pink?" Bella asked with an affronted sniff. "The bridesmaid dresses I'm leaning toward for my wedding are pink."

"We know," Chrissy said.

"We've been suffering in silence," Emma said.

"They're teasing," Angel said. "But about all that poof..."

Eighteen

Bryce was off his game. Yes, he was jetlagged and exhausted from the additional drama of his uncle's heart attack. But it was more than that.

Somewhere between slipping that ring on Georgie's finger and nearly getting his head bashed by his trophy-wielding wife, Bryce fell in love. One minute he was dodging tender feelings. The next he was neck-deep in bone-deep adoration. Her meltdowns were weirdly endearing. She kept him on his toes—unbalanced and intrigued. They'd had more awkward moments in one day then most couples had in a week and yet he'd never felt more at ease with a woman. At ease and on edge. A stimulating combination.

Heady infatuation.

He'd been in love before. He'd misjudged both relationships. Both women. One had burned him with lies and manipulation. The other with betrayal. The break-ups were messy. Hell on the ego. Hell on the heart. He wasn't big on a replay although this time was different. He hadn't misjudged the woman. He'd misjudged himself.

"You gotta tell her, man."

Bryce glanced from Mason, his friend and partner, to Joe Savage. Savage was more of an acquaintance, but he was engaged to Bella and Bella was tight with Georgie. Thus Savage had spent a lot of time with Georgie over the past year. Also, the man had already been at Mason's house when Bryce had dropped by with the twins—who were now playing in the backyard with Mason's daughter, Melody.

Georgie was in town with her friends—which included Mason and Savage's other halves.

And Bryce was sitting at the kitchen table having coffee with Mason and Savage and fielding the occasional stinker from Mason's nearby sleeping dog, Rush.

"I'm with Mason," Savage said while snatching one of Chrissy's home-baked cookies. "Secrets are hell on a relationship."

"But it's a breach of our initial agreement," Bryce said.

"The MFB thing," Mason said.

"Married friends with benefits," Savage said. "You get an amiable—and pretty in Georgie's instance—companion who'll cook and clean and take care of your kids."

"Don't forget the casual sex," Mason said while biting into a cookie.

"A nanny for them. A plaything for you. Nice gig if you can get it," Savage said. "Which you did."

"Except now you screwed it up, or think you screwed it up," Mason said, "because you broke the number one stipulation of your MFB agreement. You fell in love. Your heart's in the mix and that's a bad thing because..." He glanced across the kitchen table at Savage. "Why is that a bad thing?"

"Because it complicates matters."

"See," Mason said while nudging the cookie tray toward Bryce, "we were listening. We're on board with this marriage-of-convenience thing."

"Except it's not convenient anymore," Savage said, "because it's not just business."

"It was never business," Bryce argued because, damn, that sounded cold. "It was a mutual ass-saving."

"You get a permanent caretaker for the twins. Georgie gets a home and financial stability," Mason said.

"*And* it was a way for us to achieve our independent dreams," Bryce added because, hell, it still sounded cold.

"Georgie gets an instant family," Savage said. "You get the freedom to pursue a career in broadcasting."

"Again," Mason said as he reached for a second cookie.

"We were listening. Speaking of that sportscaster thing. How are you going to juggle that, your charity obligations, and co-managing the Coyote Club?"

"As it happens," Bryce said, "I'm looking to get out of the bar business. You've done more for Coyote's in less than a year than I did in more than four," he said to Mason. "The club's a thriving entertainment venue now. That's all you, bud."

"You're downplaying your contribution," Mason said. "Not that I wouldn't buy you out, if that's what you really wanted, but I'm not convinced it is. Let's revisit this topic when you're not so...unhinged."

"Walking away from your job in the heat of emotion is rarely a good thing," said Savage.

"You did it," Bryce said.

"I'm the exception to the rule," Savage said with a smartass grin. "Let's get back to your traumatic crisis, Morgan. You're in love with your wife."

Mason snorted. "Still trying to see the bad in that."

Bryce dragged both hands down his unshaven jaw. "Why the hell am I talking to you two about this? Why am I talking about this at all?"

"Venting your personal spleen is not your norm," Mason said. "True. Which goes to show how seriously messed up you are. Have a cookie. Chrissy's cookies make everything better."

"I'm already OD-ing on powdered sugar and pancake syrup. Thanks, but, no."

"Just tell her you love her, Morgan. Man up. Get it out there. Hell, maybe she'll say it back."

"*Dear Abby*, you are not," Mason said to Savage, then turned to Bryce. "Don't listen to biker boy. Well, half listen to him. Tell Georgie how you feel, but don't just blurt it out. Take her for a romantic walk or dinner. Chrissy and I will watch the twins. Work your way up to revealing your heart."

"Romantic seduction," Savage said. "I thought that was a given."

Mason rolled his eyes, then rose and headed for the coffee maker.

"Do you think the women are talking about us right now?" Bryce asked. "Georgie and me," he clarified.

"Gossiping over coffee and sweets at Buzz-Bee's?"

Savage raised a brow. "Really, dude?"

"They've been friends forever," Mason said. "They talk about everything."

"You're wrong about one thing," Bryce said. "If I tell Georgie I love her, she won't say it back. She loved me a long time ago. But she's over that, over me. She's gone out of her way to make that clear."

She'd even been fine with him staying over at his aunt's house instead of coming home to her on their wedding night. He wished she would have sounded disappointed or at least woken him this morning with a frisky kiss. Instead she'd been all about the kids. He'd been dealing with that ego-buster all morning.

"Georgie's over sappy-ass happily-ever-afters," Bryce went on. "She's all about happy-for-now."

"That sounds like Emma," Savage said.

"Yup," Mason said while he topped off their mugs and set a chocolate frosted cake alongside side the cookies. "What?" he asked when Bryce gave him a look. "I live with a woman who worked in a bakery for a dozen years and a kid who gets a kick out of whipping up desserts. Do a guy a favor and help me eat some of this stuff before I turn into Jabba the Hut."

Savage just grinned and sliced into the cake.

Bryce shifted and looked out the window, his heart knocking against his ribs when he saw Charlie hanging upside down from a trapeze and Chelsea swinging alongside Melody on a fairly elaborate playset. Damn if they weren't smiling and looking as if they were actually having fun. "Hey, Mason. Where'd you get that jungle gym?"

"Special order from Dickey Rhodes."

A born and raised local.

"He has a small selection of readymade models on display at Chet's Farm and Feed." Savage said. "Since we're trying to galvanize local business, I just bought one for the courtyard at Wonderland."

"Thinking about getting one for Chelsea and Charlie?" Mason asked.

"Maybe we'll visit Chet's after we leave here. Scope out the stock. See if anything floats their boat."

"Or you could surprise them," said Savage.

"I think I'd like their take on something as big as a jungle gym," Bryce said. "If we don't buy something today, at least I'll know their preferences." Even if they didn't speak their minds, he could watch and glean insight via their expressions and actions—his epiphany of the day.

He'd noted a subtle change in his niece and nephew when he'd dragged into the kitchen this morning. Something in their body language. Maybe they weren't one-hundred percent comfortable with him or Georgie, but they were comfortable in their surroundings. Bryce decided to pull back rather than risk botching his dad's progress. He could do slow and easy if that's what it took to win the trust of his niece and nephew.

Georgie, on the other hand, had filled the silence with nervous small talk about big boisterous affairs he was certain the children weren't ready for.

Co-parenting for less than a day and they were already at odds. Not that Bryce voiced his concern to Georgie. He wasn't sure how to phrase it without sounding critical. Plus, what if he was wrong and she was right? Maybe her balls out enthusiasm would work like a charm. Her sunny determination was just one of the things he'd always admired about his new wife. The least he could do was ride out the day.

Just then his phone chimed. He glanced at the screen, thinking it was Arlo or Georgie.

It wasn't.

Nineteen

FROM THE HEART OF ANGEL DRAKE
SUNDAY, JUNE 21

I told myself not to write another word in this blasted journal. It's like tempting fate. When I think about how close ~~Ryan~~ he came that night to reading my private thoughts. But he didn't and it's not like he'll stop over again anytime soon. If ever. So here I am spewing my thoughts and worries and concerns because if I don't get them out of my head I'll go crazy.

Normally I'd vent to a friend. I am fortunate to have several. The closest of course being the Inseparables, but I can't talk to them—specifically Emma, Bella, Chrissy, and Georgie—about Sinjun's role in Impossible Dream.

A) I don't fully understand how she does what she does.

B) Sinjun vowed me to secrecy and I always usually keep my word.

I consider myself the soul of discretion so imagine my surprise when I bumbled the promise I'd made to Georgie, exposing the name of the doctor and her missed opportunity via ID.com

I was mortified. But when she pushed about ~~Ryan~~ him, she pushed the wrong button. I snapped which was wrong and stupid because it opened the floodgates and talk turned exclusively to Impossible Dream. I had to bite my tongue when Bella touted the wonders of the enigmatic matchmaking company. I don't think any of us ever thought real magic was at play. We assumed it was a marketing ploy and that the results and suggested prospects were based on hardcore research and technology. Not that "visions" are magic per se, but they're not scientific. Although Sinjun did say her psychic abilities are connected to the on-line applications. Whatever that means.

And then there's the whole matter of Sinjun keeping her foretelling dreams under wraps. By not telling us about her whopping strange "gift", something she's been experiencing and utilizing for years, it's like she's been living a lie. She was always a bit of a mystery, but now I feel like I don't know her at all. Also, I'm not totally sold on the psychic-facilitator thing. I mean how does it work? Really?

If Sinjun wants me to keep her secret, I need more answers. And who knows when I'll get those? She hasn't returned one of my five calls or any of my texts. And the ID website is down on top of that. It's like she's gone into hiding. But why? It only heightens my fear that we botched things big time for Georgie and Bryce by finessing that London affair. And what about poor Dr. Ryder? Talk about a sweetheart. He would have been perfect for Georgie. Not that Bryce isn't a sweetheart, but his motive for marrying Georgie wasn't exactly noble.

I feel guilty and worried and here I am venting my frustration in this journal because I can't talk about it with the Inseparables. Not that they're available right now anyway. Everyone has Sunday evening plans with their family or significant other or, in Emma's case, with the Z-Crew Stormchasers.

So it's me and you, Journal, and then me and the TV and dinner for one. Which I'm usually fine with, only tonight I'm not. So screw it. I'm going out.

Yours not so truly,
Angel Kane-Barnes-Drake

* * *

Angel slammed shut her journal.

Rather than eating alone at home, she'd grab a bite at Café Caboose. She'd sit at the counter and chat with...whoever. It's not as if the Inseparables were her only friends in the world. They were simply her closest. Surely she'd spot a familiar face at her favorite eatery. At the very least she could count on Laura to bend her ear about her impending marriage to Carson. At this point, any conversation was preferable to the drone of the television.

Irritated and restless, Angel pushed away from her desk and nabbed her purse from the macramé hammock chair. She picked her way across the cluttered and colorful living room she'd so lovingly decorated in her own unique style.

When she'd been married, she'd felt compelled to take her husband's taste into consideration. Neither Eddie nor Baxter had been fans of *bohemian chic* so, as a courtesy, Angel had tempered her predilection for gypsy décor.

Ryan hadn't blinked at her clashing wall art, hanging paper lanterns, and mountains of Moroccan-inspired accent pillows. Ryan had finessed his way into this apartment and casually cocked a hip on her desk. He'd been comfortable in his surroundings, comfortable with her. So much so that he'd followed her into the kitchen and stolen a kiss. He'd only had eyes for her, even though she hadn't looked her best.

The intensity of that kiss, of their brief connection, still hummed in Angel's heart and mind. Not to mention how it affected her intimate parts. Yet Ryan had accepted her rejection without question. He'd given up on her, on them, without a fight.

Or had he?

Instead of fleeing her whimsical sanctuary, Angel stood frozen on the threshold, sifting through erratic thoughts.

Had Ryan thrown in the towel or was he merely switching tactics? Maybe he wasn't as out of touch with the dating game as he claimed. By backing off, he'd only made her more aware of his absence. Of what *could* evolve between them if she abandoned her fears. If she took a leap of faith.

Did she want to explore a relationship with Ryan McClure? Did she want to risk falling in love? Could her heart withstand another loss?

"Am I making a mountain out of a molehill?"

Maybe a second kiss would fall flat. Maybe they'd fizzle after one date. She couldn't remember the last time she'd had an extended one-on-one conversation with Ryan. She wasn't even sure they had much in common! The least she could do was find out, right? A casual meeting. Two friends shooting the breeze over a shared meal.

"That's if he's available tonight. Or if he's even interested. Because maybe I'm wrong. Maybe he's not waiting for me to make the next play."

Angel thunked her forehead against the door. *Once. Twice.*

Breathing deep, she pulled her phone from her purse, feeling as though she was prepping to fling herself from a plane with a potentially faulty parachute. Would she land in an exhilarating, but safe relationship? Or perish from the fall?

"Derring-do or die of wondering."

* * *

When Angel arrived at Café Caboose, Ryan was already seated in a booth, drinking coffee and texting on his phone. Had she spent too much time primping or had he been overly anxious? He looked handsome and intense and she suddenly wanted to turn tail and run. But then he looked up and saw her and, damn, busted, she had no choice but to follow through on her insane invitation.

"Don't look so spooked, Mrs. Drake," he said while standing and tucking away his phone. "It's only dinner."

She tried to smile only that didn't work. She was too tense, too excited, and too worried about her mental status. She'd called and invited the man she didn't want to have an affair with to dinner.

"Just to reiterate," she said while dropping into the seat across from him. "This is just two people who didn't feel like eating alone eating together. It's not a date." *This from a woman who'd refreshed her make-up and swapped jeans for a sundress.*

"Got it."

"So don't try to pick up the tab at the end."

"Yes, ma'am."

"Because that would be just like you. Always a gentleman. I mean, you even stood before I sat. Who does that anymore?"

He didn't answer so she answered for him. "Men with manners. That's who," she said while skimming the menu. "A man who takes a shine to another woman but doesn't act on it because he's married. A man who gives his wandering wife a dozen second chances because he thinks, hopes she's capable of change and because he puts his daughter's happiness above his own. A man who waits almost a year after he's divorced to approach that woman he took a shine to way back when. And then when he kisses her and sets her world ablaze and she slaps him for the effort, he calmly backs off. Giving her time to adjust to the idea of them. I assume," she said while glancing over the top of the menu. "Because that's just the kind of thing a guy like you would do."

Her recent musing had given her a whole new perspective. "You didn't give up on me," she said, skin flushing with suppressed desire. "You gave me time to stew on that kiss."

He gestured toward her menu. "Ready to order?"

She held his smoldering gaze while tempering the urge to leap over the table and onto his lap. She hadn't felt this stoked, this reckless, in a very long time. Now that she was here, in his company and under his spell, food was the last thing on her mind. "What I want isn't listed."

That coaxed a hot-as-sin smile out of him. "You sure about this?"

"I haven't had sex since Baxter," she blurted.

Ryan relieved her of the menu, placed money on the table for his coffee, then rose and pulled her into his side. "It's been a while for me, too. I'll try not to disappoint," he said while nuzzling her ear and smoking what was left of her ever-loving senses.

Twenty

By the time evening rolled around, romantic seduction was the last thing on Bryce's mind. In one afternoon, he'd fielded three calls that affected his and Georgie's collective lives. It wasn't something he wanted to discuss in front of the children.

Unfortunately, he hadn't gotten two minutes alone with his wife. Her energized agenda had kept Bryce and the kids fully engaged for the bulk of the afternoon. He appreciated her creativity. He enjoyed exposing the kids to new activities. What he questioned was Georgie's relentless merry-making. As if she could erase the twins' dark past by saturating their present with sunshine.

Super-nanny-on-steroids.

At this rate she'd burn out by week's end. Either that or she'd alienate the kids, and Bryce, with her exhausting pace and abundant cheer.

Even now she was encouraging the kids to join her in song as they prepared for supper. A whistle while you work approach that Chelsea and Charlie ignored. When she realized she was the only one singing, Georgie trailed off with a frown.

Bryce wanted to tell her to give it a rest. Instead, he tossed the carrots he'd chopped into the salad bowl and gave her a nudge. "Don't take it personally. They're focused on their task at hand."

Pauline had taught them how to set the table and though they were slow as mud about it—overthinking the placements of forks and spoons and folding the napkins just right—they seemed to take pride in the chore.

The elder Morgans had worked wonders. Now it was up to Bryce and Georgie to continue their efforts, bolstering the twins' confidence and providing a happy nurturing environment. Something that, by all accounts, his sister had failed to do.

Something Bryce was struggling with given the nature of those phone calls.

Georgie pulled baked mac and cheese from the oven, filling the kitchen with lip-smacking aroma and memories of his own childhood. A childhood influenced by two hands-on parents.

Bryce set the salad on the table. Words crowded his tongue. Scenarios clogged his brain. He needed to spill his guts sooner than later. Supper would have to wait.

After praising the kids' painstaking efforts, he caught Georgie's eye. "Talk to you outside for a sec?"

"Sure. Just let me cover these dishes with foil. Guys?" she said to the kids. "When you're done, slip into the living room and look through those movies I brought home. Pick one and we'll watch it later tonight with popcorn."

As always, the twins did what they were told without a contrary word. There was, however, a bounce in their steps. For them, Bryce was learning, it was the small stuff that made a difference. Movie night with popcorn. Spending two hours trying out various jungle gyms. *As a family.* Had Marla ever put these kids before her own selfish needs?

Conflicted, Bryce moved onto the porch and gazed at the sunset. He breathed in familiar country scents, grounding himself as he assessed and reassessed recent twists in his game plan.

A few seconds later, Georgie joined him on the front porch, looking flushed and concerned. "I told the kids to chill in front of the TV until we came back in. I didn't know how long we'd be." She swiped her hands down her stained apron. "You think I'm overzealous."

"I think you could crank it back a notch," Bryce said kindly. "Rome wasn't built in a day. But that's not why I asked you out here."

"Oh." She looked relieved for all of ten seconds then frowned. "Is it about your uncle? Did he take a turn for the worse?"

"Sam's home and resting and the latest prognosis is encouraging. So much so, Dad's coming home in a day or two. It's all good."

"Then why do you look so tense?"

Because I'm in love and your heart's off-limits. Because I've been offered two possible jobs—one that would perpetuate my dream and one that would ensure yours.

"Ryan called about Jimmy Trent." The least surprising call of the day.

"With his report?" Georgie stiffened. "What did he say? What are we dealing with?"

"A recovering alcoholic with a gambling problem."

"He traded one addiction for another?"

"He's also a drifter. Bounces from job to job. Town to town."

"So we have nothing to worry about," Georgie said. "No court would award a man like that custody or even visitation. He's played no part in their lives. He—"

Bryce squeezed her shoulder. "Easy, mamma bear." Her protective streak reaffirmed her extreme devotion to Chelsea and Charlie. Endearing except it bordered somewhat on obsession. In giving her all to the kids, she'd had little to no private time for him. In London, he'd felt like the center of Georgie's world. Now he was fading to the fringe of her universe. To be fair, she'd been perfectly civil all day—talkative, funny, interesting. The F in their MFB was strong and true. Problem was, Bryce wanted more.

"I'll talk to my lawyer tomorrow," he said, "but, no, I don't think Trent is a threat in that way. But he might try to shake us down for money."

"He'd use his own kids to...to...support his gambling habit?"

"It's possible." Bryce scratched his jaw. "This is one of those times when my career in the pros is a drawback. He probably thinks I'm swimming in millions."

"Maybe he did more research. Maybe he knows..."

"I almost claimed bankruptcy last year? Maybe." Bryce

glanced toward the house. "Trent told Dad he'd be in touch. Assuming he follows through, I'll suggest a meeting on neutral ground. But if that bastard shows out of the blue and I'm not here—"

"I'll call you right away."

"Me or Ryan. Or both. As backup, I'll dig up a baseball bat."

Her lips curved. "Because you don't want me to bloody your trophy?"

"Because you can do more damage with the bat."

"I could do even more damage with a shotgun."

"Don't think it hasn't crossed my mind. Arlo locked away his firearms when the kids moved in, but they're still on property."

"That settles it then," Georgie said hands on hip. "If Trent shows his face and poses a threat, he'll get a butt load of buckshot."

The ferocity of her stance would have caused Bryce to smile if he weren't concerned about her and the kids' safety. "On second thought, maybe I'll cut to the chase and confront Trent on my own terms. Settle this sooner than later."

"I'm not sure I like the sound of that."

Unwilling to waste another breath on the dirtbag who'd deserted his pregnant sister, Bryce plowed on. "There's something else. Kathryn called earlier today."

"Wow. Big day." Georgie shifted, crossing her arms and raising a brow. "So, what? She was curious as to whether or not you followed through?"

Bryce had called Kathryn when they were still in London, a courtesy call to tell her he was getting married. He needed the closure and, also, it seemed the decent thing to do. She'd been surprised, but unruffled, saying now that he had someone to look after the children he was free to pursue professional opportunities. He knew that. He and Georgie had discussed that. But for some reason when Kathryn said it, it pricked his conscience.

"It was a professional call," he said. "A tip regarding a commentary position on a new football show."

"Well, that's...that's great, Bryce. This is what you wanted, right? Do you have to audition? Submit a resume? What show? What city? Is it part-time? Full-time? Seasonal? I'm so thrilled for you!'"

Her enthusiasm caught him off guard, especially since it could mean his prolonged absence. Or uprooting the family, something he was fairly sure she wasn't keen on. Would her attitude shift when he shared specifics? Would she make a sarcastic crack? Give him the cold shoulder? Flush with anger? Anything at all to suggest she was jealous or concerned? Because that, by God, would intimate her feelings ran deeper for Bryce than she was admitting.

Throw me a bone, sweetheart.

"The first step is an in-person interview," he went on. "The job is seasonal only, but it's in Los Angeles. Part of a new CSN lineup."

Georgie blinked. "Wait. Isn't that—"

"The network Kathryn signed with. Yeah."

"So you'd be working for her? With her?"

"Mmm."

"Huh." Georgie dipped her chin and whistled low. "CSN. Wow. National exposure and I'm guessing it pays well."

"Extremely well." If she was jealous she didn't let on. Mostly she seemed stunned and impressed. Pretty much his reaction when Kathryn had relayed details. "The biggest perk involves on-air interviews with some of the most influential players and coaches in football history." His adrenaline surged. Talking football with the greats and getting paid for it. Sweet. "I told Kathryn I'd think about it and get back to her."

Georgie gawked. "What's there to think about? It's your dream job."

"That doesn't make it the right job."

She narrowed her eyes. "Oh, no you don't. Not this time."

"What are you talking about?"

"You're worried about how this job would affect me and the kids and Arlo. You're blowing off your heart's desire in order to be a standup guy. We talked about this, Bryce. You always do the right thing for the people in your life, even when it's wrong for you."

"Georgie—"

"You're going to that interview. You'll regret it if you don't. I'll regret it. Seasonal isn't the same as full-time. Maybe episodes are filmed back-to-back in a short time frame and aired over a span of weeks. Maybe it wouldn't involve relocating the family as much as some creative scheduling on our part. At the very least the interview will give you a feel for that kind of work. Who knows? Maybe you'll decide you'd rather work for a smaller station. There's probably a lot of politics with a national network like CSN. But you won't know unless you go."

He worked his jaw—touched, but unconvinced.

She reached out and grasped his arms. "This was part of our MFB arrangement Bryce. I got my dream—a family. Now it's your turn."

Bryce stared down at his new wife. His best friend's sister. A girl who'd been under his nose for years, wondering—again—how he'd been immune to her unique spirit and subtle beauty for so damned long. In this moment, he loved Georgie as deeply as if he'd loved her forever.

Then it occurred to him. Maybe these feelings had been simmering for a long time. Since that moment, fifteen years ago, when she'd charmed and embarrassed him with a babbling, inappropriate declaration of love after one of his mom's shindigs.

His pulse raced along with his thoughts. Did a sunset conversation on the porch count as romantic seduction? Because, dammit, there was no turning back and he wouldn't move forward with a lie. "About the MFB thing—"

"The benefits part. Awkward, right? I'm glad you brought it up." Georgie sagged against him with a sigh. "I thought we covered everything when we hashed out this arrangement. But we didn't touch on the potential weirdness of showing affection with kids around. It obliterates spontaneity. Not that I planned on jumping your bones in front of Charlie and Chelsea, but now I'm even stressing about what goes on at night in the privacy of our bedroom. I mean, what if one of them has a bad dream or feels ill and walks in on us? Talk about mortifying."

Bryce smiled into her lopsided ponytail. He hadn't thought of that.

"I'm even self-conscious about kissing you in front of them because who knows what they witnessed between Marla and her various partners and what if it triggers bad memories?"

He definitely hadn't thought of that.

"On the other hand, I've been giving it a lot of thought and I truly believe they'd benefit from seeing a healthy, caring relationship—based on mutual respect and friendship—in action. Maybe we just need to take it slow. A hug here, holding hands there. And as for what happens behind closed doors, we'll play it by ear. Couples don't stop having sex just because they have kids. Surely there'll be a moment when it happens, you know, naturally. Stressing about it will only make things worse, right?"

He kissed her then. More deeply and thoroughly then he'd ever kissed any woman. His senses buzzed with the intensity and novelty of true love. The sappy-ass, always-and-forever kind of love that struck a man stupid.

Georgie trembled in response, fueling his passion, stoking his hopes.

Until she broke away.

Breathless and misty-eyed, she touched her fingers to her kiss-swollen lips. "What was that?"

Her distressed expression was as good as a kick in the nads. "I'm sorry, Lou. I know I promised to keep my heart out of the equation, but—"

"Don't say it. Don't go there. I can't... I don't..."

"You're so far over me you're on the far side of the moon. I know. You don't love me, but somewhere along the way I fell in love with you, Lou. I'm hoping, with time, you'll take the same fall." Cupping her elbows, he dropped his forehead to hers. "That kiss said there's hope."

Slipping free of his grip, she stumbled back and shook her head. "I'm hot for you, Bryce. I've always been hot for you. I won't deny your kisses turn my insides to mush, but I won't fall. I can't. Trust me. It's for the best. "

He would've felt gutted if she didn't look so damned panicked. She wasn't angry. She was afraid.

"We should get back inside," she said in a clumsy bid to change the subject. "Dinner's getting cold and..."

"...the kids are waiting." Time to fall back and regroup.

She faltered on the threshold. "We agreed to a logical strategic plan geared to fulfil everyone's needs on a drama-free, long-term basis. Can't we just stick to the agenda?"

Bryce had never felt so conflicted and driven at the same

time. "No, Georgie. We can't."

Twenty-One

Once upon a miracle...

"This can't be happening."

"It can and it did."

Angel stared into the soulful eyes of the Dawes County Sheriff. Stripped of his gun and uniform, stripped of *everything*, and he still exuded a hypnotic mix of gentle warrior and fierce protector. He'd overwhelmed her last night, all night.

Waking in his arms only made it worse. He didn't have to be inside her to turn her world upside down. "Maybe we're confusing great sex with—"

"We're not." Holding her close, Ryan stroked a warm palm down the curve of her bare back. A soothing gesture as if he worried she might bolt.

That was the problem. Angel didn't want to leave this bed.

Even though his daughter was spending the week with her mom, last night they'd escaped to Angel's small apartment. Ryan had shared his country home with his ex. His place had history. Angel hadn't shared this space with anyone. Now she couldn't imagine occupying it alone or with anyone but Ryan.

Head tucked beneath his chin, she reveled in his strength

and heat. How on earth had she lucked into love a third time? She kept waiting to feel guilty, as if she'd somehow betrayed her deceased husbands. And yet there wasn't a remorseful bone in her body. They'd known Ryan. They'd liked Ryan. And most of all, they'd want her to be happy. "Eddie and Baxter were good men."

"Yes, they were."

"I loved them very much."

"I know."

"They showed me the stars, but you," she said knowing now what Chrissy had meant about cosmic, love-fueled sex, "with you I circled Mars."

Ryan laughed. "I think I actually know what you mean by that. Thank you and my pleasure."

"This. Us. It feels different. But no less powerful and every bit as wonderful."

"Is this where you remind me that you're supposedly cursed? Because you kissed the hell out of me last night and I gotta tell ya, hon, I've never felt more alive."

Heart swelling, Angel eased back and caressed her lover's stubbled jaw. "I fought this for all I was worth and now I don't have an ounce of fight in me. God help you, Ryan. I'm head over heels in love."

He smoothed her curls from her face, his dark eyes bright with emotion. "I would have waited a lifetime to hear that."

"How do you think Sienna will feel about you having a woman in your life? Someone other than Lacey?"

"Sienna's dazzled by her mom, but she's not blind to her faults. Not anymore. We'll take it slow. It'll be okay."

Angel's soul danced, her body burned. For Ryan McClure. Georgie's big brother. She knew him almost as well as Georgie, which probably intensified her hard and fast fall. Once she stopped fighting the attraction—*whoosh!* "I'm not sure I can take it slow with you, Ryan."

He smiled then. That same ornery grin that preceded cosmic sex. "Then we'll go full out. That'll be okay, too. I promise."

Feeling lighter than she'd felt in years, Angel waggled her brows. "My shop's closed on Mondays."

"I'm off today, too."

"Well, woo-freaking-hoo, Sheriff McClure."

Ryan rolled on top of her just as their ring tones blared in tandem. "Damn," he said. "I need to look. Sorry."

Could be about his daughter or work. Angel got it. She took the opportunity to glance at her own incoming call. *Sinjun*. Finally. "I need to take this, Ryan."

Ryan rolled out of bed, phone in hand. "It's Bryce," he said while nabbing his jeans. "I'll take it in the kitchen."

Angel watched his sexy butt go, then thumbed connect. "Where the heck have you been?" she asked in a hushed voice. "Are you okay?"

"I'm fine. Well, not really. Complications with the company. But never mind that. I had a dream."

Angel pushed herself up, sheets clutched to her breasts. "Should I be worried?"

"I don't know. I don't know what to think. I saw Dr. Ryder again. With Georgie. Only this time you were there. You were in his arms, Angel, and Georgie...Georgie was crying."

Angel palmed her forehead. "What the hell does that mean?"

"I told you, I don't know."

"Can't you interpret your own dreams? I mean, isn't that part of what you do? Part of your ID-tuition?"

"Yes. Usually. But...everything has been off with Georgie. Or maybe it's me that's off. I just... I have a bad feeling and now you factor into it. I'm sorry, but I can't be any more specific."

"Well, that's just frickin' great. Wait. I called Ryder. Georgie was worried that Impossible Dream wouldn't follow through with her cancelation. Since I feel somewhat responsible for the glitch, I offered to contact him myself."

"You spoke with Dr. Ryder?"

"Yes. Just long enough to tell him Georgie got married. He was a really nice guy. I liked him a lot. I—"

"Oh, no."

"What?"

"You don't want to know where my brain just went."

"Actually," Angel said, unable to contain her sarcasm. "I do."

"You connected with Ryder. What if that was the start... What if he calls you back or you run into one another and hit it off? What if Georgie has second thoughts about Bryce and then she walks in and finds you in the arms of her dream man—meaning Dr. Ryder?"

"Whoa, whoa, whoa. That is *not* going to happen. Georgie and Bryce are happy and I'm..." Angel glanced toward her bedroom door. "I'm involved."

"Since when?" Sinjun asked. "With who?"

"I have to go," Angel said as she caught sight of Ryan. "I'll call you later." She placed her phone on the nightstand and drew her knees to her chest.

Clad only in jeans, Ryan moved in and perched on the edge of the mattress instead of climbing back into bed. "I need to go, babe."

Angel tensed. "Everything okay?"

"Bryce asked me to drive down to Chandler to give Arlo a lift home. He's going out of town for a couple of days and he'd feel better if Georgie and the kids weren't alone."

"I thought his obligations with the charity circuit were over until the fall."

"This is unconnected. Sort of. First he's flying to Vegas for a one-on-one with the kids' birth father. Then he has a job interview in LA. With CSN. Under the direction of Kathryn."

Angel blinked. "His former—"

"Yup."

"It's Kathryn's way of winning him back, I'll bet. Offering Bryce his dream job. Well, that conniving..."

"I know Bryce has judgment issues, but he won't betray his vows. He's not built like that."

"Kathryn may not seduce him personally, but that job?" Angel's stomach dropped. "It would entail Georgie moving away."

"According to Bryce, Georgie's not going anywhere."

"What does that mean?"

"I'm not sure. He may be one of my oldest friends, but Bryce holds his cards close to his chest. I can tell you one thing, day three into their marriage and they've already hit a rough patch. What is it with those two? Even when you set them up for success—"

"Maybe we never should have set them up," Angel said, feeling sick with dread.

"What do you mean, we? Arlo and I played matchmaker."

"Never mind. I—" Her phone rang again. "It's Georgie."

Ryan nodded, grabbed his shirt, and slipped into the bathroom.

"I'm sorry to call so early," Georgie started.

"It's nearly nine. Not so early."

"Yes, but it's your day off and I know how you like to sleep late, but I didn't feel right calling anyone else and I had to talk to someone. I don't trust myself not to screw this up, although I think I already did."

"Slow down and speak up," Angel said as she pulled on a robe. "Why are you whispering?"

"I don't want the kids to hear."

"So move into another room or step outside."

"I am outside. Just being extra cautious. Last night Bryce told me he's in love."

"With you?"

"Yes, of course with me!"

"Well, it could have been Kathryn," Angel said in her defense. "You know. Bryce's former fiancé. I mean that would explain your distress. Otherwise, I don't get it. Bryce loves you. His wife. Isn't that a good thing?"

"It's a *horrible* thing!"

"Why?"

"Because I can't love him back."

"You're kidding, right? You've carried a torch for Bryce since—"

"If I love him... If I tell him I love him... If I go all in... I'll lose him. It never fails."

Angel palmed her brow, trying to make sense of her friend's jumbled thinking. "Oh, wait. I get it. You think you've loved and lost a dozen times before—"

"I have love and lost."

"But none of those men were Bryce."

"I keep trying to do the right thing, like sending him off to a job interview with my blessing because I know how badly he wants that job. In truth, I hate that he's going because I'm worried Kathryn will try to steal him away. And why wouldn't he be tempted? She's beautiful and successful and his spaz-a-zoid wife just spurned him!"

"Are you telling me Kathryn offered Bryce a sportscaster job?" Angel asked, not wanting to let on that Bryce had already called Ryan.

"Haven't you been listening to me?"

Angel rolled her eyes just as Ryan emerged from the bathroom, fully clothed and looking handsome as sin. She pointed to the kitchen, mouthed "coffee" then got back to Georgie.

"I've been listening to a crazy person. Tell Bryce how you feel, Georgie. Before he goes to that interview."

"I thought I'd be okay with it, but then he was so distant last night, and then this morning... He didn't even kiss me goodbye."

"He left already?"

"A few minutes ago. He needed to stop by his old apartment first. His dress suits and shoes are still there."

"Then you've still got time. Load the kids in the car, Georgie. Drop them off here then haul your ass over to the club."

Silence.

The smell of brewing coffee roused thoughts of Ryan and how scared Angel had been to give love another go. She knew all about loving and losing in a far more painful way than Georgie had ever experienced. On the other hand, fear was fear, and everything was a matter of perspective. As for Dr. Ryder and Sinjun's mysterious visions... Any doubt Angel had about Georgie being with the right man evaporated the moment she learned Bryce voiced his love. Yeah, boy, love was a game changer.

"Fine," Angel said, changing tactics. "Let Bryce fly off feeling like a schmuck for bearing his heart and not winning yours in return. I mean nothing ever goes right for him anyway, right? So what if he succumbs to a pity boink with Miss Snooty-Pants. It's not like you're really his wife," Angel said, going in for the kill. "You're just an MFB."

If angry silence sizzled, Angel would be toast.

"I'll be right over."

Smiling, Angel joined Ryan in the kitchen for a quick cup of java.

"So what's up with my sister?" he asked while searching out two mugs.

"Let's just say I'm not the only one who thinks she's jinxed in matters of love."

"Bryce and Georgie are in love?"

"Apparently so."

"Can't say I'm surprised. Although it went down faster than I imagined."

"Like with us?" Angel teased while nabbing a carton of milk.

Ryan caught her waist and pulled her against him. "Time to put that jinxed business to rest, Angel. I'm in for the long haul."

Trembling with an equal mix of dread and lust, Angel melted in the sheriff's arms. "Don't tempt fate, Ryan. And don't make promises you can't keep."

"Never."

Twenty-Two

Bryce couldn't decide which had been tougher. Maintaining physical and emotional distance from Georgie throughout the night and morning, or saying goodbye to the twins for the third time in less than two weeks. The second time in two damned days.

Once again, he'd endured that heartbreaking look from Chelsea who clearly struggled with abandonment issues.

"*I'll be back*," he assured her. Only this time instead of touching her head in a reassuring gesture, he stooped and gave her a brief, tight hug. She didn't hug back, but she didn't stiffen or squirm either.

He hugged Charlie as well, stepping up his game, making his intentions clear. He cared. And he'd be back.

As for Georgie... He was at a loss. So instead of doing or saying the wrong thing, he held his tongue and kept his distance. The next move was hers.

Scaling the steps that ascended the left side of Coyote's, Bryce entered his second-floor apartment for the first time in several days. Even though he'd moved back to the ranch a few months ago, this place still held the bulk of his furniture and other domestic belongings, as well as the portion of his wardrobe more suited to special affairs. He'd intended to move back after Arlo had fully recovered from his hip injury, but that process was ongoing and now that Georgie and the twins were in the picture this place was out of the question. He'd clear it out, eventually. This particular visit was an in-and-out. He had two days of travel ahead of him.

Tossing his suitcase on the bed, he moved to the closet and fingered his way through jackets, trousers, suits, and ties. He didn't care about impressing Jimmy Trent, although he was intent on making an impression. As far as the CSN interview, in spite of his reservations, he took the opportunity seriously. The sharper he looked, the sharper he'd feel.

Because he was obsessing on both meetings, coordinating his wardrobe took longer than usual. When he got to the point where he was waffling on whether or not to pack the tie Kathryn had bought him—the tie she loved, the tie he hated—Bryce closed the suitcase and swung it to the floor. He chucked the tie in the waste bin.

At the same time, someone pounded on the door. "Coming," he shouted when the banging grew louder. His pulse quickened when he opened the door and saw Georgie— alone and flustered.

"I know you have a plane to catch," she said, "so I'll make this quick."

"The kids?"

"With Angel."

Bryce stepped back, inviting her inside and bracing for a rant regarding the guidelines and rationale of their MFB agreement.

She caught him off guard with a full-frontal assault.

He stumbled back, landing ass-first on the couch with a lap full of Georgie.

Straddling his hips, she plowed her fingers through his hair while blindsiding him with a deep, soulful kiss. Reminiscent of their sunset kiss on the porch, only this time she was the one in control, the one baring her heart. Cradling his face, she eased back long enough to gaze into his eyes and—*frick, yes*—he got her message loud and clear.

Heart full, Bryce managed to finesse them off the couch and into his bedroom. He eased her onto the mattress, feasting on her lips and tongue, reveling in the heat and wonder.

Georgie loved him.

She pushed at his shoulders, signaling him to roll onto his back. She rolled with him, once again in the position of control. Her fingers crept under the hem of his shirt, skimming his abs, his chest.

Bryce was primed for hot and heavy, maybe even wild, but then she froze.

"This is wrong," she said.

"Feels right to me."

"You'll miss your flight."

"I'll catch another."

She pushed into a sitting position, still straddling him (that was something), but looking on-edge instead of turned-on. "I just wanted you to know. I didn't want you to fly to LA thinking I don't care. Thinking I don't..."

She licked her lips. "I'm afraid to say it, Bryce. I know I told you I've fallen for half the men I've dated, but this is different. Has always been different." She slid away, giving him her back as she settled on the edge of the bed.

Bryce ached to touch her, but sensed she needed the distance to get out whatever she was gearing up to say. The tension, her tension, was tangible. As a countermeasure, he relaxed against the pillow, offering calm and patience.

"The thing is," she said, while staring down at her clenched hands. "I sort of lied about being over you. I never stopped crushing on you, Bryce. Not even after you broke my teenage heart. But I did suppress my feelings. I mean, what was the point? You went off to college then joined the pros and, even after you moved back to Nowhere, you never gave me a second look.

"I wrote you off as an extremely romanticized unrequited love and I tried my damnedest to nurture that same kind of breathless attachment to someone else. I tore through relationships like I tore through jobs. One night I hit the wall and vowed to settle for an amicable union with a widower or divorced man with children. An instant family. I applied to Impossible Dream.

"When I suggested the nanny gig," she said, "I wasn't trying to trick you or snag you. I honestly wanted and needed the job. I didn't think you'd hire me if I admitted I was hot for you. I made light of my crush, because I honestly thought I could manage it. Plus, I thought it would be temporary.

Even though it had been four months, I still hoped to hear from ID-dot-com.

"But then you whisked me overseas for a magical getaway," she barreled on. "Being with you twenty-four-seven, sleeping in the same bed, getting to know you, really know you. Hooking up? Oh, God. Sex with you was beyond what I'd ever imagined and believe you me, I imagined a lot. Even so, I kept the "love" notion at bay. Especially after you suggested a marriage-of-convenience. I talked myself into believing that we'd shine as married-friends-with-benefits. I was determined to keep my heart out of it Bryce, because every time I love, I lose."

She peeked over her shoulder, eyes bright with tears. "I don't want to lose you."

Chest tight, Bryce slowly shifted so they were sitting side-by-side. "For what it's worth, Lou, I don't feel trapped, manipulated, or bamboozled. I feel like the luckiest son of a bitch on the planet. If any one of those relationships would've worked out, I wouldn't have gotten this chance with you."

"But what if I screwed up your future by making my own magic?"

"I don't follow."

"What if you were meant to reunite with Kathryn? Or what if you were destined to meet your true love at an upcoming charity event? A woman more suited to rearing Chelsea and Charlie? What if I made the wrong choice? A selfish choice?"

Confused, Bryce raised a brow.

"Impossible Dream contacted me with my dream job."

Ah. "When?"

"Moments before we got married. That is, they sent it early that morning, but I didn't see it until I was in the bathroom with Angel. They matched me up with a doctor, a surgeon, a widower with three children. They live near Chadron and on paper they're a loving and well-adjusted family."

Bryce's pulse spiked as her words sunk in. "You picked me—a guy who's floundered financially, a man who's wrestling with a career crisis as well as his new and unexpected role as father—over him? A stable, successful, no doubt wealthy, surgeon, with a loving, well-adjusted family?"

Talk about a risky life choice. That accounted for her recent erratic behavior. "I'm guessing Angel argued for the doc," he added.

"Kind of. In the beginning anyway. Especially since Impossible Dream was responsible for matching up Bella and Savage and Chrissy and Mason. And look how happy they are."

"But you chose me," Bryce said. "Why?"

"I told Angel it was because I'd already given you my word. But that was only part of it."

He clasped her left hand and thumbed her wedding ring. Pre-game jitters paled in comparison to what he was feeling now.

Georgie met his gaze dead on, her green eyes bright with affection. "I chose you, Bryce, because I love you."

He knew what it cost her to say the words, making them all the sweeter. Cupping her cheeks, he kissed her with gentle passion while easing her back on the bed.

"Your plane," she said in a breathless voice.

"Next plane," he said while peeling away their clothes. "I'm making love to my wife."

Twenty-Three

It was the sunniest day in Dawes County history. Or at least in Georgie's recent history. She couldn't remember the last time she'd felt this happy, this content, this hopeful.

Yes, she was concerned about Bryce's meeting with Jimmy Trent. Yes, she was on pins and needles regarding his interview with Kathryn and CSN. But she was too jazzed to obsess on worst-case scenarios.

Even though she'd parted ways with Bryce more than two hours before, her senses still reeled from their lovemaking. His touch...gentle, yet passionate. *Possessive.* He'd claimed her body and soul. He loved her for all her quirkiness and faults. And she loved him back. Truly and madly. All in.

She'd practically floated back to Angel's apartment, her spirits soaring even higher when Charlie and Chelsea proudly modeled their new *dos.* Angel had given Charlie a blue faux-hawk. ("It'll wash out.") Chelsea sported three purple feather extensions ("Also temporary.") and cute, blunt bangs. Georgie applauded their fashion statements and they actually smiled. *Smiled!*

As if that wasn't thrilling enough, Charlie voiced a wish. "Can Miss Angel come with us for our adventure? She doesn't have anything to do today."

Not that Angel looked bored or lonely. In fact, she fairly

vibrated with good cheer.

"What put the pep in your step today?" Georgie asked.

"Knowing you and Bryce moved beyond MFBs," Angel answered. "Also I've decided to date Ryan, but let's not jinx it by talking about it. Let's just see how it goes."

Her friend and her brother hooking up. Finally. A positive step for Ryan and an amazing leap for Angel, considering her kiss-of-death phobia. Aside from a tiny happy dance and one gleeful squeal, Georgie refrained from making a big deal out of their delightful impending coupledom.

So now here they were. Georgie and Angel and Charlie and Chelsea on a *Jeep* tour of the area surrounding Eagle Butte with their very own professional guide, Emma. On this, the sunniest day in Dawes County history—according to Georgie's heart.

"Lots of people think that all of Nebraska is as flat as a pancake," Emma said to the twins as she expertly steered the *Jeep* over a rutted country road, "but as you can see, that's not true. Look at all the dips and peaks in this region. Canyons and creeks. Lots of ponderosa pine. That tall, rocky, mountain-like thing? That's called a butte. There are several in this state, but this is one of the tallest. All sorts of cool critters live in these parts. Bighorn sheep, elk, mule deer, eagles, turkeys. If we're lucky, maybe we'll spy one."

Georgie, who was sitting in the back with the twins, smiled as they passed a landmark and her friend segued into a watered-down version of a historical battle between two Indian tribes. Knowing the twins were wary of their new surroundings, she was tempering her normally more colorful points of interest. She'd even omitted bobcats, mountain lions, and coyote from her list of notable wildlife. When her lecture turned to the butte and the challenge in reaching its summit due to the sheer sides, Georgie chimed in to brag about Emma's job as a trail guide for hikers. "She's an expert rock climber, too."

"Unlike me," Angel said.

"Or me," said Georgie.

Out of all the Inseparables, Emma had always been the most athletic. An adrenaline junkie, she was also the most adventurous.

Angel, who was riding shotgun, looked over her shoulder

and grinned at Georgie. "Remember the time you tried to climb that ridge on the eastern face?"

Emma snorted. "I told you there was too much soft rock."

Even back when they'd been kids, Emma had been an expert on the region.

"Chrissy double-dog dared me," Georgie said.

"And Lord knows you rarely shy from a challenge," Emma said while tugging at the brim of her Z-Crew ball cap. "Gotta love that about you, Georgie."

"What happened?" Charlie asked as they bumped slowly along the road.

"I slipped," Georgie said.

"Bounced and skidded several feet on her, um, behind, and landed, splat, in a gooey mess of mud," Emma answered with a good-natured laugh.

"Don't worry," Angel told the twins. "The only thing she bruised was her pride."

Georgie rolled her eyes, welcoming the change of subject when Emma mentioned a possible eagle sighting and pulled to the side of the road.

"There's an extra pair of binoculars under your seat," she said to Georgie. "Nab those, will you?" Emma hopped out of the *Jeep* and, in one swift move, unbuckled Charlie's seatbelt and hefted him over the side. "We'll get a better view clear of these trees, little dude."

Georgie was still fishing for the binocular case as Angel hoisted Chelsea out and into her arms. The little girl's, "Oh, no!" caused Georgie to sit up so fast, she banged her head on the side of a roll bar.

"I'm sorry, honey," Angel said to Chelsea. "Don't worry we'll get it."

"What happened?" Georgie asked as she scrambled to the ground.

"Chelsea dropped her bear," Angel said just as they were joined by Emma and Charlie.

"Where?" Georgie asked then looked to where Chelsea pointed. "Oh." The bear's blue coat and red hat made it easy to spot amongst green grass and brown twigs. It had tumbled over the side of a small slope, landing inches from a sparkling creek.

"I'll get it," Emma said.

"On it," Georgie said, wanting to look like a champ in Chelsea's eyes by rescuing the bear Bryce had bought her in London. A bear Chelsea had been carrying around like a security blanket since this morning when Bryce hugged her goodbye.

"Watch your footing," Emma said.

"It's not like I'm climbing into a canyon," Georgie called over her shoulder. "It's just a little ditch."

But the toe of her sneaker caught on an exposed branch and suddenly she was falling forward and tumbling down the grassy slope. In a blur of an ungraceful somersault, she miraculously snagged the bear as she rolled by and splashed into the creek.

Shaking off the shock, Georgie marveled that she'd somehow saved the bear from a watery demise. She, on the other hand, was soaked. Sitting waist-deep in the babbling brook, she waggled the bear high above her head and shouted, "Saved!"

Emma doubled over with robust laughter while Angel pumped a fist in the air. "Woot!"

Squinting against the sun, Georgie brightened when she saw her friends weren't the only ones who delighted in her comical rescue. Chelsea and Charlie were laughing. Laughing!

"Are you okay?" Angel called between snorting giggles.

"Never better," Georgie said with a face-splitting grin. On this, the sunniest day of sunny days.

* * *

Because of Ryan's background search, Bryce had a lock on James B. Trent's home and job situation. He had phone numbers and addresses. He'd considered showing up unannounced and catching the man off guard. Instead, Bryce called ahead of time and, with minimal discussion, set up a time and place to meet. Not surprisingly, Trent was anxious for the one-on-one. The question was (in the words of Arlo), was he a money-grubbing weasel or an ass-hat skunk?

Bryce was about to find out.

Two hours after landing in Vegas, he entered the '50s themed diner and was promptly approached by a thirty-something man. The retro eatery met Bryce's expectations. Jimmy Trent did not.

Bryce slid into a booth, second-guessing his assumptions, while the birth father of the twins ordered a pot of coffee. Instead of looking like a desperate, down-and-out addict, Trent looked fairly respectable in his rumpled shirt and tie. His gaze was clear. His hands were steady. And the only thing he reeked of was tobacco.

"Let's cut to the chase," Trent said while stirring sugar into his mug. "I'm assuming you dug up dirt on my less than respectable lifestyle. Or maybe your sister painted an ugly picture. I'd bet—although I'm trying to abstain—that you don't like me, Morgan."

"Based on the facts as I know them," Bryce said carefully, "I wouldn't want to see Chelsea and Charlie in your care."

"I always knew Marla would place those kids with you if anything happened to her. That's why I didn't worry about them. Much." He shifted and loosened his tie. "I was a mess when we were together, but so was she. We would have been a disaster as parents."

"So you just walked out?"

"It was more complicated than that. And it's not something I'm compelled to rehash or explain to you. Honestly, it doesn't matter. What matters is that those kids get a better break the second time around. When I heard about Marla, I thought, damn, but then I learned the twins were with you and I thought, good."

Confused, Bryce eyed the man hard. Trent currently hawked cars at a prime dealership. That meant he was probably gifted with blowing smoke and talking in circles. "Yet you called my dad and made threats."

"After I learned you ditched one woman at the altar and ran off with another. That's right," he said. "I was keeping tabs on you. Or rather, on the designated guardian of my kids. And before you make some crack, I did try to do right by them a couple of times. Marla shut me out. I don't expect you want me to talk poorly about your sister, so let's not go there."

Instead of correcting Trent's misinformation regarding the details of his breakup with Kathryn, Bryce angled for the heart of the matter. "Back to the phone call. You intimated you'd take legal steps."

"My way of scaring you straight."

"Sorry?"

"Former pro ball player. Semi-celebrity. Bar owner. Forty and never married. The thought of you parading woman after woman in front of those kids the way Marla..." He scrubbed his hands over his face and shook off the anger. "I told you. I wanted them to have a better break this time around, not a repeat performance. Just because Marla idolized you—"

"You're wrong about that."

"You were the good one, the strong one, the successful one."

Bryce swallowed hard.

"If Marla talked about you to those kids the way she did with me, they probably think you're a god. And if they're even a little bit like Marla, they're worried about disappointing you."

Jesus.

"I wanted to meet you in person. Wanted to know you're at least half the man Marla described you to be rather than a figment of her intoxicated imagination. Other than that all I have to go on is media accounts and what little that cheap-ass investigator learned. I don't want to interfere in Charlie and Chelsea's lives. They don't need to know me. But I'd like to know they're well cared for in a stable home with a stand-up family."

Was it possible he'd misjudged this man? "That PI, did he or she report back that I married after all?"

Trent nodded. "Said she's rumored to be a nice girl."

"She is." Bryce drank from his mug, his mind working the puzzle of his sister and Trent. At this moment, only one thing was clear. "The stable home and a stand-up family is a done deal. Can I ask you one thing? Was Marla good to those kids?"

"They weren't physically abused to my knowledge and they didn't go hungry, but they weren't the center of her world. Not even close. They played second fiddle to her needs and her man of the moment."

"Considering she shut you out and given your transient lifestyle, you're awfully enlightened about the particulars of

Marla's home life. Another PI?"

"A mutual friend."

Bryce drummed his fingers on the table, deep in thought. Even though he'd been a self-admitted "mess", Trent cared enough to keep tabs on his kids. That had to count for something. "If you want to establish some sort of contact with Charlie and Chelsea—"

"I don't." He looked out the window, worked his jaw. "I'm in the process of atoning for some...regrets. The best I can do in regards to Marla and the twins is this."

Sensing the conversation had reached its limits, Bryce laid enough cash on the table to cover the coffee and tip. "The private-eye—"

"I'll call him off." Trent met Bryce's gaze. "I'm a decent judge of character when I'm sober. My gut says Marla wasn't exaggerating as much as admiring. She wished she could be more like you, but it wasn't in her. Not that she was all bad. You just had to look deep." He raised an assessing brow as Bryce slid out of the booth. "Bryce-the Bullet-Morgan. Must have been hell growing up in your shadow."

* * *

Georgie was in the midst of cutting a freshly made lemon poppy cake when her phone rang. Expecting a call from Bryce, she'd kept her phone nearby throughout the day. Her spirits dipped when she looked at the screen. "It's my mom."

"Ignore it," Angel said.

"I can't. What if something's wrong?"

"Something's always wrong." Angel sighed. "Go on. Take it. I'll serve dessert."

"Start without me," Georgie said as she pushed out the kitchen door onto the back porch. "I'll join you in a sec." She thumbed connect. "Hi, Mom."

"My daughter gets married and I have to hear about it from someone else?"

Georgie flushed head-to-toe. "It was only a couple of days ago." As if that made the oversight forgivable.

"I know things are strained between us, Georgina, but you could have at least texted me."

"You're right. I'm sorry. It happened so fast—"

"—and you didn't give me a second thought. Or maybe you did and that's why you didn't tell me. Maybe you thought I wouldn't approve and you're right. Why in the world would you want to tie yourself to a loser like Bryce Morgan?"

Georgie's pulse slowed, her heart pounding in slow, angry thuds.

"And taking on two kids of Marla's? That girl was a walking disaster. Given her genes and influence, they're bound to be hellions."

A hundred bitter thoughts begged to be voiced, but Georgie rose above. "Oh, I don't know. Considering my influences, I turned out okay."

Silence.

"I love Bryce for who he is, Mom. Not for what he does or doesn't do or how much money he does or doesn't make. If life gets a little boring or tough along the way, I'll ride it out and look for ways to make it better. That's what responsible, caring adults do."

"Are you through?"

"Not quite. Bryce and I are throwing a party next weekend. A post wedding celebration. If you'd like to fly up—"

"I have plans with Damion."

Her latest live-in. "Well, if they change, the invitation stands." In her heart of hearts, it would mean the world if her mom went out of her way to celebrate Georgie's happiness. But she didn't say that out loud. It was too much like begging. No child should have to beg for their mother's attention and love.

Just now Charlie and Chelsea were seated at the dining room table with Arlo and Ryan and Angel. Every particle of Georgie's being ached to be with her chosen family. "I need to go, Mom."

"Goodbye, Georgie."

Her tone suggested an ominous finality. As if the distance that had always existed between them was now insurmountable. Georgie tried not to care.

* * *

Flying to Los Angeles to interview for a job he had no

intention of taking—should it be offered—seemed like a waste of everyone's time. But Bryce knew if he passed up the chance, he'd wonder if he had what it took to nail the gig. And Georgie would worry he passed on his dream. He'd made too big of a deal out of wanting to get back in the game. Specifically as a commentator.

He realized now that part of that narrow focus was wrapped up with Kathryn. She planted the seed when they first hooked up and watered it liberally over the course of their torrid affair. He couldn't see the forest through that one tree. Yesterday morning, Coach Hamilton, the senior coach at Bryce's high school alma mater, had planted a new seed and the more Bryce thought about it, the deeper it rooted. He hadn't mentioned that phone call to Georgie because he was certain she'd think he was settling—a noble way to reconnect with sports that wouldn't entail relocating the family.

"You always do the right thing for the people in your life, even when it's wrong for you."

Except Hamilton's job offer didn't feel wrong. It just wasn't highly profitable.

Before his discussion with Trent, Bryce had been of the mind that he now had a wife and two kids to provide for, in addition to watching Arlo's back. Financial security was paramount and the CSN job tied neatly into his drive to be in the spotlight.

After his discussion with Trent, his thinking swung to, *I now have a wife and two kids to care for.*

Care as opposed to *provide.*

A subtle distinction, but one he pondered during the short flight to LA. Along with Trent's parting observation regarding Marla living in The Bullet's shadow. That off-hand comment kicked his brain into overdrive.

By the time he reached his hotel and checked into his room, he was mentally wiped. He wanted to do the right thing for all concerned, including himself. And he burned to somehow rectify his massive fumble of Marla's happiness and wellbeing. No, he wasn't wholly responsible for his sister's troubles, but he sure as hell contributed.

He planned to order room service and to make an early night of it. But first he texted Kathryn, confirming the time of the next day's interview. He also owed Georgie a call. He'd touched base briefly after parting ways with Trent, assuring her the man posed no threat. He'd promised to call later to catch up on her day and to wish the kids goodnight.

Snagging a bottle of water and toeing off his shoes, Bryce flopped into an oversized club chair and placed a call to his wife. The angst of the afternoon faded as he reflected on the morning. Georgie in his arms, in his bed, in his heart. "Hey, Lou," he said when he heard her sweet voice.

"Are you settled into your room?"

"Pretty much."

"You must be beat."

"Not physically."

"Speaking to Trent must've dredged up all sorts of sadness about Marla."

"It did." Bryce swigged water then sprawled in the chair. Exhausted. Remorseful. Yet there was something oddly comforting about confiding in Georgie—his friend, his lover, his wife—someone who'd circled in his universe for years. "Remember when I told you about my obsession with being a source of pride for Mom and Dad?" Not to mention his friends and schoolmates and every team he ever played on.

"Nothing wrong with wanting to excel in your friends and family's eyes, Bryce. Especially your parents. I think that's natural. I mean, I've always felt like that. At least you succeeded."

"Yes, but while all eyes were on me, Marla struggled in the shadows."

"It's not like your parents ignored her. You certainly didn't ignore her."

"No, I lectured her. And I sure as hell didn't understand her. I thought she was rebellious and petty. Reckless and unmotivated. I pointed out the pain and troubles she inflicted on Mom and Dad, harped on the potential scandal that could affect my career. Everyone describes me as generous and salt-of-the earth. At that point in my life, Georgie, I can assure you I was massively self-absorbed.

"I can't turn back the clock. I can't make things better for Marla," he said, "but I can ensure a better life for her children. I can afford them the attention they deserve. Speaking of Charlie and Chelsea, you promised to tell me about a breakthrough today. I need a pick-me-up, Lou. Let's hear it."

The tension in his shoulders eased as he listened to Georgie's animated replay of their *Jeep* tour around Eagle Butte. He busted his first smile in hours when she described her tumble and the kids' subsequent reaction.

"Doesn't bother you that they were essentially laughing at your misfortune?" he asked with a smile in his voice.

"Are you kidding? It was the best! I'm thinking I need to watch some old Marx Brothers movies. Bone up on some prat falls."

Bryce laughed at that. "I'm guessing today was an ice breaker. Should get easier from here on out. Sorry I missed the big moment."

"Speaking of big moments, you'll never guess who's dating who? Hint. They ate dinner here tonight with Arlo and me and the kids."

Bryce thought back on his earlier discussion with Georgie. "Ryan and Angel?"

"They couldn't keep their eyes off of one another the whole time they were here."

Knowing their history, Bryce applauded, what he considered, a perfect match. Ryan deserved better than the hell Lacey had put him through and Angel pretty much lived up to her name. "Maybe we'll see another wedding soon."

"I don't know that Angel would ever take it that far. She's superstitious about the husband thing. But that doesn't mean they can't live long and happy lives as lovers."

"You don't know your brother very well if you think he'll settle for that."

"Speaking of family," Georgie said in a more somber tone. "My mom called tonight. It was awkward."

"Isn't it always?"

"Yes, but, well, I invited her to our wedding celebration. I hope you don't mind. It's not like she'll come."

Bryce thought about Erica Jones. A woman who'd been in and out of probably as many relationships as his sister. Multiple husbands. Several children. Always in debt and always mooching off of someone else. What makes a woman like her tick? What made Marla tick?

"Trent mentioned that Charlie and Chelsea played second fiddle to Marla's own needs," he said, "but that didn't make her all bad. Sometimes you have to look deep, honey. Don't lose faith."

Don't give up on your mom, the way I gave up on Marla.
Georgie released a long, wistful sigh. "I wish you were here."

He grinned. "We could go the next best route."

After a thoughtful pause she feigned a shocked gasp. "Why Bryce Morgan, are you suggesting phone sex? Aren't players supposed to abstain the night before a big game?"

"If you're referring to the interview—"

"I am. It's huge and we all wish you the best. In fact, the kids peeked in and they want to wish you luck."

"Ah. The kids. That's why you're rejecting my advances."

"The real thing is worth waiting for," she said with an ornery smile in her voice. "Hold on. Here's Charlie. Chelsea and Arlo are waiting in the wings."

The phone conversation with his family brightened Bryce's mood and reinforced his decision. After saying his goodbyes, he left a message for Coach Hamilton then dialed room service, ordering the biggest steak on the menu.

Thirty minutes later, he emerged from the shower feeling refreshed and famished.

The knock on the door coincided with him pulling on a complimentary thick, terry robe. "Perfect timing." Towel-drying his hair with one hand, he padded barefoot across the lush carpet, expecting to greet a waiter.

Instead, Kathryn stood on the other side of the threshold, looking sexy and polished in a form-fitting dress and heels. "I got your text."

Bryce raised a brow. "I know. You texted me back, confirming tomorrow's meeting. You didn't say anything about dropping by."

"This was an afterthought." She smiled one of her killer smiles. "Aren't you going to invite me in?"

"What about if I meet you in the lobby in ten?"

"Oh, stop being a wuss, Bryce. It's not like I'm going to seduce you." She crooked a finely shaped brow. "Unless you want me to."

His dick didn't as much as twitch.

Since he hadn't shifted to allow her in, she rolled her eyes. "Seriously," she said after patting the designer satchel hanging from her shoulder. "You don't want to do this in the lobby."

Intrigued, Bryce stepped aside. He threw his towel on the bed and tightened the robe's sash as his former lover and short-time fiancé sashayed across the suite.

It occurred to him that he'd never seen Georgie sashay. She sort of bounced or blew or plain old walked into a room. She also didn't spend her time and money at ritzy boutiques and pricy spas. The more Bryce drank in Kathryn's polished veneer, the more he hungered for Georgie's earthy charm.

"Can I offer you something from the mini-bar?" he asked as she poised on the edge of a seat.

"Depends on how this goes," she said, still smiling. "So. How are the kids?"

"Good."

"Arlo?"

"Cranky, but good."

"Your wife?"

Eyes narrowed, Bryce sat in the opposing chair. "Why are you here, Kathryn?"

"Because I like you, Bryce. And I wanted to save you some embarrassment. Unless you already know about this and don't care."

She pulled a file out of her satchel and placed it on the table between them. "Don't get your jock strap in a twist but, as part of the interview process, we conducted background searches on all of our potential hosts. This show is geared to shine the light on legends in the industry. It's a feel-good show. Apparently we need more of those," she said with a condescending snort. "At any rate, we'd like to avoid any scandal or potential scandal surrounding the four hosts of the show. Everyone has skeletons in their closet, even squeaky clean golden boys like you, Bryce."

Blood simmering toward boil, he rolled back his shoulders and summoned calm. "If this is about my sister—"

"Actually," Kathryn interrupted while pulling an 8x10 photo out of the file and sliding it under his nose. "It's about your wife."

Twenty-Four

Once upon a disaster...

Georgie woke to gloomy skies. Thunder rumbled in the distance and she instantly skimmed her phone for weather alerts. Severe storm warnings, but nothing tornado related. Not yet anyway. She imagined Emma, camera in hand, anxiously awaiting a call from Zeke and the Z-Crew inviting her to join them on some insanely dangerous chase. Emma was warped like that.

Georgie, on the other hand, willed the ominous weather to pass quickly or to blow in another direction altogether. As backup, her mind turned to indoor activities—games and crafts and maybe a movie. Things to keep the kids entertained in lieu of the picnic and outing she'd planned for the city park.

Breakfast whizzed by—a wonderfully, moderately lighthearted affair—even though they were all on pins and needles regarding Bryce's interview. In order to fill the anxious silence, Georgie brought up the need to sort through her boxed up belongings. Most of her personal possessions were still in the barn—exactly where her friends had stored them a few days before. She needed to decide what to keep and what to give away or sell. As it stood, they'd be merging three collections of household items. Hers, Bryce's, and Arlo's. No need for three toasters, three vacuums, three sets of silverware...

According to the latest weather report, a tornado watch had been issued, but no *warnings*. It simply meant conditions were ripe and a tornado *could* develop, but no guarantee. As long as they kept an ear and eye on the weather, no reason they couldn't spend an hour or so in the barn sifting through boxes.

But then, in between stuffing his face with waffles and sausage, Arlo shared an idea he'd been gnawing on for the past couple of days.

"I'm thinking about moving into the guest cabin."

Georgie was horrified. "But this is your home, Arlo. You've lived in this cabin, the main cabin, all my life."

"Longer than that," he said. "I'm thinking I'd like a change. A bit of privacy. Leave the big house to the newlyweds and young'uns."

"Arlo—"

"I'm only moving a few yards away. Don't worry. I'll join you for meals." He winked while wiping a napkin over his greasy lips. "That's what you get for being such a good cook. Leave the dishes for later and let's hop over for a looksee. You can help me decide what furniture I want to tote over and what goes where."

Georgie wasn't sold on the move, but she didn't argue. Bryce would be home late tonight. They could hash it out then.

After clearing the table, she and the kids followed Arlo across the side yard. She noted he'd nabbed his battery-powered all-weather radio—a recommended possession for people who lived out of hearing distance of the town's tornado sirens. They hadn't discussed the possibility of a twister—why alarm the children?—but she knew it was on his mind.

While the kids skipped ahead, Georgie peered at the skies. She wasn't particularly fond of the dappled cloud formations or the vague greenish tint. Although, according to Emma, scientifically speaking, tornadoes weren't necessarily results of green thunderstorms.

"No need to panic," she mumbled to herself. And besides,

in addition to the automated weather alerts via her phone, Emma always gave the Inseparables a heads-up when she joined the Z-Crew on a chase specific to Nowhere. After ensuring she had no such message, Georgie tempered her cyclone phobia and turned her attention to Arlo's potential new home.

In the past, the modest five-room cabin had served as the residence of the ranch foreman. The interior needed a facelift. New area rugs, fresh paint, but essentially it was clean and cozy. Georgie was inspecting the kitchen appliances when Arlo called out.

She peeked into the living room and saw him looking out the screen door. Every muscle in her body tensed as she readied to grab the kids in order to seek shelter from an oncoming twister. "What is it?"

"Not what. Who. Bryce."

Chelsea and Charlie scrambled toward the door, following their grandpop onto the porch.

Georgie slumped against the fridge in relief. *Thank God.*

But wait. It was only eleven a.m. Bryce should've been in the thick of that interview.

Perplexed, she stepped onto the porch just as he met the kids half way across the yard. Confusion morphed into joy when she realized the twins were excited to see him. *Progress.* He caught them in an easy hug. *Be still my heart!* But then Bryce made his way to the guest cabin, and her stomach pitched. He didn't look happy.

"Dad, will you take Chelsea and Charlie into the main house. I'd like to speak with Georgie in private."

"Sure but—"

"I'll explain later."

The kids left with Arlo and Georgie felt the world tilt. A storm was coming all right but not in the way she'd anticipated. In all the years she'd known Bryce she'd never seen him lose control. She'd never witnessed his fury. Sometimes she wondered if he'd ever truly lost it on anyone as he always seemed to take even the worst news in stride. This moment, however, he vibrated with an eerie calm that rattled Georgie as surely as a deadly twister.

"What is it? What's wrong?" she asked as he ushered her into the small, stuffy cabin.

Had CSN changed their mind about him and canceled the interview? Had he flown all that way for nothing? Had Jimmy Trent done a one-eighty? Had he made some sort of threat? Had Bryce misjudged his feelings for Kathryn? Had something happened between them? Was he angry with himself? With circumstances? With Georgie? She couldn't tell.

Up close and personal, she noted little details. Like his bloodshot eyes and unshaven jaw. Had something or someone kept him awake? Instead of a suit, suggesting he'd come here directly from the interview, he was dressed down in jeans and his polo shirt was somewhat rumpled. His laptop satchel hung from his shoulder. Why hadn't he left it in the car?

Georgie watched as Bryce pulled something from the pocket of his leather case. He handed her a manila folder.

Assuming he wanted her to open it, she did. The world didn't just tilt, it careened.

Heart pounding, hands trembling, she flipped through four different photographs. She stared at her younger self in various skimpy combos of satin and lace. The biggest bonehead indiscretion of her life had risen from the grave to bite her in the ass. "Where did you get these?"

"CSN did an extensive background search on potential hosts. One that extended to family members."

"Is that even legal?" If nothing else, it struck her as a severe invasion of privacy. Instead of worrying about how many eyes had been on this file, Georgie tried to absorb the fact that these pictures even existed. "They must have dug really deep. I don't understand... The photographer assured Ryan he'd destroyed any trace—"

"Ryan knew about these?"

Georgie met Bryce's disappointed gaze and winced. "I was only nineteen and in between jobs," she rushed to explain. "I thought it was a legitimate fashion shoot for an east coast lingerie catalogue. I didn't imagine anyone who knew me would ever see them. Even if they did, it didn't seem any more risqué than posing for a swimsuit layout. But then the outfits got a little racier and the photographer a little more hands on, if you know what I mean."

Bryce didn't respond, but she swore his eye twitched.

"Richard, the photographer, became more aggressive with his physical advances and I got a little scared. I was in over my head. I'd only confided in the Inseparables and they convinced me to confide in Ryan. He was furious, not so much with me, but with the photographer. He dug around and guess what? The guy had a disreputable reputation. Ryan had a talk with Richard and the next thing I know, Richard packs up and moves on. Ryan assured me he obtained and destroyed all the prints as well as the memory card."

"We're talking digital, Georgie. *Richard* could have downloaded the files to another device and obviously he did."

"But Ryan was so sure."

"Ryan was wrong. What I want to know," Bryce said, "is why you didn't tell me. In the past two weeks we've had at least three or four discussions where we talked about skeletons in our closet or things we weren't proud of. You obviously regret that shoot. Why—"

"Because I was embarrassed!" Georgie exploded, near tears. "Not so much because of the photos themselves. I mean I'm not naked in any of them and they're not Playboy material, exactly. Although, I admit, depending on how prudish a person is, some of them could be construed as provocative, I guess. What bothers me most was the situation itself. I was desperate for money and so flipping naïve and...and needy. Richard made me feel beautiful and alive when my self-esteem was at a low. I allowed myself to be charmed into something that turned sleazy! Surely you can imagine why I wouldn't want to share that with you."

"Love implies trust. You should have trusted me with this, Georgie." He angled his head and studied her hard. "What if Trent had hit me with these instead of CSN? You knew I was concerned about him trying to blackmail or smear us in some way in order to take the kids and yet you let me walk into that meeting unarmed."

"I didn't think—"

"Anything else you want to tell me?" he ground out. "Strike that. Anything else I should know?"

Implying she was harboring a slew of dirty secrets? "Like what?" she snapped then slapped her hands to her sides and sighed. "I thought this was history, Bryce. It didn't occur to me that Trent would find these. That *anyone* would find these. I'm sorry, but it's not the end of the world."

Although maybe it was the end of them.

Georgie's cheeks burned under his ice-cold glare. Is this how he'd been with Marla? Puritanical? Unforgiving? It was a side of Bryce she'd never seen and it rattled her to the core. He didn't just slip off that pedestal. He plummeted. Obviously, she'd fallen from grace as well. Tears burned her eyes as she struggled to understand the extent of his upset and damn if those tears didn't flow.

She expected him to reach for her, to soothe her distress because that would be so Bryce. Putting her distress above his disappointment. But he stood there, rigid.

She realized then that she'd instigated something he'd always avoided. *Scandal.* Or at least something that could be construed as scandalous and maybe for those who were speculating, damning. Did they fear these photos were just the tip of the iceberg? "Oh, God. Did I... Did these... Did I cost you the commentator job?"

"As it happens, I was more interested in another job opportunity. Now I'm in the position of having to meet with Coach Hamilton to tell him why I can't take his place as senior coach at the high school."

Georgie felt sick. "When did that offer... Wait. You mean you'd rather coach kids than host a football show?"

"Not as lucrative, I know," he said, sounding bitter. "But, yes, for me, it held surprising appeal. Not that it matters now," he said while turning to leave.

Oh, my, God. She not only ruined his chance at his dream job, but the perfect job. Palming her throbbing head, Georgie marveled at her ability to screw up, not only her own life, but the life of the man she loved. Instead of listening to her heart, she should've followed Impossible Dream's lead. "I should have chosen Ryder."

"I'm sorry you feel that way."

He walked out before she had a chance to elaborate.

Pride and frustration kept her rooted. Okay. Maybe she should have told Bryce about the lingerie shoot, but his level of anger was unreasonable, wasn't it? She flipped through the pictures a second time. Honestly, they weren't as tawdry as she'd built them up to be in her mind. Could they really reflect that badly on Bryce?

By the time she made it to the screen door, he was already driving off. She reached in her pocket for her phone, intending to call Ryan. It rang from an incoming call from Bella. She answered automatically. "Hey."

"Is Bryce home yet? Is he okay? Are you okay?"

Swiping tears, Georgie battled for focus. "What are you talking about?"

"Joe called me. Actually he called twenty minutes ago, but it rolled to voicemail. I just now—"

"Could you get to the point?" Georgie blurted. How was Savage mixed up in this? Or was there something more?

"Anything else you want to tell me?"

"Right. Okay," Bella said in a rush. "Joe was at Tank's— he drove his motorcycle in for repairs—when Bryce rolled in to gas up his car. Unfortunately, Tom Rhodes was filling up, too. They had words, Georgie. Loud words. Joe overheard Tom say some nasty things about you."

"Like?" Georgie asked through gritted teeth.

"Like how you finally tricked some gullible bastard into marrying you. And some other really unflattering stuff that made you sound like a gold digger. Oh, and he called you a prick teaser. I mean, how awful! I don't blame Bryce for socking him."

Georgie blinked. "They fought?"

"Joe said he had to pull Bryce off of Tom."

She couldn't believe it. In all the years she'd known Bryce, she'd never heard about him getting into a fistfight. Breaking them up, yes. But not engaging!

"So he didn't come home yet?" Bella asked.

"He was here."

"Was? Oh, Georgie. He didn't believe those awful things Tom said. How could he?"

"Unfortunately, unwittingly," Georgie said, "I gave Bryce reason to doubt me."

She stepped outside just as the first raindrops fell, her mood as volatile as the crack of distant thunder. Tom's lies didn't hurt nearly as much as her husband's lack of faith.

Twenty-Five

Bryce peeled away from the ranch with a dagger in his heart.

"I should have chosen Ryder."

Had Georgie spoken out of anger or did she seriously regret not choosing the wealthier man? Tom Rhodes would argue the latter. Then again, Rhodes was a vindictive jerk.

Bryce banged his hand on the steering wheel. The one-two punch from Kathryn and Rhodes had warped his logic. By the time he confronted Georgie, he'd worked up a head of steam and rolled right over her. Even now, even though he knew he'd been an ass, he couldn't temper the sting of being blindsided.

He'd circumvented an awkward meeting with the CSN executives by passing on the interview. They'd only pepper him with questions he had no answers to while ogling photos of his scantily clad wife. Considering he'd already written off the job, why subject himself or Georgie to the scrutiny?

He planned on walking away from the coaching job, too. What if down the line those photos somehow became public? What if they went viral? The biggest allure of that coaching job—aside from immersing himself in football—was making a positive difference in local teens' lives. If Marla's teachers and counselors would have been more attuned to her specific problems, if they would have looked deeper, maybe they could have helped her early on. Bryce wanted to be that authority figure. The one who looked deeper. The one who steered a lost kid straight.

Georgie was right. Those photos weren't the end of the world, but they could potentially stir up a firestorm of controversy. They exploited a teenage Georgie in skimpy lingerie and playful poses. It only took one radically narrow-minded parent to twist those sexy images into soft porn. Georgie would be mortified by talk like that and what if it reached the twins' ears?

On the other hand, if Bryce wasn't in a teaching position, if he continued on course as a bar owner, those photos seemed far less threatening. He wasn't happy about backing out of the coaching job, but protecting his family trumped professional satisfaction. Whatever his reasons, he owed Coach Hamilton an explanation face-to-face.

Bryce was contemplating that explanation as well as replaying his confrontation with Georgie when the skies darkened and rain poured.

He switched on the wipers and frowned at his ringing phone. *Ryan.* Probably calling on his sister's behalf. The question was, would his friend offer calm perspective or rip him a new asshole. Holding firm to the wheel, Bryce tripped the hands-free speaker. "Hey, bro. What's up?"

"Tom Rhodes just left my office sporting a busted lip and a grudge against you."

"Did he file charges?"

"A restraining order. Did you really threaten to—"

"Yes."

Ryan groaned. "Listen. Friend to friend, I appreciate you protecting my sister's honor, but you can't wail on every dickwad that insults your wife."

"I'm surprised he repeated the conversation."

"I got Tank and Savage's input, too. Since when are you so thin-skinned? And hot-headed? Everyone in Nowhere knows Rhodes is a blowhard."

"He caught me at a bad time."

"Just tell me you didn't repeat that crap to Georgie. She's sensitive about talk that puts her in the same league as my stepmom."

"I didn't mention my fight with Rhodes, no. But we did go round about something else."

Bryce shared what he knew about the lingerie shoot, how he'd come into possession of the photos, and how he'd passed on the interview rather than having to explain those photos to the CSN execs. He hadn't even had an explanation for Kathryn who had, surprisingly, downplayed their relevance.

"These are pretty tame in the scheme of things," she'd said. *"Hell, did you see last month's bathing suit feature of McClusky's new supermodel wife? The point is these photos suggest Georgie had a wild side and the question is, is there something even racier floating around out there?"*

Bryce didn't know at the time. And he didn't want to have that conversation with Georgie over the phone. *Was* there something more controversial in her past? Unfortunately, he stewed on the possibility through the night and on the flight home. After all, she'd been cagey about her attraction to him and that Impossible Dream response. Who knew what else she was holding back for whatever the hell reason?

In light of her tearful explanation, he doubted there were similar "embarrassing" experiences in her past, but then she'd skewered him with that parting barb about the surgeon, the *rich* surgeon, reigniting the embers of doubt inflicted by Rhodes.

"Man, you've really got it bad," Ryan said.

"What are you talking about?" Bryce asked as the rain eased and something harder smacked at his windshield.

"Angel told me you and Georgie moved beyond that MFB nonsense. The fact that those photos and Rhodes's taunts got bone-deep under your skin shows how deeply you love my sister."

Bryce couldn't argue that. For one, it was true. Secondly, he was in a sparse hail storm and... *Oh, hell.* He pulled to the side of the road and squinted in every direction. The hail dissipated and he caught sight of something ominous to the south. "Oh, hell, no."

"Deny it all you want," Ryan said. "But... Oh, shit."

Bryce dialed up his radio. He heard the alert from the National Weather service in tandem with the tornado warning blaring in the background over the speaker phone.

"I've got a visual," he told Ryan, while swinging his pickup around one-eighty. "Southeast of Eagle Butte and heading our way."

* * *

Locals had two choices when it came to professional hair services. Elroy's Cut & Shave Emporium, owned and operated by—you guessed it—Elroy. And Heavenly Hair, an all-service salon and Angel's pride and joy.

Although Elroy was favored among several farmers and ranchers and radical teen boys, there wasn't a woman in Nowhere who'd risk her hair to a barber who specialized in Crew Cuts, Princetons, and Head Shaves. Therefore Angel's salon was always busy. If a client was desperate enough, she'd risk just about any kind of inclement weather in order to get her hair colored and/or cut and styled by Angel and her talented team.

Chrissy was no exception.

She'd braved stormy skies in order to keep her scheduled appointment. "Why did I ever let you talk me into cutting my hair into such a drastic style? The upkeep's a bitch."

"It's not drastic," Angel said, while snapping a cape around her friend's neck. "It's trendy. And you're the one who chose the style."

"Yeah, but I didn't know I'd have to come in for a trim every six weeks."

"A small price to pay to look like a kick-ass rock star."

Chrissy rolled her eyes. "If you say so."

"If it's such a pain, let it grow out."

"Mason loves this cut. Says it's sexy."

Angel's lip twitched as she picked up her scissors. "Ah. So this is for Mason."

"And me." Chrissy crooked a begrudging grin. "Who doesn't want to look like a kick-ass rock star?"

Smiling full out, Angel flashed on the day she'd first given her friend this shaggy, sassy do. The same day Chrissy had slipped about Ryan's longtime crush on Angel. "It's almost been a year," she reflected out loud. "I opened the shop especially for you."

"I remember it well," Chrissy said while flipping through an arts and crafts magazine. "Bella had just moved in with Savage. I hadn't reunited with Mason yet. And Ryan was still married to Lacey."

"There was talk of circling Mars," Angel said in a near whisper. Chrissy's code for mind-blowing orgasms that included shattering stars and imploding planets.

"Yeah," Chrissy said in a similar hushed tone. "And the fact that you've never had the pleasure of that trip. In spite of being in love and married twice."

Her husbands had gifted her with many an orgasm, but nothing compared to the all-consuming, out-of-this world experience she'd experienced with Ryan. "I was going to share this with all of the Inseparables at the same time. Not the details per se, but..."

Chrissy caught Angel's gaze in the mirror. "Spill."

Bursting with girlish infatuation, Angel almost giggled. "I recently rocketed to the red planet and back."

"Shut up!"

Angel shushed her.

"With who?"

"Ryan."

"Shut the frick *up*!"

This time it wasn't Angel who quieted her friend but the heart-tripping, ear-splitting sound of tornado sirens. The sustained blast wailed in tandem with alerts from multiple cell phones. Stylists and clients alike scrolled through their weather apps.

"Stay calm, everyone," Angel said even as her pulse raced, "and gather your purses. We're moving this party to the basement."

After locking the front door, Angel shifted to the rear corridor and calmly ushered clients and co-workers past her and down the stairwell. Tornado warnings were common in these parts, although the last time one touched down and caused damage in this region was five years back.

Everyone flowed into the brightly lit basement—a safe area that also served as a supply room for hair products as well as a laundry room for Angel's personal and professional needs. Of the six women, including Angel, three of them were clients.

Darla, a part-time employee of Buzz-Bees, was frantically air-drying her freshly painted yellow nails while Holly, their resident manicurist/receptionist scrolled through both of their phones.

Janeen, Angel's longtime fellow stylist, guided Mrs. Cartwright to a utility sink in order to rinse the bold color from her hair rather than risk fluorescent calamity.

Certain everyone was accounted for, Angel turned to Chrissy who was also glued to her phone. "Where's Melody and Rush?"

"With Mom and Dad. They just texted they took shelter."

"They'll be fine."

Chrissy nodded although she didn't look convinced. "Mason's at Coyote's. No. Crap. He's driving over here. What the hell is wrong with him?"

"He's only a couple of blocks away," Angel said. "He'll be fine, Chrissy. Tell him to come in through the back door. I'll go unlock."

"Give me your keys," Chrissy said. "I'll do it. You stay here and monitor this crew. Make sure everyone steers clear of those windows."

Angel glanced up while passing Chrissy her keys. Two skinny windows several feet above their heads. If they blew, shards could fly. Angel repeated Chrissy's warning while scrolling through her own texts. Emma was on a chase with Zeke. Homes in the immediate danger zone included those belonging to Bella's dad, Bella and Savage and, oh, hell, the Morgans.

"According to the Z-Crew Twitter feed," Holly said, "tornado damage confirmed."

"It's going to barrel through my lavender farm," Mrs. Cartwright said in a wobbly voice.

"And this town," said Darla.

"Unless it veers off," Angel said, forcing calm. "It could even double back." Wishful thinking, but according to Emma, possible. Engrossed in her own phone, Angel was trying to check in with everyone, including Ryan. When his name popped up as a call, she took it. "Where are you?" she asked. "Are you okay?"

"I'm fine. Where are you?"

"Holed up in the basement of the salon with co-workers and clients."

"Stay put until you get an all clear from me. We've got a rain-wrapped funnel."

"Emma's with Zeke. Says it's a twister intense enough to inflict severe damage, but not total devastation. Still, it could intensify and for those in its path..." Angel's heart nearly pounded through her ribcage. "Where are you Ryan?"

"Taking care of business."

Police business. Emergency business. No doubt heading into the fray. "Damn you, McClure."

"Hang tough and have faith, babe. I have to go."

He disconnected and Angel fought the urge to retch.

* * *

It loomed on the horizon like the devil commencing to knock on their door. A wall of dark clouds and a spiral of destruction. Georgie had seen lots of photos of tornadoes, compliments of Emma, compliments of the news, and she'd caught a glimpse of the twister that bounced through this countryside five years back. But she'd never felt this kind of raw fury up close and personal. The prospects were terrifying.

"What is it?" Charlie asked in breathless wonder as Georgie half-carried the children the short distance from the cabin to the garage.

"A bad storm," she said, her voice sounding eerily calm to her ears considering she was scared out of her gourd. "No worries. We're going to ride it out in grandpop's nifty new underground shelter."

"Had it made special after a twist...er...after a storm a few years back!" Leaning heavily on his cane, he race-wobbled into the bombastic wind, that battery-powered radio gripped tight between his gnarled fingers.

Georgie's own hands were full of the children and one ineffectual umbrella. She'd grabbed it, hoping to shield the kids from any hail. It had blown inside-out almost as soon as they stepped into the bluster. Chelsea buried her face against Georgie's neck and Charlie held tight to Georgie's free hand.

Georgie took one last look at the whirling monster—*Where are you Bryce?*—then hurried into the garage and jerked her attention to Arlo. He tossed his cane and dropped to the cement floor, unlatching and sliding open a steel door. "Come on!" he shouted while switching on a light and illuminating the compact room below.

"It'll be fun," Georgie assured the twins. "Like camping out." She crouched next to Arlo and together they lowered the children in first.

"Never seen a twister develop so fast," he said close to her ear. "And it's closin' in."

Georgie shivered with dread, but steeled her spine. "You next!" she ordered as the building groaned with the force of the winds. No way was she leaving him up top with that faulty hip. "Don't argue!"

He didn't, but he did grumble.

Once he was clear of the small ladder, Georgie scrambled to follow—her tattered umbrella abandoned next to her father-in-law's cane. Since the garage door was open she got a parting shot of the landscape. Tree branches and unidentifiable debris blew past the barn. Would that barn and the cabins still be standing when they emerged? *If* they emerged?

The second she'd learned about the tornado, she'd fired off a text to Bryce letting him know they were headed for the shelter then shoved her phone in her pocket. Fumbling for it now, she winced at its absence. She must have lost it during her chaotic sprint for the garage. Had Bryce made it to the high school safely? Was he still on the road? When the alerts went off had he veered back for the ranch? That would be so like the man she knew and loved. Risking his neck to make sure his family was safe.

Heart in throat, Georgie squinted into the chaos, the wind roaring in her ears.

"We gotta seal that door!" Arlo shouted from below.

She willed Bryce to scramble into the garage in the nick of time. But all she saw was the fury of the storm.

"That boy can take care of himself," Arlo said as if reading her mind.

Her father-in-law joined her on the last rung and together they slammed shut the door. He secured the dead bolts from the inside while Georgie slumped to the floor, her wobbly legs no longer able to support her weight. The children squeezed in on either side of her as Arlo rifled through a rubber bin of supplies and tossed them a blanket. "So what'll we do to pass the time?" he asked in a jovial voice.

Georgie blinked and channeled Bella. Bella who was hopefully hunkered down safe in the bowels of Wonderland. "What about a story?" She couldn't think about Bella or any of her friends—other than to wish them safe from harm. Thinking would lead to fretting and she had to keep it together for Chelsea and Charlie.

"We don't have a book," Chelsea said in a small voice.

Georgie gave her a hug. "We can make up a story."

"Or tell one from memory," Arlo said as he passed everyone a bottle of water.

Bottled water, blankets, a battery-powered lamp and radio. What else did he have in that survival bin? Enough to keep them going for a couple of days if they got trapped inside?

"*Mary Poppins*," Arlo said, jerking Georgie out of her morbid thoughts. He looked at twins. "That was your mama's favorite story when she was a kid."

"She got us the movie," Chelsea said, sitting straighter.

"We seen it a lot of times," Charlie said with a smile.

"Then you know it," Arlo said. "We can tell it together."

And just like that the subject of Marla was no longer shrouded in misery. It was as if she'd swooped down from heaven and cocooned them in love.

Above them the door rattled and even though they were ensconced in asphalt and steel, the vibrations and noise were intense.

"Sure is loud," Charlie said.

"You know," Arlo said. "Sometimes good things blow in with the wind. Like that nanny in the movie," he said with a bolstering smile for Georgie.

"She flew with an umbrella," Chelsea said.

"Bet if we had some umbrellas," Charlie said while staring up at the door, "we could do some flying out there."

"You're probably right," Georgie said.

Latching onto the whimsical thought, she kick-started the story of the nanny who changed the lives of a family for the better. But somehow, while the merry tale tripped from her tongue, her mind froze with ominous images of Bryce and her friends and everyone in Nowhere. She prayed for a miracle, for minimal damage and no loss of lives. She prayed for another moment with Bryce. She mourned the ugly way they'd parted.

Please give us another chance.

Her frantic heartbeat pounded in her ears as she rambled about the story's featured characters. "Mary and Bert and the little boy and girl hopped into a chalk drawing and emerged in a fantastical land where sheep sang and an umbrella and cane danced midair." Oh, to have the power to conjure a happy ending for everyone in Nowhere.

Especially this family, Georgie thought while thumbing her wedding ring. *Especially me and Bryce.*

"Then Bert gave Mary a bunch of wildflowers that turned into butterflies," Georgie said. "Remember how—"

"Georgie," Arlo interrupted. "Listen."

She stopped mid-sentence, but all she heard was the pounding of her heart. No, wait. A pounding from above.

Arlo was on his feet and up the ladder. "That you, boy?" he shouted while shoving at bolts.

The kids bounced up as the door slid open and Bryce's face appeared surrounded by a halo of daylight.

"Thank God," he and Georgie said in tandem.

She realized suddenly that the tornado's roar was gone.

Arlo noticed, too. "We in the eye?" he asked still poised on a rung.

"No," Bryce said. "It's northwest of us now."

Heading for Nowhere, Georgie thought.

"It's safe to come out," Bryce said, his voice tight with emotion. "Just watch where you walk. Lots of debris."

"The cabin?" Arlo asked as he stepped back down and urged Charlie up the ladder first.

"Still standing," Bryce said.

"Aunt Georgie carried me all the ways here," Chelsea said as Bryce lifted her out.

"She told us a story so we wouldn't be scared," Charlie said. "I wasn't scared. Well, maybe a little."

"That makes two of us," Bryce said.

"Our Georgie girl was a champ," Arlo said as he climbed out.

"I don't doubt that for a second," Bryce said.

The *champ* was frozen. Georgie could scarcely breathe, let alone move. She heard Arlo whisper something to Bryce, before urging the children outside.

Bryce lowered himself into the shelter. He stooped next to Georgie then pulled her into his arms.

All the fear and emotions she'd stuffed down, welled up and over. Hands balled in Bryce's shirt, she sobbed against his neck. "I'm so sorry I screwed things up."

"I'm the one who's sorry, Lou. I overreacted. It'll be okay. We're okay."

"What I said about Dr. Ryder. I only meant if I'd chosen him I wouldn't have messed things up for you. I don't care about his money. I'm not a gold digger. I'm not—"

"I know, honey. Everything got twisted in my head. I'm clear now. We're good."

"But the photos. The coaching job..."

"We'll sort it out."

"I love you something fierce, Bryce. If anything had happened to you—"

He cut off her words with a kiss—a deep and loving melding that slid through her being like liquid sunshine. "I love you, Lou. I'm here for you. Now and always. Do you believe me?"

She nodded while sniffing back tears.

"I need you to pull it together again," he said while finessing her to her feet. "I need you to hold strong."

Hearing the strain in his voice, she looked into his eyes and braced for bad news.

"Ryan's car was blown off the road en route to an emergency. He's been shuttled to Chadron Medical."

Twenty-Six

Once upon a dream...

Angel nearly wore a path in the tiled-floor of the building's basement. Like everyone else in the room, hers eyes were glued on the *Twitter* feed of the Z-Crew Stormchasers. It's how she knew Emma and Zeke and team were unharmed even though they were in the thick of things.

She also knew that Bella and Savage's house had sustained severe damage, along with Bella's dad's house, and the Cartwrights' lavender farm. The twister clipped the Morgan Ranch, but missed the Mooney Ranch altogether. That meant Chrissy's parents and her daughter were all clear and that Georgie and gang were probably shaken but okay.

According to the Z-Crew reports, the twister was losing steam but still on ground and slanting toward Nowhere.

Angel glanced over and saw Chrissy huddled in Mason's arms.

Bella had texted that Savage was with her and that they were hunkered down in Wonderland along with three other families.

Angel had yet to get an update from Georgie and Bryce

and she hadn't heard from Ryan.

The fear she'd been trying to suppress since he'd last called clawed at her being. She didn't want to think the worst. She didn't want to think she'd once again loved and lost. But the notion clung like the sickening scent of funeral lilies.

Her morbid thoughts blurred when the overhead lights flickered then died, plunging the basement into darkness.

At the sound of a freight train, Angel dropped to the floor like everyone else and covered her head as the room shook and the tornado roared.

Thirty seconds.

It lasted all of thirty seconds, maybe forty, and then stillness and quiet.

"Was that it?" Janeen asked.

"Wasn't that enough?" Holly asked.

Chrissy stooped next to Angel. "Mason and I are outta here. We know Melody's okay, but we need to see it with our own eyes." She squeezed Angel's shoulder. "Are you okay?"

Angel nodded. "Go, but be careful. It's probably a mess out there."

Everyone else scrambled up the stairs as well.

Her heart went out to Mrs. Cartwright and Angel realized she should offer to drive the shaken woman home rather than allowing her behind the wheel. Bella's dad would need help, too, yet Angel, who rarely crumbled in a crisis, stared at her phone, unable to move. According to the news feed, Nowhere was now in the clear. Moderate wind damage to assorted buildings. Patches of flooding.

Her phone rang, startling Angel out of a paralyzing fog. Bryce's phone, but Georgie's voice.

"Are you okay?" her friend asked.

"It just barreled through," Angel said while pushing to her shaky legs. "I haven't looked outside yet, so I don't know what kind of hit the exterior took, but I'm okay. You?"

"Rattled, but unharmed. Thankfully, I can say the same for Bryce and the kids and Arlo."

"The property?"

"Took a beating. Both cabins are still standing and so is the garage, but there's major roof damage and several windows blew out. Unfortunately, the barn's history."

"But everyone's okay," Angel said, sensitive to the strain in Georgie's voice.

"Not everyone."

* * *

Angel didn't ask Bella and Joe for a lift. They had worries of their own. If aging Mrs. Cartwright could drive under extreme stress, so could Angel.

It was the longest forty-minute drive of her recent life.

She'd barely been aware of the damage to the businesses and streets as she drove her sportster out of Nowhere. Oh, she noted mangled roofs and missing shingles, bent sign posts and broken windows, but the overall severity didn't register. Her mind was full of Ryan who was, at this moment, in surgery.

At this point she didn't know details. Only that he'd been heading toward a bad storm-related accident when the tornado veered slightly and his sheriff's pickup got caught in the fray. A paramedic truck had been following but managed to steer clear. Apparently, Ryan's vehicle rolled several times before landing upside down in a gully. Thank God for those paramedics. While calling in backup, they'd gotten Ryan out of the wreckage and safely to Chadron Medical.

By the time Angel walked through the hospital doors, she was soaked with nervous sweat.

By the time she made it to the waiting room, she was trembling head to toe.

Georgie flew out of her chair and across the room, grabbing Angel in a crushing hug. Her slender body shook with sobs.

"Oh, God," Angel croaked. "Is he—"

"No, no. He's fine. I mean, he's alive. Still in surgery. I'm just... I'm worried sick about him and so relieved to see you."

Bryce walked up behind Georgie, finessing her into his arms while giving Angel a reassuring squeeze. "According to the nurse, Ryan's in expert hands."

"That's another thing," Georgie said, while drying her eyes. "You won't believe who those hands belong to. Dr. Benjamin Ryder."

Angel blinked.

"The Impossible Dream surgeon," Bryce clarified.

The surgeon Sinjun had seen in a vision, not once, but twice. Angel swiped her clammy palms down her dress. Ryan hadn't been in those dreams. Was that because he wouldn't survive? Lightheaded, she swayed.

"Whoa, hon." Bryce caught Angel by the arm and eased her into a chair.

Georgie sunk down beside her and fanned her with a magazine.

Just then Zeke and Emma rushed in. Dressed in muddy jeans and t-shirts and matching ball caps, they looked equally shaken and frazzled. An unusual state for the daredevil weather enthusiasts.

"Heard about Ryan on the police scanner," Zeke said. "Would have been here sooner, except..." He tore off his cap and slapped it against his thigh. "How damned bad is it?"

"At least one broken leg," Bryce said. "Head trauma. Busted ribs. We don't know the full extent."

"Shit." Zeke wilted into a chair. He was as close to Ryan as Bryce was. All three went way back.

Just like the Inseparables.

Looking abnormally pale, Emma sat and draped an arm around Georgie. "Your brother's tough stuff. I know it sounds bad, but he'll be okay." Then she frowned over at Angel. "Why do you look so green? Buck up, Buttercup. Georgie and Ryan need us strong."

"She's in love," Georgie said.

"With who?"

"Ryan."

"Since when?"

Angel cradled her spinning head as Georgie blurted what details she knew about Ryan and Angel as a couple. That was fair, she thought distractedly, since she'd spilled the beans to the Inseparables about ID.com and Dr. Ryder.

Feeling more ill by the moment, Angel excused herself. "I need fresh air. And privacy," she added when her friends rose to join her.

A basket case of knotted emotions, Angel left the room. Borrowing a pad and pencil from a receptionist, she slipped outside, breathed deep, and started scribbling.

FROM THE HEART OF ANGEL DRAKE
TUESDAY, JUNE 23

This is crazy. Ryan is inside fighting for his life and I'm outside pouring my thoughts onto a scratchpad. But if Sinjun was right, if journaling has a positive impact on one's physical and emotional being, then I'm going to scribble until I've purged every negative thought from my brain.

Jinxed. Cursed. The kiss of death. Every man I love dies. Yeah. THOSE negative thoughts.

Ryan needs good energy, positive energy, so I'm swinging things around. I can almost hear Eddie and Baxter urging me to do just that. I know. That's crazy, too. But it's not like I'm hearing voices or conversing with spirits. What I'm listening to is my heart. Eddie and Baxter are tucked in there forever and always. But there's room (or maybe it's that they made room) for Ryan because he's an exceptional man, a good man, and absolutely the RIGHT MAN FOR ME.

If I was lucky enough to fall in love with a third incredible man and for that incredible man to love me back... THAT'S something to fight for.

Buck up. Be strong. Have faith.

Ryan's going to live and I'm going to be there for him. I'll love him and care for him and nurture a loving relationship with Sienna. We will live a long and happy life TOGETHER.

Yours truly,
Angel Kane-Barnes-Drake (maybe-someday-McClure)

She glanced up at the heavens and smiled. "Okay. I've got this. I'm good. I'm better than good."

Vibrating with positive energy—for Ryan, for them—Angel tore her scribbled words from the pad and tucked them into her pocket.

She returned the pad to the receptionist then hurried back into the waiting room. *He's fine. He's fine. He's fine.*

At the same time, a physician in surgical attire entered from the opposite end.

Angel recognized the good-looking doctor in a heartbeat.

He looked exactly as he had in the emailed photo she'd seen on Georgie's wedding day, except he was wearing scrubs instead of a suit. "The McClure family?" he asked.

Everyone stood.

"How is he?" Georgie asked.

Angel closed her eyes. *He's fine. He's fine. He's fine.*

"Considering the severity of the crash, Sheriff McClure is a very lucky man," Ryder said. "He's got some physical therapy ahead of him, but I anticipate a full recovery."

Georgie burst into fresh tears—happy tears.

Unable to help herself, Angel rushed Dr. Benjamin Ryder and hugged him for all she was worth. "Thank you. Bless you."

Sinjun's voice rang in her ears. *"I saw Dr. Ryder again. With Georgie. Only this time you were there. You were in his arms, Angel, and Georgie... Georgie was crying."*

Gasping, Angel eased back. "This is why she dreamed about you and Georgie."

Ryder scrunched up his handsome face. "Excuse me?"

Angel flushed. "I'm sorry this isn't the time..." She smoothed the scrubs she'd rumpled then offered her hand in greeting. "I'm Angel Drake. We spoke on the phone."

His expression telegraphed recognition as his gaze flicked across the room. "Georgie Poppins?"

"Ryan McClure's my stepbrother. And it's Morgan now. My last name, I mean," Georgie said with an arm locked around Bryce. "This is my husband. Bryce Morgan."

"So you're the lucky man," Ryder said with a smile.

"That I am," Bryce gave Georgie a squeeze then moved forward to shake Ryder's hand. "I'm also a close friend of Ryan's. Thank you for what you did in there, Doctor."

"You're welcome." He turned to Angel then. "And you're connected to the sheriff how?"

"We're, um... He's my, well, boyfriend. For lack of a better term."

Zeke's brows shot up. "Since when?"

"Another Inseparable bites the dust," Emma said with a grunt.

Ryder took in all the faces and the unlikely connections. "Small world."

"And getting smaller all the time," Georgie said. "Thanks

to Impossible Dream."

"It's getting a little weird, if you ask me," Emma said.

They had no idea how weird, considering all the connections were based on Sinjun's ID-tution. Angel intended to have a long talk with their long-distance friend, but until then she'd stay mum as promised. Besides, right now her heart and head were with Ryan.

An hour later, a nurse finally ushered Angel into his room. Seeing him bruised, battered, and bandaged wasn't easy, but she didn't tear up.

Until they locked gazes and he smiled.

Eyes burning, heart bursting, she gently took his hand.

"Is this where you cite that kiss of death crap," he asked in a slurred, croaky voice, "and break off with me for my own good?"

"No. This is where I tell you I'm moving in for a while to take care of you and Sienna—for your own good."

"And when I'm healed and thriving?"

Now it was Angel's turn to smile. "I can tell you one thing for certain, Ryan McClure. I'm in this for the long haul."

Epilogue

Once upon a wedding celebration...
Two months later

After years of waffling through life, Georgina Poppins-Morgan found peace and joy in the aftermath of her worst fear. She also found her true calling.

The tornado that rocked their region didn't steal any lives but it did create chaos.

When she learned it would take weeks if not months to repair the damage of the worst hit rural homes, she spearheaded a relocation plan for her friends and neighbors.

After ensuring Arlo would be staying in the main cabin with Georgie and Bryce and the twins, she appointed the guest cabin to Bella and Savage and their cat, Killer.

Bella's dad, Archie, was living in a guest cabin on the Mooney Ranch. That one was a no-brainer considering Roger Mooney (Chrissy's dad) was Archie's brother.

The Cartwrights' home and business was in tatters so they proved a double challenge. Georgie not only arranged accommodations, she found them temporary employment—something to keep them afloat and in decent spirits during what would be a slow renovation period.

Georgie made it her mission to visit every business in Nowhere to determine who needed what in terms of supplies and repairs. In some instances, she was able to provide hands-on assistance with the help of the Inseparables, significant others, and various other locals. Sometimes she had to reach out to regional professionals.

Years of bouncing from one job to another had gifted Georgie with various skills and her resilient nature helped her spin new possibilities when others fell through. For the first time in her life, she was making a positive, worthwhile contribution to the community and, per that longtime pact with the Inseparables, she was helping to keep Nowhere alive and on the map.

Speaking of the Inseparables, their brush with disaster instigated the notion that *life's too short*. Actually the twister had that effect on a lot of Nowhere locals. As a result, people were living full out, embracing joy anywhere they could find it, and following through with commitments and goals sooner rather than later.

Which brought them to today.

After a two-month delay, Georgie was hosting the wedding celebration of all wedding celebrations. Instead of throwing a party in honor of her and Bryce's civil service wedding, they renewed their vows in front of friends and family in a sunny outdoor affair at the Morgan ranch.

As if that wasn't perfect enough, Bella and Savage and Chrissy and Mason, who'd been engaged for almost a year, and Angel and Ryan, who'd been living together for two months, all took their vows alongside Georgie and Bryce.

A quadruple wedding. A Dawes County first.

As if *that* wasn't perfect enough, Sinjun flew in for the festivities, which made this the first time all the Inseparables had been together in almost twenty years. Georgie and friends were dying to finally learn the details of Sinjun's association with Impossible Dream—something she'd promised to reveal over the weekend when they met for a reunion at Café Caboose. Yes, Sinjun was staying in town for a while!

It would have been even *more* perfect if Emma had caught one of the four bouquets the brides tossed her way. However, in her typical single and happy-for-now fashion, Emma folded her arms as the petals flew by. "Like that's ever going to happen."

"Happy?" Bryce asked close to Georgie's ear.

"Let's see," she teased. "I'm wrapped in my husband's arms and swaying to a slow song on my re-wedding day, surrounded by friends and family and three quarters of Nowhere—all of who seem to be enjoying the food, music, and company."

"Mom would be impressed."

"Also," Georgie went on with a smile, "Charlie and Chelsea are blossoming more and more, Arlo's finally free of his cane and therefore less grumpy. And, because we succeeded in muting the potential scandal of the photo snafu, you're joining the high school staff as a sport's coach and social counselor which I know means a lot to you and will definitely benefit Nowhere. So, yes. I'm happy, Bryce. Deliriously happy."

He smiled down into her eyes, kissed her deeply, then angled his head toward the house. "I've got a surprise for you."

She waggled her brows. "Does it involve spontaneous sex?" They'd indulged in quite a bit of that lately, stealing secret moments every chance they got.

"No," he said with a grin, "but I promise you'll like it."

He took her hand and led her through the crowd.

The twins were dancing with Melody and Sienna. Arlo was shooting the breeze with Archie. And from what she could tell, Emma had wrangled Sinjun and the other newly wedded couples into doing shots. Georgie had sworn off drinking today, telling everyone her stomach was too jittery, which it was. But not due to nerves like everyone believed.

Bryce led her into the main cabin, across the living room, and into the dining room. Georgie saw the breathtaking bouquet of poppies and assorted other wildflowers on the table and gasped. "Oh, Bryce. They're gorgeous."

"They're not from me." He reached for a card tucked behind the lovely vase and passed it to her. "They were delivered to me earlier today, but I was instructed not to give them to you until after the ceremony."

"Curiouser and curiouser," Georgie said, still smiling. But then she opened the card and tears filled her eyes.

"Dear Georgie," she read aloud. "I'm sorry I can't be there today, but I want you to know how happy I am for you and Bryce. And how proud I am of you for all you're doing for the people of Nowhere. You're a very special woman. Make your own magic more often. Love, Mom."

Georgie stared at the typewritten note.

"I know you would have preferred her actually being here," Bryce said.

"No. This is fine. Honest." After the tornado scare and following Bryce's advice to "look deeper", Georgie had put more effort into staying in touch with her mom. The phone conversations weren't all that warm or long, but they were something. *Where there's a connection, there's hope.* "These flowers, this card... She loves me. And well, this makes this day almost perfect."

"Almost?"

"I was going to wait until tonight but... You know how after the storm we decided to live full out? To forego birth control and let nature take its course? Life's too short and all that?"

Bryce raised a brow.

"And you know how we've been trying for two months and waiting and waiting?"

He caught her hand and tugged her close. "Something you want to tell me, Lou?

"I took an early pregnancy test this morning." Heart bursting with contentment and joy, Georgie smiled up at the one-and-only true love of her life. "The wait is over."

teaser from

no place like nowhere

An Impossible Dream Novella

~book four~

One

Once upon a nightmare...
Nowhere, Nebraska

"We got rotation."

"We got more than that, Zeke. Pull over."

"Is that... Yeah. I see it. Funnel. We got a funnel!"

"Look at that beauty. Getting a shot."

"Submitting report. Funnel two to three miles southeast of Eagle Butte. What the hell? Come on. Come on. Submit. Live cone. Shit. Okay. Submitted. "

"Touch down! Dust! Debris!"

"Moving northwest. According to the radar..."

"Get in the truck, Emma. Son of a... Stop texting and haul ass!"

"Weather service still reporting a watch. Update to a warning, dammit."

"Punch it, Zeke!"

"Video streaming. Look at that spin."
"Check out these readings—"
"Call it in, Dewey."
"Tornado on the ground. Reporting tornado on the ground. Cutting across Cartwrights' Lavender Field. Heading toward Nowhere."
"Copy that Z-Crew. Law enforcement aware."
"We've got debris and downed poles in this location. Tornado damage confirmed!"
"Oh, God. Bella and Joe. Georgie. The Morgans."
"Passing in front of us."
"Frickin' hail."
"Slow down, Zeke. Visibility sucks."
"Gotta get on the other side of this."
"Police scanner."
"Heard it. You don't think they're talking about Ryan, do you?"
"Turn it up."
"Dammit!"
"Debris. Watch it. Jesus, Zeke!"
"Holy crap!"

Emma Sloan jackknifed and bolted out of bed. She stood in the middle of her room, drenched in sweat, half-asleep, and battling for calm.

"Just a dream. Just a dream."

Only it wasn't.

Heart pounding, she padded barefoot across the hardwood floor and wrenched open her bedroom window. She thrust her upper body into the night, into the fresh air. Breathe. She gaped at the starry sky—so brilliant, so calm. So unlike that moment two months back when a twister ripped through this countryside and grazed the town.

A town she was desperate to escape.

Guilt and frustration welled. Feeling trapped, she eased out of the second-story window, settling on the portion of the roof that jutted over the screened-in front porch. No fear. She'd been doing this since she was a kid. Raised by her aunt and uncle, she'd lived much of her life in this old farmhouse.

She'd lived all of her life in Nowhere.

A photographer, weather freak, and outdoorsman rolled

into one, Emma dreamed of trotting the globe in a series of adrenaline-charged adventures. In a perfect world, she would have escaped the limitations of this speck on the map long ago. But in addition to wanderlust, she also suffered from extreme loyalty to family and friends as well as a sorry-ass budget.

She'd taken up storm chasing to make a few extra bucks. Mostly she did it for the thrill. Only now the thrill was gone. This tornado twisted her insides and haunted her nights. This tornado was personal.

Tilting her face to the moon and stars, Emma channeled her frustration and anger into steely resolve. Time to act.

Luckily, she knew a *facilitator* of impossible dreams.

NOTE TO READERS

This series comes from the heart and a longtime love affair with fairy tale romances. I hope I provided you with a bit of joyous escapism! If you enjoyed MARRY POPPINS please consider writing a review on any e-tailer or review site (such as Goodreads). Spreading the word helps me to share the love. Your support is very much appreciated!

Follow the adventures of the Inseparables in the next installment of Impossible Dream—NO PLACE LIKE NOWHERE. For a glimpse of something different, visit my website to explore my many worlds. From steampunk to paranormal to contemporary. Something for everyone!

www.bethciotta.com

ACKNOWLEDGMENTS

It takes several professionals to bring a book to life. Special thanks to *EJR Digital Art* for the fabulous cover art and formatting! My appreciation to my critique and editorial team—Elle J Rossi, Cynthia Valero, Deidre Motto, Mary Stella... and Melissa Norr of *Brazen Pen Editing*. A huge thank you to my marketing advisers: Bards of Badassery. And my everlasting gratitude to my husband, Steve, for supporting my not-so-impossible dream!